TRUST ME, I'M LYING

MARY ELIZABETH SUMMER

TRUST ME, I'M LYING

DELACORTE PRESS

Text copyright © 2014 by Mary Elizabeth Summer
Jacket photograph copyright © 2014 by Carrie Schechter

All rights reserved. Published in the United States by Delacorte Press,
an imprint of Random House Children's Books, a division of Random House LLC,
a Penguin Random House Company, New York.

Delacorte Press is a registered trademark
and the colophon is a trademark of Random House LLC.

randomhouse.com/teens

Educators and librarians, for a variety of teaching tools, visit us at
RHTeachersLibrarians.com

Library of Congress Cataloging-in-Publication Data
Summer, Mary Elizabeth.
Trust me, I'm lying / Mary Elizabeth Summer.
pages cm
Summary: Having learned to be a master con artist from her father, Julep Dupree pays expenses at her exclusive high school by fixing things for fellow students, but she will need their help when her father disappears.
ISBN 978-0-385-74406-5 (hc : alk. paper) — ISBN 978-0-375-99151-6 (glb : alk. paper)
— ISBN 978-0-385-38288-5 (ebook)
[1. Swindlers and swindling—Fiction. 2. Fathers and daughters—Fiction. 3. Organized crime—Fiction. 4. High schools—Fiction. 5. Schools—Fiction.] I. Title.
PZ7.S953935Tru 2014
[Fic]—dc23
2013037937

The text of this book is set in 11.75-point Goudy.

Printed in the United States of America
10 9 8 7 6 5 4 3 2 1
First Edition

Random House Children's Books
supports the First Amendment and celebrates the right to read.

For my first reader, Miranda,
and my future reader, Caelan

THE STRATTON JOB

I can't say I have much personal experience with conscience. I wasn't born with that particular cricket on my shoulder. But people who believe in conscience seem to think it has something to do with compassion. And it could, I suppose, if you tilt your head and squint at it in just the right light.

The truth is, conscience exists because everyone has something in their past they're not proud of. And if you're smart enough to use that to your advantage, you can stay one step ahead of the consequences. Any good con man with the right kind of rope can hang an entire mob.

But my story doesn't start with the mob. It starts with a pair of borrowed pumps and the front walk of a black-shuttered Colonial.

I am Ms. Jena Scott, the youngest attorney at Lewis,

Duncan, and Chase Law. Or at least, I am for the next thirty minutes. Then I'll turn back into Julep Dupree, sophomore at St. Agatha's Preparatory School and all-around fixer. (Julep's not my real name, either, but we'll get to that later.)

It's the officially unofficial talk around school that I'm a solver of other people's problems. And I am. I just happen to charge a respectable sum for my services. St. Aggie's isn't cheap, and a job at the local deli isn't going to cover the cost of toiletries, let alone tuition. Luckily, my fellow students can more than afford my rates.

My talent is the one thing I can leverage. I'm a grifter, a con artist, and a master of disguise. I'm the best, actually, because I was taught by the best—my dad, Joe. Never heard of him? Well, you wouldn't have, because he's never been caught. And neither have I. The best grifters are ghosts.

For the newbies out there, a grifter is a person who specializes in selling people something that doesn't exist. At the moment, I'm selling my client Heather Stratton's parents on the idea that she has applied to New York University. Which, of course, is a load of crap.

Heather doesn't want to go to NYU; she wants to be a model. But since her mom won't bankroll that endeavor, my job is to grease the wheels, so to speak, so everyone believes she's getting what she wants. It's a win-win-win, really. Heather is happy, Mrs. Stratton is happy, and I get paid. When you look at it like that, I'm in the making-people-happy business.

Heather's paying for a full pig-in-a-poke package: fake application, fake interview, fake acceptance. And it's going to cost her. I've already had Sam, my best friend and partner in crime, build a fake NYU website showing Heather's application status. Then came the official-looking brochures and letters on NYU stationery Sam and I spent an afternoon making. And that was easy compared to getting the envelopes to sport a postmark from New York.

Now I'm doing the interview bit. Ms. Scott is a new creation of mine. A lawyer by way of NYU undergrad and University of Pennsylvania law school. She works at a big-deal firm here in Chicago and occasionally does admission interviews for her alma mater.

I straighten my suit skirt in the perfect imitation of a lawyer I saw on television last night. There's a good chance nobody's watching, but it never hurts to get into character early. I touch my hair to make sure the longish brown mess is still coiled into a tight French roll. I adjust the thin, black-framed glasses I use for roles both younger and older than my near-sixteen years.

Then I remember my gum—doesn't exactly scream professionalism. Lacking an appropriate disposal option, I take the gum out and stick it to the bottom of the Strattons' mailbox. I walk up to the covered porch and rap smartly on the blue door. A few moments later, a brittle, middle-aged woman with a too-bright smile and Jackie O style opens it.

"Mrs. Stratton, I presume," I say in a slightly lower pitch than usual. People assume you're older if your voice is deeper.

"You must be Ms. Scott," she says. "Please, come in."

She's easy enough to read. Nervous, excited. She's an easy mark, because she wants so much for me to be real. I mean, look at me. This disguise is a stretch, even for a professional grifter. But she won't doubt it, because she doesn't want to. No disguise is more foolproof than the one the mark wants to believe. I might feel a little bad for her if I were a real person. As it happens, I'm not a real person, and she is not my client.

I cross the threshold into an immaculate foyer. The living room opens off to my left, rich and inviting but lacking in the warmth the plush upholstery implies. It's a gorgeous room, beautiful and cold, like an ice sculpture in the sun.

Mrs. Stratton motions me into the room and I sit in an armchair next to a brick hearth that hasn't seen a fire in years. Julep would have chosen the couch, with its army of throw pillows, but "Ms. Scott" is here on business and doesn't approve of all the touchy-feely nonsense that comes about sitting next to people.

"Would you like something to drink?"

"A glass of water would be most appreciated," I say.

Mrs. Stratton leaves the room, returning a few moments later with a precisely cooled glass of water. She places a coaster on the polished end table next to me. I smile my approval, and her smile widens.

"I'll go get Heather," Mrs. Stratton says, and calls up the stairs for her daughter, who is expecting me.

Heather enters the room in what I can only assume is her Sunday best. Her family is Episcopalian, I'm fairly sure. I can usually tell by the decor of the house, the mother's clothing choices, and the books on the shelves in public spaces. For example, you can always tell a Baptist household by the oak dining room table, the spinet in the living room, and the variety of Bibles on the shelf next to the television set. Episcopalians don't often have televisions in their living rooms. Don't ask me why.

"Hello, Heather," I say, standing and extending my hand. She shakes it, shooting me conspiratorial glances while acting fidgety, and overall doing a lousy job of pretending she doesn't know me. But her mother will chalk it up to nervousness as long as I do my part right.

I sink back into the armchair, and Heather sits across from me on the couch. She looks tense, but then, she would be. Heather's mother hangs around for another moment or two before realizing she is supposed to leave and finally whisking herself away to some other part of the house.

I raise my hand when Heather opens her mouth. So many of my clients foolishly think we don't have to go through with the scam from beginning to end. They assume that once they can no longer see the mark, she's not still around listening. My dad calls it the ostrich syndrome.

"Tell me about yourself, Heather," I say. "What do you want to study at NYU?"

What follows is a yawn-fest of questions and answers. I couldn't care less about Heather's GPA. And student government? Really? But I'm helping her swindle her parents—I'm hardly in a position to judge.

At the end of the interview I cut her off almost midsentence and stand up, not having touched my water. I'm out of the house and at the door to Sam's Volvo, proper good-byes offered and promises to put in a good word for Heather with the admissions office made. I open the driver's-side door and slide into the leather seat, exhaling as I settle in. It's a far cry from the hard plastic chairs on the "L," which is my usual form of transportation.

I sense more than hear the purr as the engine turns over. I pull away from the curb cautiously, not because I'm a cautious driver by nature, but because I am still in character. Once I've turned out of sight of the house, I crank the radio up and slide the windows down while I push the gas pedal to coax the car to a peppier speed. It's a warm Sunday in early September, and I want to milk it for all it's worth. With one hand, I pull out the pins holding my hair back, letting the tangled tresses fall naturally to my shoulders.

Sam knows I'm not a legal driver. We've known each other since fourth grade, when we started pulling the three-card monte on our classmates, so he's well aware of my age. You'd think he'd be more nervous about lending his brand-new Volvo to an untried, untested, unlicensed driver. But then, I'm the one who taught him how to drive.

Ten minutes later, I pull into the parking lot of my local coffee haunt, the Ballou, which is half a block from the St. Aggie's campus, and claim a space next to a souped-up seventies muscle car. Chevelle, I think, though I'm hardly an expert. Black with two thick white racing stripes down the hood and windows tinted black enough to put Jay-Z's to shame.

I take off my jacket and untuck my blouse. Kicking off the heels, I flip open my ratty old canvas bag and take out my well-worn Converse high-tops. I wriggle my feet into them as I tie my hair up again. Then I toss the glasses into the bag and grab my dad's old leather jacket.

The Ballou is pretty much what you'd expect a coffee shop to be: wooden tables, scuffed and stuffed chairs, a lacquered bar polished to within an inch of its life, a smattering of patrons sipping lattes and reading Yeats. You see lots of MacBooks and iPads, and the occasional stack of textbooks gathering dust while their owners text or surf the Web.

Sam is sitting at our favorite rickety, mismatched table with the cardboard coffee-cup sleeve under one of the legs.

"To the minute," Sam says, spotting me over the top of his graphic novel. "I'll never know how you can guess that close."

"Just have to know the mark."

"That's what you say for everything," he says, smiling and moving his bag aside.

"Well, it's true for everything," I say while I casually steal his cappuccino.

Sam has a gorgeous smile. I often tease him about it, which he hates, or at least pretends to hate. But I think he secretly appreciates being noticed for something besides his status as the only son of Hudson Seward, board chairman of the Seward Group and the richest black man in Chicago. Sam wants to escape his father's name as much as Heather wants out from under her mother's iron fist.

Everyone wants something, I suppose. Me? I want a full ride to Yale. Hence my internment at St. Agatha's.

"How'd it go?"

I yawn.

"That good?"

"Cake," I say. "But we prepped well this time." I take a swig of his coffee.

"As opposed to any other time?"

"Granted." I set his keys on the table. "Thanks for the car."

He pockets the keys. "And you're thanking me because . . . ?"

"Hey, I say thank you sometimes." I cradle the cup between my hands to warm them.

"No you don't," he says.

"Yes I do."

He plucks the cup out of my grasp and leans back. "No you don't."

I've just conceded when Heather appears. I don't love that she insisted on meeting up with us, but she's the sort who needs to know each step of the plan in detail. She's more her mother's daughter than she thinks. She slips gracefully into the chair next to mine.

"That went . . . well?" she says with a slight question at the end, like she's asking for confirmation.

"It did," I say. I make it a policy to avoid hand-holding. But she's my client, and far be it from me to begrudge her a bit of customer service.

"So what now?" She huddles into herself and lowers her voice to a whisper. Really, how my clients keep anything a secret when their body language continually screams *Look at me! I'm planning something nefarious!* is beyond me. I guess it's true what the French say: fortune favors the innocent. Lucky for me, it also favors the moderately dishonest.

"Now I welcome you to NYU," I say.

Then I detail the rest of the plan, which involves sending Heather a fake internship offer from a modeling agency to raise the stakes. Mrs. Stratton will be so desperate to secure Heather's spot at NYU she won't think to question our irregular instructions for sending the tuition check. In my profession, this is called the shutout, and it works every time.

"But how do I cash a check made out to NYU?" Heather asks.

"It won't be made out to NYU. It will be made out to me. Or to Jena Scott, actually."

"You think she'll fall for that?"

"Fall for it? She'll be the one suggesting it. Trust me, the check is the easy part."

Heather's doubt is evident, but she's not the one whose confidence I'm trying to steal.

A half hour later, Sam drops me off at my apartment building.

"Catch you on the dark side," I say as I get out and head to the front door.

"The dark side is a bad thing," Sam calls after me.

I wave while he pulls away from the curb, shaking his head at me.

"Hi, Fred," I say to the homeless man sitting between the row of mailboxes and the radiator in the entryway.

"Hey, Julep," he says in his Dominican accent. "How's shit going?"

"Shit's good," I say, and open our mailbox. I pull the comics out of the paper and hand them to Fred. If anyone needs a laugh, it's him.

In case the homeless guy hasn't given it away, my dad and I live deep in the West Side slums—the same apartment building we've been in since my mom left us. I was eight at the time, so that's, what? Seven years? Well, in all that time I've seen neither hide nor hair of any maintenance personnel beyond the very occasional plumber.

I'm so used to it, though, that I climb the narrow stairs without seeing the fuchsia and black graffiti or the grime in the corners. In fact, I don't even notice when I get to our apartment that the door is slightly open. When I try to put my key in the lock, the door swings away from me. Still, I'm distracted by a tuition bill from St. Aggie's, so I walk right in.

The first thing I notice is my dad's chair tipped upside down, the stuffing from the cushion littered around it like yellow sea foam. My lungs constrict as I take in the rest of our belongings: Pictures torn down to reveal stained walls. Drawers pulled out and overturned. Even some of the linoleum flooring in the kitchen has been ripped up and left in curling strips.

"Dad?" The sound of my heart hammering is probably carrying farther than my voice.

This makes no sense. We have nothing worth stealing—no one breaks into the apartments in our building for monetary gain. Not that there isn't violence; it's just usually domestic or drug-related.

I push open the door to my dad's room and it gets stuck about a third of the way open. This room is in even worse shape than the rest of the apartment. Books and papers and blankets and broken bits of furniture cover the ratty carpet like shrapnel from a bomb blast. But still no Dad. At this point, I'm not so sure that's a bad thing.

Not as much damage in my room, but it's still trashed. Curtains trailing along the floor. Desk knocked over, the bulb from the lamp shattered and ground into the carpet.

I pick my way back toward the kitchen as I study what was left behind. I'm certain someone was looking for something, but I have no idea what. It's not like we stashed a Monet under the floorboards.

My dad does have a gambling problem. He's the best grifter you've never heard of, like I said, but we're still living in the ghetto. I'm sure you're wondering why, since I keep telling you he could con Donald Trump out of his toupee. Well, that's the reason. No sooner does he get a "windfall" than it gets spent on the ponies.

But he never borrows to bet. He bets everything we have but nothing we don't. His bookie's his best friend. Ralph even comes to my birthday parties. So I seriously doubt it's a payment problem.

It has to be a con that's gone south somehow. Which means my dad's in trouble. He has something his mark wants. And not just any mark—a mark willing to break in and do this. That means a mark on the shadier side.

I reach the kitchen and tip a chair upright. What could my dad be into that would have resulted in this? What could he have that somebody would be looking for? The answer is lots of things: forged documents, information about something incriminating, who knows? The two bigger questions, though, are did the person find what he was searching for, and why didn't my dad tell me what he was doing?

My dad is not the sort to shelter his offspring. We're a team. I sometimes help him brainstorm when he's planning a con. He doesn't often use me as a roper, mostly because I'd stick out like a sore thumb in the circles he tends to work. But he always tells me his angle.

I lean against the wall, surveying the destruction in the kitchen. Something tells me that whoever tossed the place did not find what he was looking for. That might very well be wishful thinking, but I decide to act on the hunch anyway. Can't hurt to do a bit of searching of my own.

But before I turn over even a plate, two thoughts occur to me. One, I should call the police before I tamper with any potential evidence. Two, if the home-wrecker didn't find what he was looking for, he might come back.

I reach for my phone and tap a nine and a one before I come to my senses. I can't call the police. Police plus abandoned minor equals foster care. Hello! I let out a shaky breath at how

12

close I came to screwing myself nine ways to Sunday. I delete both numbers and quickly pocket the phone, as if my fingers might somehow betray me.

I'm sure you think I'm being melodramatic. But I'm not an idiot. Everyone knows that foster care is a prison sentence. Umpteen thousand crime procedurals cannot be wrong. Besides, my dad and I are our own system. I'm the only one who knows him well enough to figure out where he's hidden whatever the intruder was searching for. If the police get involved, they'll be the ones ruining the crime scene, not me.

I picture my dad, every detail from his thick brown hair to his scuffed oxfords. If I were my dad and I had to hide something . . .

What hasn't been touched? I turn in a slow circle till I find it—the perfectly upright, not-even-a-millimeter-out-of-place trash can.

Only cops dig in the garbage, Julep, and even then, only on TV.

Before considering the consequences, I yank the bag out of the can and empty it onto what's left of the linoleum. Last night's chicken bones come tumbling out, along with several plastic wrappers and a lump of grease-covered foil. Gross, yes. Illuminating, no. I root around in it anyway, holding my breath and hoping. But there's nothing in the bag that can remotely be construed as valuable. No pictures, no papers, no money, nothing.

I plop on the floor next to the mess, swearing to myself. I mean, who am I kidding? How am I supposed to find my dad in a pile of half-eaten chicken? The trash can mocks me with its dingy plastic lid. Still upright, it is the only thing in the apartment that's exactly where it should be.

I kick out and knock it over. Might as well finish the job, right? But as it falls to the floor, I hear something bang around inside it. I pull the mouth around to where I can see. Inside the can is a padded envelope.

Ignoring the muck, I reach in and grab the envelope. As I rip it open, I have this strange sense of doom, like liberating its contents is some kind of point of no return. I ignore the feeling. He is my dad, after all.

But when I pull out said contents, I'm even more unnerved. In one hand, I hold a note:

BEWARE THE FIELD OF MIRACLES.

In the other, I hold a gun.

THE GEEK JOB

"Julep!" Sam shouts as he flies through the door.

I realize what I must look like, sitting next to garbage with my back against the battered cabinets, holding a gun. Before his eyes find me, I set the gun on the floor behind me. I'm not trying to hide it, but a person can only take so many shocks at once.

When he sees me on the floor, he rushes over.

"Are you okay?"

"I said as much on the phone, Sam."

"You don't look okay."

"You really know how to compliment a girl."

He tries to pull me to my feet, but I don't let him. First, because there's really nowhere else to go. Second, well, I'm not sure my legs will hold me just yet. He sits down next to me instead.

"You know what I mean," he says.

I pull my knees in closer. I could still call the police, I suppose, but I know I won't.

"Is this like last time?"

I shake my head. But it's a fair question. This isn't the first time my dad's disappeared.

When I was thirteen, I came home from school one day, finished my homework, made myself my standard mac-and-cheese dinner of champions, and watched five hours of television before I realized my dad wasn't coming home that night. Nor did he come home the following night, or the night after that. No note, no call, nothing.

I was petrified. But when I told Sam, he assured me that if my dad didn't come back, he and his parents would take me in. Just having that safety net calmed my panic. My dad eventually came back, two weeks of peanut butter sandwiches later. He's never really explained where he was, but I got the impression it had to do with a job that went bad.

At the time, I was angry with him for scaring me. But looking back, I'm certain he was trying to protect me from someone who might have tried to hurt me or use me against him. Had I been him, I'd have done the same thing. Still, everything changed after that. Or rather, I changed. I no longer wanted my father's life.

But this disappearance is different. This time someone's destroyed our apartment.

"He's still not answering his cell?"

"I haven't tried again since calling you," I admit. "But I called seventeen times. If he hasn't answered by now, he's not going to."

"His circumstances might change," Sam says, choosing his words carefully. I appreciate the tact, but let's call it as we see it, shall we?

"Look at this place, Sam." I gesture at the mess. "This is not the work of his usual kind of mark. This is something else."

Sam scans the room, shoving shards of a plate out of the way with his foot.

"Well, you can't stay here."

"That's not what I meant," I say. A flash of fear spikes through me as I realize he might out me to the cops. "You have to promise you won't tell anyone."

"Julep, you aren't actually considering staying here—"

"Of course I am. He might call or come back."

"But—"

"Sam, please. You can't tell anyone or I'll get shipped off to some foster farm. No more St. Aggie's."

Sam opens his mouth to protest but closes it when he realizes I'm right.

"You still can't stay here," he says after a pause. "You can stay with us."

"Your mom thinks I'm a 'bad influence,' remember?" I put air quotes around *bad influence* to soften the sore point he hates talking about.

"She'll just have to deal." He's irritated despite my air quotes.

"We're not in grade school anymore, anyway," I say. "Sleepovers aren't exactly kosher."

"This is serious, Julep. You can't just brush it off. What if whoever did this"—he nods at the linoleum strips—"comes back?"

I hate to admit it, but he's right. If the thugs decide to try again, it will be tonight.

"Fine. I'll stay with you for one night."

He lets go a breath I didn't realized he was holding.

"Good," he says.

I give him a sour look. "Just one. I'm pretty sure they won't come back. Why would they waste their time? They either found what they were looking for or they didn't because it isn't here."

"What would they be looking for?"

"No idea. Maybe nothing. But I found this." I show him the note. Then I slowly pull out the gun. "And this."

His expression turns stormy again, and he takes the gun from me, dropping the note into the chicken drippings.

"Hey!" I say, rescuing it.

He ignores me, ejecting the bullet-holder thingy and checking the chamber with expert skill.

"Since when do you know anything about guns?" I glare at him as I wipe off the note.

"The colonel's been taking me shooting since I was twelve, Julep."

Sam's dad, who he lovingly refers to as "the colonel," in addition to being a CEO, is a retired army colonel with the military bearing, ambitious drive, and strict governance of Sam to go with the rank. Of course the man would teach his son how to shoot a handgun.

"I thought it was, like, duck hunting or something."

He shakes his head. "Sometimes I wonder if you know me at all."

I wrinkle my nose, not wanting to admit that I might be a little hurt by that, mostly because there's a chance it's partially true. Very partially. Like, a minuscule amount.

"Anyway, it's not loaded," he says.

"My dad gave me an unloaded gun?"

"So it appears." He puts the gun back together and hands it to me. Then he reaches for the note. "What does it say?"

" 'Beware the Field of Miracles.' "

He scans the note. "What do you think it means?"

"I don't know," I say. "But it's just like my dad. Riddles."

"Do you think it'll lead us to whatever it is these people want?"

"Possibly," I say, shifting uncomfortably.

"But . . . you think it leads to something else?"

"It could lead to the missing millions or whatever. Or it could lead to my dad. But the note is definitely from him, and he clearly wants me to do something."

Sam sighs and takes my hand. I let him keep it.

After I pack a bag and we move our party to Sam's house, Sam and I have a perfectly uneventful sleepover, involving sneaking me in through his bedroom window and arguing over who'll be taking the bed versus the Star Wars beanbag chair.

I win the argument for the beanbag chair and yet somehow wake up in the bed anyway, and so I am extremely grumpy the next morning. I then sneak back out his bedroom window when the maid knocks on his door. I give half a thought to hot-wiring Sam's car and taking off without him, but he shows up with the keys and drives us to school.

St. Agatha's Preparatory School, fondly referred to as St. Aggie's by most of its attendees, was Chicago's first private all-girls academy. But due to various recessions and other natural catastrophes over the years, it became a coed institution. It's still true to its Catholic roots, however, holding Mass on Wednesdays in the chapel, lighting candles for every holy day, and passing the presidency from nun to nun.

The campus itself is gorgeous. Several turn-of-the-century buildings form a perimeter around a large, grassy quad complete with fountain and triumphal arch. The southern side is bordered by Holy Mother of God Church, while the northern end is bound by the gymnasium and theater building. The other two buildings house the classes as well as the administrative offices for the various school authorities.

The smallish parking lot is tucked under the shadow of the church's steeples, adding to the chill I feel through my wool coat and school-mandated tights. Despite the warmth yesterday, September is fast fading into October, and Chicago's famous wind is already starting to blow.

Sam tugs one of my braids and I smack the back of his head, which is our loving way of saying "See you later." I need a coffee and some research time before starting my day. First period is one of those things I consider optional. Like nuts in brownies. And flossing. So as Sam goes into the nearest building, I head in the direction of the Ballou.

"Hey, Julep. Got a sec?" Murphy Donovan—a soft, bespectacled nerd from my biology class—stops me before I get very far.

"You happen to have a decent cup of espresso on your person?" I say.

"Not on me, no."

"Then if you want to talk, you'll have to walk me."

He falls into step like a well-trained puppy, but he seems to need a little prodding in the talking department.

"So is this a social call?" I ask.

"No. That is, um, I'd like to"—he lowers his voice and looks over his shoulder at the students flitting hither and yon around us—"hire you."

"I see. How can I be of service?"

"I want you to get Bryn Halverson to go to the fall formal with me," he all but whispers.

I consider his request as I shift my bag. I could do it. Easily, in fact. All it takes is a modified fiddle game. My brain is already spinning the con, assessing resources, gauging the mark. But I'd like a little more information before I take the job.

"*The* Bryn Halverson?" I say. "Head JV cheerleader, homecoming court, failing Spanish—that Bryn Halverson?"

"She's failing Spanish?"

"Focus, Murphy."

"Yes, her," Murphy answers.

"Do you mind if I ask why?"

He drops his gaze to his hands. "I like her," he mumbles.

"You and every other straight, red-blooded American male," I say, more truthful than kind. I don't need to drag this out of him. I can do the job without it. But how I approach the job affects him, and understanding his motivations lets me know how far I can go.

"I liked her before. I've liked her since middle school, when she had braces and frizzy hair and was whipping all our butts at algebra."

I sigh and give him a sympathetic look. I'm going to take the job, of course, but I'm not thrilled about it. Not because I'm opposed to manipulating Bryn, but because I already know Murphy's going to get trampled. And since Murphy's a tech-club buddy of Sam's, Sam is not going to be pleased if I help Bryn break Murphy's heart.

"Honestly, Murphy, it would be easier if you just wanted the social status."

"So you'll do it?"

I nod reluctantly. "Yes. But you'll probably regret it."

"How much?"

"Depends on how much you like her."

"No, I mean—"

I wave him to silence. "I know what you mean," I say, calculating the fee in my head. What is the going rate for breaking somebody's heart? This is one of those questions that make me reconsider my line of work.

"Five hundred. Cash. Plus the standard proviso."

"What proviso?"

"You owe me a favor."

"What kind of favor?"

"The kind where you don't know what it is until I ask it," I say, pausing at the door to the Ballou. "If it's any comfort, it's usually something pretty tame, and generally in your area of expertise."

Murphy mulls over my terms for all of half a second before forking over the cash. I'd never pay that much for a school dance, but then most of the students at St. Aggie's have money to burn. Even worse is the threat of an unspecified favor to be called in at a later date. But I've never had anyone protest. I guess that's what comes of having unlimited access to whatever you want—when you need something you can't get, you're willing to put everything on the line. Maybe the opportunity to confess your undying love is worth it. I've never felt that way about anyone, so what do I know?

"When should I ask her?" he says.

"A week from tomorrow," I answer as I open the door. "That gives us time to lay the groundwork, but still gives her a few days to buy a dress. Assuming she doesn't have a closetful already."

"What if she says no?"

"You should be more worried about her saying yes."

He gives me a confused look.

"I'll take care of it," I say, stepping into the warm glow of the Ballou.

It takes me longer than most people to order coffee, because

I'm chatting up the cashier to finagle a free drink. It's not hard. Especially at a chain, which is more likely selling the coffee-shop experience than the coffee. But even indie-shop baristas are given a lot of leeway. All I have to do is determine what pushes the buttons of the person who pushes the buttons, and bingo—all the macchiatos I can drink. But it does take a little more time than fishing for cash.

"You new?" I ask as I step up to the counter.

I'm a regular at the Ballou, so I know all the baristas. I've never seen this guy before, so I already know he's new. It doesn't really matter whether you're a regular or not, though—just have a spiel handy for either possibility.

"First day," he says.

Stocky and bald and built like a linebacker, the forty-something man looks more like he should be on the set of an action flick than wearing a barista apron.

"Like it so far?"

"Manager's nice enough."

"I'll have a triple soy caramel macchiato, please." The *please* is essential when angling for a free drink. "My name is Julep," I continue, offering a hand while flashing him a dimpled smile.

"Mike," he says as he shakes my hand.

"I know all the baristas' names," I tell him. "Have to put something next to their numbers on my speed dial. You never know when you're going to have a caffeine emergency."

He laughs and starts making my drink without charging me first, as he can see that I'm winding up for a full-on conversation.

"Have you been in the barista game long?"

"My first time, actually," he admits with a smile. On him, it looks like a piece of granite cracking in the middle. "Tell me if I mess it up and I'll try again."

"Oh, I'm easy," I say. "As long as it's got loads of caramel, I'm a happy camper. Besides, you look pretty confident back there. I'm sure you've got it down."

Compliment, compliment, compliment. But keep it focused on the job at hand. Telling him he looks great in that shirt sounds like you're flirting rather than impressed with his handiwork. Flirting has its place, for sure, but not in this situation. You need generosity, not a date.

"That'll be four-fifty," he says, putting the cup of caffeinated sugar rush on the counter in front of me.

I rummage around in my bag. "Oh, jeez. Looks like I forgot my wallet. I guess I should cancel the drink order."

"Might as well take it since I already made it," Mike says, pushing the drink toward me. "Call it practice."

"You're a gem, Mike. You have no idea how much I need this coffee."

"I've been there," he says, smiling and wiping his hands on a caramel-smudged cloth.

"Thanks. I won't forget this!"

I take a seat on a ratty sofa that's been through the Goodwill mill a time or two and then pull out my phone. I left the gun in my apartment last night. I can't tell if it's a clue, a warning, or a loaded (ha) attempt at offering protection. If it's a clue or a warning, I can puzzle it out without the actual gun;

if it's protection, well, it's not going to do me much good. I've never even seen a gun—loaded or not—in real life, let alone fired one. My dad's a con artist, not a thug, and he always says: *Your story is your best offense; your disguise is your best defense. Weapons will only get you killed.*

A clue, then. But I have no idea about what, so I set aside the gun conundrum for now and pull out the note.

I type "Field of Miracles" into my search engine app. The first page of hits all seem to be related to Pisa. As in, the famous leaning tower. I click on a link titled "Why is the area behind the Tower of Pisa called the Field of Miracles?" The answer has something to do with the Italian poet Gabriele D'Annunzio. I'm pretty sure my dad is not suggesting I take up Tuscan poetry. So what else could Pisa mean? Maybe there's a museum display somewhere in Chicago showcasing blunders of an architectural nature? Another search dead-ends that theory.

Maybe Italy is the key. I look up the number to my father's favorite Italian restaurant and tap Send. But a five-minute conversation confirms that the restaurant manager hasn't seen my dad in weeks, and there are no reservations for him on the books.

I disconnect, discouraged but far from throwing in the towel. I scan the Wikipedia entry for Pisa, but nothing grabs me. I change tack and look more into the building itself, the design, the flaw, the man who built it. But there's nothing that leads me to my dad.

Problem is, my dad is a voracious reader. He'll read anything from physics texts to pulp private-eye novels. And he never reads a book twice, because his mind's like Alcatraz—once something's in, it never gets out. All good con artists are like that. We need to be knowledgeable on a thousand different subjects in order to convince a thousand different marks of our authenticity. So my dad might have been reading up on some obscure piece of Pisa history and it didn't occur to me to notice. Or Pisa could just be a red herring.

I sigh and put down my phone, rubbing the bridge of my nose to ward off a sudden prickling in my eyes. It's just hit me—what an impossible task this is. The note could mean anything, or nothing at all. I could be looking in the exact wrong direction. He could be anywhere, waiting for me to figure it out and lead in the cavalry. But what if I don't figure it out? What if he's waiting for reinforcements that never come?

I tamp down a wave of nausea and try to rein in the fear galloping through my chest. Having a mental break is not going to do my dad any good. I count silently back from ten, forcing myself to breathe. To think. There's got to be something I'm missing. And then I look at my phone again and realize that I'm going to be missing the beginning of second period if I don't get moving.

I force myself to my feet and nod a final thanks to Mike as I head back toward campus and, more specifically, my locker. I need to switch out a couple of books before heading to my morning classes. Plus, I need to set Murphy's job in motion.

As I pass the girls' bathroom, I duck in and dig in my bag for a pocket mirror. I lean back against a sink and check the reflection of the back of my head, fluffing my hair and waiting for an opportunity to present itself.

Luckily, I don't have to wait long. A couple of girls walk in, gabbing about boys. Not surprising, really, since everyone's obsessed with the upcoming dance. Heather's one of the organizers, so she's been subjecting Sam and me to gossip about it for the last month. In any case, I can use the conversational topic to my advantage.

"Who are you going with?" Paula, a thin, reedy girl on the cheer squad with Bryn, asks Harper, a curvier girl on the dance squad.

"Matt, of course," Harper says. "You?"

"Well, I'm throwing hints at Sebastian, but he's not getting it."

"I wonder who Tyler is going to ask," Harper says, referring to the masculine object of every St. Aggie's girl's (and some of the guys') fantasies.

"And how he's going to ask," Paula says. "Jack's formal proposal to Elise last year was epic."

I clear my throat, pulling out a tube of lip gloss. "You know, Murphy still hasn't asked anyone."

"Murphy? The AV nerd?"

"Geek is the new black, you know," I say, hiding a smirk behind the applicator brush. "Besides"—I lower my voice to conspiratorial—"I hear he's the envy of the guys' locker room, if you know what I mean." Then I stow the gloss, leave the bathroom, and meander to my nearby locker.

While I twirl the locker dial this way and that, I notice

the girls from the bathroom passing by, heads bent together. They are no doubt dissecting my comment from every possible angle. I can't help but smile—easy as selling candy to a PTA mom.

Then I notice something off about my locker. It smells funny, like wet alley trash. I pull up the metal latch and swing the door open slowly.

A girl behind me screams.

THE WARNING

"You really have no idea who would have done this?"

Susan Porter, St. Agatha's bulldog dean of students, is glaring suspiciously at me as she calls the janitor on her walkie. I keep my snark in check, but it isn't easy. My relationship with the dean isn't what you'd call amicable.

"I really don't," I say. I'm not great with authority. Especially when that authority is on to me. "I certainly didn't put a dead rat in my own locker."

Her expression tightens, and since her features are already sharp enough to cut, the effect easily cows the more naive students. She's wasting it on me, but I suspect it's not something she can turn on and off. Her face just looks that way when she's aggravated, and she's almost always aggravated. Don't get me wrong; she's great at her job. She somehow manages to keep twelve hundred or so teens from outright revolt without getting so much as a strand of her titian bob out of place. And she's perpetually suspicious of me, so she must be doing something right.

She scribbles something in a Moleskine notebook with a tiny pencil, both of which she carries in her navy-blue suit-jacket pocket. I'm sure whatever she's noting is going straight into my file. The dean's been on my case almost since I started at St. Agatha's. She can't have anything substantial against me or she'd have used it by now, but her ability to sense the criminal element is uncanny. I have yet to get a connection to the dean's office, but when I do, I'm going to prioritize pilfering said file.

"Rest assured, Miss Dupree, that I will find the culprit," she says, and stalks off.

It sounds more like a threat than a promise, but I'll take what I can get. If it's a student prank, she'll find out. If not . . .

The janitor arrives, and I move out of his way to give him full access to my gore-covered locker. I try not to watch as he wraps the furry corpse in a piece of brown butcher paper before detaching its tail from the coat hook. I'm not really an animal person, but I still feel sorry for the little guy.

The puddle of guts on the floor of the locker is going to take the janitor longer to clean, so I decide to give up on my books. I turn to head for class and run smack into a hard, warm pillar.

"Are you all right?" asks the pillar.

I step back in surprise and look up, immediately recognizing Tyler Richland, the St. Aggie's demigod/senior Harper name-dropped in the bathroom. He's captain of the fill-in-any-sport-here varsity team, he's popular, and he has a hotness factor that approaches solar levels. You don't go to St. Agatha's and not know Tyler Richland. In fact, you don't live in Chicago and not know Tyler Richland. His dad's a senator.

"Fine," I say, and move to go around him.

"I meant about your locker. You must be pretty shaken up."

I frown at him. I don't like people telling me how I should feel. And it's weird that he's talking to me at all. I'm a sophomore, on top of which I've gone to a lot of trouble to stay relatively anonymous. But then, maybe he has a job for me.

"I'd be shaken up," he continues, turning his charm up a couple of notches. "I'd probably faint."

"I suppose it's not the nicest present someone's ever left me," I say. My chilliness is starting to thaw under the onslaught; that's how powerful those molten-chocolate eyes are. But I am nothing if not professional, so I keep my expression neutral.

"Do you know what it's about?"

"I have an inkling," I admit, thinking about my trashed apartment. Coincidences are like unicorns—you can believe in them all you want, but that doesn't make them real.

"Why didn't you tell the dean?"

"Because it's none of her business." I start again in the direction of class. Tyler slides into step next to me. "Can I help you, Tyler?"

"I think I may have seen something."

I nearly trip over my own foot. "What? Who?"

"I only saw him from the back. Long black coat, black boots. He didn't look like he belonged here."

"Do you think you'd recognize him if you saw him again?"

"Honestly, I don't know. Maybe."

"Why didn't you say anything to the dean?"

"I was about to, but it seemed like you didn't want her involved. I won't tell her what I saw if you don't want me to."

"That's weirdly thoughtful of you," I say. "Why so chivalrous?"

He shrugs and smiles. "It's what I would want. Besides, I'd hate to be on your bad side. It looked like you were on the verge of going for her jugular."

"That is possibly true," I say with a half smile. "So, yeah, if you could keep what you saw between us, I'd be grateful."

"Grateful enough to clue me in?"

I study his face, trying to make out the reason for his interest. Simple curiosity? Concern for my, or his, safety? Something else? I do see concern, but I'm more worried about the curiosity.

"It's too dangerous."

Wait, what did I just say? Crap! I meant to say "it's nothing" or "just a prank" or anything else that would put him off. Not "it's freaking dangerous and you should definitely be interested now." Is some errant part of my psycho-girl psyche trying to show off for him? *Without permission?* I mentally smack that part of me back in line. Unfortunately, it's not in time to avoid piquing Tyler's curiosity even more.

"Really?" he says. Yep, definitely more interested. "Well, if it's too dangerous for me, it's certainly too dangerous for you."

I glare at him, though it's hardly his fault that some ridiculous pubescent impulse hijacked my mouth.

"Maybe I should tell the dean," he says. His expression reads as cagey. He might not have any intention of telling the dean, but then he steps back a pace or two like he's going to make good on his threat.

"Wait," I say, and then change my mind. "Maybe I don't care that much if you tell the dean."

"If that were true, you wouldn't have asked me to wait."

Ugh, what is wrong with me today? Maybe the rat spooked me more than I thought. Or it's hormones. Stupid fear-triggered hormones! My dad's out there. And there are dead rats in my locker. I do not want a rookie, cute or otherwise, underfoot. But the last thing I need is to have the dean breathing down my neck.

"Look, I appreciate your concern, Tyler, but I can handle it."

He bends his head closer to mine. "You shouldn't have to. At least, not without help."

There's something unreadable in Tyler's expression, which bugs me. People are generally open books. You can tell what their motivations are in a single exchange, if you know what to listen for. That said, I'm used to being the pursuer, not the target.

"Do you even know my name?" I ask.

"What does that have to do with accepting my help?"

"It has to do with me trying to figure you out. Why are you so insistent on helping me?"

He doesn't answer right away, but it's not because he doesn't have an answer. I can see it there, hovering just behind his eyes.

"Honestly?"

"Yes, please."

"This is going to sound kind of strange, but . . ." He pauses, and . . . blushes? Really? There's only a hint of pink, but it's definitely there, on his perfectly sculpted cheekbones. "You didn't scream."

"I didn't scream?"

"When you saw the rat."

I struggle and fail to come up with why this is a compelling reason to want to help me. Not just want to, but *really* want to. Enough that he's blackmailing me for the privilege.

My doubt must be evident on my face, because he continues his explanation. "There's something about you. Something different." His eyes linger on mine too long. "I want to find out what it is."

Okay, that's unusual. As is the way my heartbeat stumbles when he says it.

"I don't need help," I say, and swallow. It's a losing battle at this point, but so was the Alamo.

"Not even from someone who can potentially ID the guy?"

"You haven't given me any reason to trust you," I say.

"I haven't given you any reason not to, have I?" he says.

I remain skeptical, but he does have a point.

"Besides," he says, softening his tone. "If something like that happened to my sister and some guy could help her out and didn't, I'd have a problem with that."

And my insides have officially melted. For those of you keeping score at home, that's game, set, and match to Tyler. My inner grifter throws her hands up in disgust.

"What exactly did you have in mind?"

"Meet me tomorrow at the Ballou? I can ask my wide receiver to sketch the guy in the black coat. His senior project is figure drawing."

"What time?" I ask.

"Four?"

I nod reluctantly. His smile widens, flashing his blindingly white teeth. The late bell rings and students scramble into classrooms.

"See you tomorrow, then," he says with a wink. "Julep."

• • •

"It's time to call the cops."

Around five o'clock the Ballou rapidly loses patronage. St. Aggie's folks have, for the most part, all shuffled home for dinner and family game night and the perpetual gloating that comes with the extremities of privilege. No one else in the surrounding community seems to need overpriced, froufrou stimulants, or at least, not of the coffee variety. My own coffee was legitimately purchased this time—by Sam, but it counts.

"So you said." I roll my eyes at Sam over his double-chocolate-hold-the-whip mocha. "But we both know why I'm not going to. It was just a rat, Sam."

"Yeah, now. But what happens when you ignore the warning? You have to assume the worst."

"Whoever's behind the redecorating of my apartment can't possibly know about my dad's note." I lower my voice in the unlikely event someone is around to hear us. My new friend Barista Mike is the nearest human, but he's wiping down the bar and seems lost in his own thoughts.

Sam leans forward, lowering his voice to match mine. "They apparently don't need to know about it to think you have something they want."

"What if they're just trying to keep me quiet rather than trying to get something from me?"

"It doesn't matter why they're harassing you. It just needs to stop."

"It does matter if I intend to stop them myself. If I can figure out what they want, I might be able to find out who they are."

"Find out who who is?" Heather Stratton slides into the seat between me and Sam at the small wooden table. "Are you talking about the rat thing? Paula filled me in. She said Rachelle had a fit."

Rachelle must have been the one who screamed. Figures. She's always such a drama queen.

"It was more of a surprised squeak," I say, taking a sip of my coffee. Bleh—hazelnut. Barista Mike is still on the steep syrups learning curve, apparently.

"Do you know who did it?" she asks in full gossip mode.

It's clear she thinks our business relationship gives her a backstage pass to Team Julep, which would be annoying if I actually knew anything. Since I don't, it's merely amusing.

"No," I say.

Sam gives me a meaningful look, which Heather correctly interprets to mean that I'm holding out on her. I'd say he's getting sloppy, except I think he's done it on purpose.

"But you know why it was put there?" Heather leans forward.

"Just a prank," I say, adopting the defense I should have used with Tyler.

"Pfft." She waves a hand. "Val said Tyler saw the guy who put it in your locker."

Fabulous. Valerie Updike, Heather's BFF, is only the world's most proficient gossip. I would know, since I've used it to my advantage a time or two. So much for keeping it between us.

"Tyler?" Sam says. "Tyler who?"

"Tyler Richland. Jeez, Sam," Heather says.

"Yeah, jeez, Sam," I repeat, smiling.

"Julep's going to have Tyler identify the guy in a lineup or something."

I refrain from banging my head on the table. It would only draw more attention to this fiasco of a conversation.

"I'm not putting anyone in a lineup, and I'm not calling any cops, Sam, so just forget it."

Sam, who opened his mouth to interject the bit about calling the cops again, closes it in favor of a reproving frown.

"What I am going to do is track down our homicidal Pied Piper of Hamlin and tie what's left of the rat carcass around his neck."

They both stare at me like I've gone nuclear, but I've had it with the peanut gallery for the day.

"And how do you plan to do that, exactly?" Sam's the first to recover because he knows me best. He knows I don't bite. Usually.

"Tyler's going to give me whatever he can on rat boy, and I'm just going to . . . keep digging, I guess." I don't want to mention my dad's note with Heather sitting right here, and Sam knows better than to bring it up.

Heather looks disappointed, but I'm not responsible for entertaining her, just defrauding her mom.

"Don't you have somewhere you need to be?" I ask.

"Not really, no."

We study each other in silence for a moment.

"Why not?"

"I have an appointment with the dean in half an hour."

I freeze, alarmed. But after taking a breath, I realize the dean can't possibly know what's going on with Heather's NYU scam. It doesn't involve the school in any way.

"What for?"

"I'm interviewing for the student-assistant position. My mom insists it will beef up my NYU admissions profile." She huffs and twists a long, maple-colored curl around her finger. "I wish I could tell her that I'm guaranteed to get in."

"Don't even think it," I say, suddenly nervous for a whole different reason. "Early decision doesn't go out for another four months."

"I know," she says, annoyed, like she's the one who told me in the first place. "I'm not going to blow it."

"Good."

"So I'm stuck with this dean interview, hoping like hell I don't get the job."

Then it hits me—the gift-wrapped opportunity I'm being handed here.

"Yes," I say quickly, finally warming to the conversation. "I mean, yes, take the job. It's perfect."

"Uh . . . am I missing something?" Heather says.

"I'm calling in my favor."

• • •

Later that evening, I let myself into my apartment. I keep my eyes downcast as I cross the room and drop my bag onto a kitchen chair. I'm afraid that if I put my bag on the floor, the mess will swallow it whole.

I start clearing the kitchen, putting chipped dishes back in the cabinets, throwing the shards of broken plates in the newly scooped and bagged garbage. I mop twice to get rid of the congealed-chicken smell.

Sam offered to hang out at home with me when his attempts to cajole me into staying at his place again failed. It was sweet of him to offer. Also unnecessary. It's just a bunch of stuff strewn around an empty room. It doesn't mean anything.

Yeah, yeah, I know. I don't think he bought it, either. But bagging the remains of one's broken life is sort of a solo endeavor.

As I trash the gutted chair stuffing, I run down a mental list of costs: rent, utilities, tuition, food . . . All of it adds up to well over what I make conning for rich kids. I need a new angle. Something that will keep me afloat until my dad gets back. Something I can work in my off hours that rakes in enough money to cover costs. Something low-profile, steady, and easy to maintain. Something different.

An idea strikes me, and I take a break from cleaning to go on a hunt for my dad's ID-forgery equipment. I unearth the printer from beneath an avalanche of books. The diffractive film and lamination pouches are on the floor of the bathroom, for no discernible reason. The laminator is upside down behind the laundry basket. The camera is nowhere to be found, though that is hardly surprising. I can use my phone's camera, anyway.

What I'm talking about is making—and, more important, selling—the one thing every teenager under the age of twenty-one would give their eyeteeth for: a grade-A, on-the-level, better-than-bona-fide fake ID. At a hundred bucks a pop, I could make a significant amount of cash in a small amount of time. Not enough, but, you know, every little bit helps.

I take a break from forgery planning and head back to the kitchen. I pick up my bag from the chair and sink into it, setting the bag in my lap. The ID job is a good idea, but it doesn't get me any closer to finding my dad. I wrestle with the doubt that's been dogging my heels all day, but my gut tells me that nothing I've considered so far is even close.

I scroll through my phone contacts list to Sam's name. I'm about to push the Call button, if for no other reason than to listen to him tell me about his latest *StarDrive* victory—anything to distract me from the darkness creeping out from the corners of the room—when just above Sam's name, I see Ralph's. My dad's bookie. If anyone would know about my dad's "field of miracles," it would be Ralph. And just like that, everything clicks into place.

Field. Miracles.

I jump up, dumping my bag on the floor. The racetrack. That must be it. I have to talk to Ralph. I call his number, but it's the store, and his voice mail picks up. He must already be home for the night. I'll have to go see him tomorrow after school. But finally—a win in the Julep column.

I feel like celebrating, so I go in search of the coffeemaker. Nothing says victory like late-night java. Besides, I have three chapters of reading for AP lit, a section review on quadratic equations for pre-calc, and a five-page French paper due by—I check the syllabus on my phone—the end of the week. Looks like it's going to be another all-nighter.

I rescue the coffeepot from under my bed, untangling the curtain from the broken lamp in the process. But as I pivot away from the window, something catches my eye. Or rather, some*one*.

My window has a street view, and there are quite a few people on the sidewalk. But there's only one person staring up at my window. One person in a long black coat with black boots and light hair. One person leaning against a black Chevelle with white racing stripes, the same Chevelle I saw parked outside the Ballou yesterday. One person who has definitely noticed me noticing him, broken lamp or no.

I race out of my apartment and fly down the stairs and out of the building just in time to see the Chevelle's taillights disappear around a corner. The roar of the engine drowns out the rest of the street noise for half a minute as my stalker accelerates through all five gears and cruises out of sight with all my answers.

THE ID JOB

"Julep, what did you do?"

Sam slides his lunch tray onto the table and sits down facing me. The rows of highly polished oak tables don't allow for much in the way of private conversation, but Sam and I tend to tuck ourselves on the outskirts of the sophomore row, almost under the mantel of the gigantic fireplace on the far end of the dining hall.

I stare at my tray with contempt, pushing at the mound of shapeless pasta slop with a fork. "I made the profound mistake of choosing the lasagna."

"I mean about Murphy. The poor kid has a permanent red face, and all the girls are staring at his crotch."

"Oh, that." I sniff at my plate and make a face. At least I managed to finagle another free latte from my good buddy

Barista Mike—too much vanilla this time, but free. "I got him a date to the formal."

"You mean you got him every date to the formal. You'd better hope he doesn't get Dumpstered by the end of the day, or he might demand a refund."

"Once you give him his geek-chic makeover, he'll be good to go. You're meeting up with him after school, right?"

"I still don't know what you want me to do. I don't know anything more about fashion than you."

"Yeah, but you manage to get to school looking better than an unmade bed, and that's what we're going for. Just glam him up enough to pass."

Sam sighs. "All right. We'll ditch seventh and go to the mall."

"Great." I give up on the lasagna and fish around in the salad instead for a piece of lettuce that isn't too wilty. "I'm having coffee with Tyler, so we can meet up after that to—"

"What?" Sam interrupts. "Why are you having coffee with Tyler?"

"To get a better description of what he saw." I find and spear a likely-looking tomato.

"Didn't he say he only saw the guy from the back?"

"Yep," I say. "But he wants to help."

I chew on both the tomato and the thought. With time and space, it seems weird to me that Tyler was so insistent. In the moment, it made sense to agree to meet him. But now that I'm telling Sam about it, I realize how thin Tyler's argument was, and how ridiculous I sound now repeating it.

"I think he wants something," I add.

"Like what?" Sam lowers his fork, his expression disapproving.

"I don't know, Sam. I'll find out when I have coffee with him. Maybe he has a job for me."

"Another job? I don't think it's a good idea to take on another job right now."

"What do you mean?"

"If it's for a job, you should just blow him off."

"I'm not blowing him off. Look, this job thing is important. You'd better not be telling people I'm on hiatus."

"I haven't been telling anybody anything, but you can't do everything, Julep. You're supposed to be going to school—not fixing everybody's problems so you can pay the rent. And why not? Blow off Tyler, I mean."

"Because he may know something important. And if I don't pay the rent, I'll lose the apartment. Without the apartment, I'm a sitting duck for foster care. Plus, I pay tuition by the semester. I owe the balance for the year in a month."

"We can find a way to fudge the records—"

"No," I say with more force than I mean to. After a breath, I continue more calmly. "No." I need St. Aggie's to get to Yale. I won't base my new life on a lie from the old one. At least, not directly.

"Then I'll get you the money. Or I'll have my dad talk to the president. And anyway, what could Tyler want with you if not your services?"

Okay, that is just offensive. "I don't know, Sam. Maybe it's all part of some diabolical plot to get me expelled. And the hell you will. I'm not a homeless dachshund or something."

"None of that is what I meant. I'm just trying to help. And I'm not saying Tyler is a bad guy. I guess I'm just surprised."

"Well, thanks, but I don't need that kind of help." I chomp a carrot that utterly fails in the crunch department. "And I'm not saying Tyler is a good guy. I just need to find out what he knows. End of romance."

Sam manages to keep his mouth shut under my acid glare. He knows when he's stepped in it, and he knows when to back out quietly. After a few minutes of furious nibbling, I relent and decide to keep talking to him.

"So I had a thought."

"Why do I always get nervous when you say things like that?"

"Can you at least hear me out before you start with the negativity?"

He shoots me a flat look.

"I was thinking about getting into a little forgery," I say, ignoring his insolence. It's so hard to find good minions these days.

"That's not really your style," he says, tipping his chair onto its back legs and crossing his arms.

"True. But it's a regular inflow of cash, which I kind of need at the moment."

"Is it worth the risk? You could get into real trouble for this—not just school trouble."

"I need the money, Sam."

"I know," he says finally. "But I don't have to like it."

Before I can respond, someone's shadow falls across our table. An enraged Murphy is looming over me.

"Julep, what the hell did you do?"

• • •

After ditching my lunch tray, I liberate a few pastries from the teachers' lounge and head to the computer lab. Or rather, the room that passes for a computer lab at St. Aggie's.

It's not that there aren't computers. There are. Rows and rows of them. But the decor makes the room look less like a lab and more like a French bordello. Red velvet drapes and lush Victorian armchairs make the clean, sleek lines of the screens and wireless keyboards seem unusually sharp.

Ms. Shirley, the pixie-spinster computer science teacher, doesn't bother acknowledging my entrance. I'm only a minute or two late. If she noted everyone who arrived less than five minutes late, we'd all have failed from lax attendance in less than a month.

A few students squeak in behind me and scurry to empty seats, slinging their designer backpacks onto their chair backs. Some of them pull out notebooks, as if they actually intend to take notes rather than surf celebrity websites.

Don't worry. I'm not stupid enough to conduct any incriminating business on a school computer. That's why god invented smartphones. I whip out mine and open a new email.

Subject: Driver's License
From: JulieCarew96@xmail.com
To: JulieCarew96@xmail.com
BCC: 12 recipients

Good news! I found your driver's license. You must
have dropped it when you were at band practice
yesterday. I'll leave it in your locker and you can pick it
up next week. Just leave me a finder's fee of $100. ;-)
Remember to email me with your info for the group
project. Have a great time in the Hamptons!

If I've lost you, let me break it down. The twelve recipients
I've blind-copied are representatives of St. Aggie's criminal
element—drug dealers, hackers, truants, thrill seekers, party
animals, and instigators.

The message isn't exactly in code, because you really don't
have to take it that far. The recipients know enough to recognize my alias email address by now. And if that isn't enough to
clue them in, the "Good news!" opener is a mutually agreed-
upon signal that the message has a hidden agenda. The rest is
decipherable enough, if you know to look for something.

The only other part that's in code is the reference to the
Hamptons. That's what we St. Aggie's crooks call the rest of
the students. My reference to the Hamptons will, I hope, clue
the guys in that I want them to spread the word to their entou-
rages, customers, and classmates.

That task done, I send a quick text to Heather, asking her
to meet me in the music room after sixth period. There are no

classes there for seventh, so we'll have the room to ourselves. I want to find out if she got the job with the dean. Plus, it gives me the chance to plant the marker for where to drop the cash.

"Dupree?"

Ms. Shirley is frowning at me through the bedazzled black frames of her reading glasses.

"Putting it away now, Ms. Shirley. Just checking the stock market."

One of Ms. Shirley's weaknesses is her obsession with the health of her investment portfolio. Her right elbow twitches as she considers going for her own phone. But she places her hands with purpose on her keyboard instead.

I slide the mouse around for effect, as if I've just been finishing up the CSS web-design project that's due. Since Sam taught me CSS in middle school, I had my project done a week ago.

After sixth, Heather is waiting for me just inside the music classroom.

"I got the job. Apparently, I was the only idiot who applied. I know you're shocked," she says.

"Congratulations," I say as I draw a small star on a cabinet in the corner. "I had every faith in you."

"I also got what you wanted," she says, pulling a thick manila folder from her bag and handing it to me.

"This is a copy, right?" I ask, noting the absence of a name on the folder's tab. Good girl.

"I do know how to work a copy machine." She tosses her head like an offended filly. "And what's with the graffiti?"

I smile at her as I slide the folder into my bag. "It's a drop-box. For payment."

"What do you need a drop-box for? Don't people just hand you cash?"

"This is for a higher-volume gig. I think the dean might get suspicious if students start flagging me down in front of god and everybody."

"And it won't be suspicious if those students start loitering around the music room?"

"You and I are loitering in the music room, aren't we? Besides, it's all about plausible deniability. Worse comes to worst and the dean finds the drop-box, I'm out a couple hundred bucks. But she catches me with a bag full of black-market merchandise, I get a one-way ticket to public school."

"What black-market merchandise?"

"You'll find out soon enough. Now, about your next assignment."

"I already paid you my favor!"

My smile turns wicked. "This is less a favor and more a performance opportunity."

She considers me for a second before responding. "I'm listening."

As I outline her new role, her expression morphs from mildly irritated to amused.

"All right," she says. "But you can't tell him it's coming."

"I wouldn't dream of it."

I check the lock on the cabinet. Easily pickable, but sturdy enough. Plus, there's still the thick layer of undisturbed dust I discovered last year when I needed to stash a phone I'd filched for another job. Mr. Beauford, the music teacher, is older than Methuselah and legally blind in at least one eye, so this is as safe a place as any. And it has a handy slot on the front.

"So have you gotten your dress yet?" Heather asks.

"You mean for the dance I'm not going to?"

"Why aren't you going?" Her face shows sincere puzzlement, as if bypassing the social event of the season is simply beyond her comprehension.

I'd normally go. I'm not averse to spending an evening floating in a sea of flounce and frippery. A lot of drama goes down at school functions, providing both free entertainment and potential new clients.

"I've got a lot on my plate and not much in the way of a costume."

She rolls her eyes at me. "Cop-out."

"You're right—it is. But it also happens to be true."

"Suit yourself." She shrugs dismissively.

I move toward the half-closed door. "We'd better get a move on if we want to make it to class before the—"

As I pull the door in, the dean appears, framed in the doorway and wearing a smile like a cat that's gotten into the cream.

"Trading secrets, ladies?"

I open my mouth to lie, but she holds up her perfectly manicured hand.

"I'd rather hear from Heather. She is my assistant, after all."

I silently will Heather to rat me out over something minor to preserve the dean's trust in her. But the chances she'll receive the message are slim, as telepathy only works in the movies, and the odds are even slimmer that she'll figure it out herself since she's not a player. And sure enough . . .

"We were looking for music. For the dance."

Not what I was hoping for, but I can work with it.

"I highly doubt the dance committee is going to approve the marching band for its entertainment."

I leap in before the dean can stop me. "The theme is 'Swing in Space' "—that part is actually true; don't ask me who came up with it, or why—"and we were hoping Mr. Beauford could recommend period-appropriate music."

The dean narrows her eyes at me. "So if I were to look in your bag, I would find a list of this 'period-appropriate music'?"

"We missed him," I say, smothering a spike of anxiety. If she finds that file in my bag, both Heather and I are toast.

"Then I suppose I won't find anything but schoolbooks." Her grin widens from tabby cat to tiger shark.

She seriously has some kind of sixth sense when it comes to rule-breaking. There's no reason for her to suspect there's anything in my bag. In fact, she probably suspects something totally different from what she'll find—unless she's been standing here the whole time, listening to our conversation.

"Open it," she says.

One thing any con worth his salt will tell you is that it's always a good idea to know the laws you're breaking, though not for the reason you might think. The laws themselves will tell you how far the people in power can go to catch you, when you can clam up and demand a lawyer, when you can plead the fifth, that sort of thing. So yes, I've read the student handbook—memorized it, even. And unfortunately for me, according to ordinance 33, section F, the dean is well within her rights to search me.

In other words, we're screwed.

"Dean Porter, you're looking lovely today, as always."

Tyler Richland, knight in shining armor, strides out from behind the dean. I didn't even hear him approach, which just shows how off-kilter I am about the stolen file.

The dean's smirk turns sour with irritation as she turns to address Tyler. "The late bell is about to ring, Mr. Richland. Shouldn't you be in class?"

"I was on my way there when I saw you," he says smoothly. "My father asked me to tell you that he really appreciated your campaign contribution."

The way Tyler emphasized the word *father* with a small pause afterward distracts the dean from her objective.

"He did?" she says, then clears her throat. "I mean, of course. I think his voting record is impeccable, and I'd like to see what he can contribute next term." She flicks a sharp look at me.

"He's hoping you'll call him so he can thank you personally," Tyler says, flashing a smile.

I'm intrigued. He seems to have a knack for the tale. I try to place why his style strikes me as familiar, and then I remember seeing his dad on TV. I'd never thought to equate politics to grifting before, but the comparison seems apt. Especially now, watching the way Tyler is playing the dean.

"I—well, I—" The dean's hands flutter as if she doesn't know quite what to do with them. "I mean, yes. I'll do that."

Then she flits off as if she never meant to check my bag. I wait till she's rounded a corner before relaxing. Heather levels a death glare at me and hustles down the hall to her own class.

Tyler, on the other hand, seems happy to see me. His smile transforms from smooth to sincere when his gaze catches mine. Seeing the contrast between the two smiles is an unexpected bonus. It helps me get a better handle on him. If it's this easy to tell when he's working an angle and when he's not, then I'll have more warning if he tries something on me.

Not that I think he will try something. There's no motive, for one thing. He may be the hottest thing to happen to the female population since hair product, but he's still just a student at St. Agatha's. He'll no doubt be someone important someday, but right now he's just a pair of amazing brown eyes and a tight— Um, well, you get the idea.

"That should give you time to hide whatever it is you don't want the dean to see," he says.

Okay, an observant pair of amazing brown eyes.

"Is it that obvious?"

"It is to the dean, which makes it obvious to everyone."

"Fabulous."

He laughs. "Don't worry. It'll take her at least an hour to get ahold of my dad."

I lean against the doorframe, frowning at him. Despite my

newfound and grudging respect for his skill, I'm still irritated about his spilling the beans to Valerie about the rat.

"So you're following me now?"

He points at a nearby classroom filling with students. "I have Grosky for Spanish seventh period. And yes, I am following you."

Cute. I make a mental note to have Sam download Tyler's class schedule. Just because there's no reason for Tyler to lie to me doesn't mean I shouldn't check.

"How did you know the dean has a thing for your dad?"

"She uses every imaginable excuse to call him personally. She goes out of her way to ask me how he's doing. She almost swooned when he complimented her suit at last year's fundraiser. It wasn't hard to figure out."

"Well, I'm impressed. I'd never have guessed she had the capacity for a crush. And you not only read her right but used it to your—well, my—advantage. I hate to say this, but I owe you one, cowboy."

"You'll owe me two when I help you catch the guy who put the rat in your locker."

"About that," I say, crossing my arms. "I'm miffed that you told Val when I asked you to keep it between us."

He shakes his head. "I didn't tell her. She was there when I saw him."

"She saw him, too?" Maybe my secret admirer isn't really all that secret.

"No. He'd just left when she came up to me. She asked what I was looking at, and I told her someone put something in a locker and took off. I didn't think anything more of it until you opened the locker and Rachelle screamed. Val must have put two and two together."

I scan his features, using my new knowledge of his tells to determine whether he's playing me like he played the dean. My gut says no—that about this, at least, he's being truthful. Still, my reaction to him is troubling.

"I told you I wouldn't tell, and I won't," he says, his voice soft, as if he's trying to coax a feral kitten from a sewer.

I gaze at him a beat too long and then break eye contact, laughing softly at myself. "You're good."

"Am I?" he says, his smile back.

The late bell rings, jarring us both out of whatever we've stumbled into. I feel flushed all of a sudden.

"*¿Quién necesita español?*" Tyler says. "Let's just go. I'm buying."

"Actually," I say, regretting the decision even as I'm making it, "I think I'll pass on coffee."

He looks disappointed.

"I have something else in mind," I say.

"Like what?"

"Like a trip to Chinatown. You in?"

THE BOOKIE

Tyler has a shiny silver sports car—an Audi R8, to be exact. With fine Nappa leather that my petty-criminal butt has no business sitting on. The word *aerodynamic* is an insult to this car's sleek, almond-shaped carapace. It looks more like a rocket ship than a car, which is why my knees are hugging the gearshift and I'm leaning toward the middle as Tyler guides it around turns at speeds that would make a Formula 1 driver sweat. I shouldn't complain, though. Tyler volunteered to drive since I lack a car and Sam's was unavailable.

Speaking of Sam, he's going to burst a diode when he finds out I'm taking Tyler to see Ralph. Not that I blame him. I've really gone off the rails on this one. And what's worse is that I have no idea why. This isn't a game. The people who trashed my apartment are not in it for laughs. If I'm really going up against them, and it seems from this trip to Ralph's that I am, then I have no right involving civilians. Especially this particular civilian. One whiff of scandal and his father could very well lose the upcoming election. Tyler certainly wouldn't thank me for getting his pretty R8 repossessed.

So why am I involving him?

I grit my teeth and grip the door handle as my internal organs are left on the sidewalk across the street when Tyler rounds another corner.

"Where am I taking you again?" Tyler asks, breaking through my rambling thoughts.

"To see Ralph, my dad's book—er, friend," I say, coughing to cover the slip. It's not that I think Tyler would tell. It's just not my secret to share.

Which brings me back to wondering why I'm sharing my own secrets with Tyler. I'm not exactly reticent, but I do tend to keep to myself. He's explained his interest. He's kept the secret I asked him to. He's even stuck his neck out to save me from the dean, or at least from my own stupidity in getting caught, and proven he has some natural talent in the grifting department. He could be—already has been, in fact—a real asset.

What makes me nervous is that I have no idea what he'll ask for in return. I deal in favors all the time, but it always goes both ways. You don't get something for nothing. Not in life, and certainly not in this business. Tyler seems content to just be along for the ride. But Sam's question, though insulting, raised a fair point: if Tyler doesn't want my services, what *does* he want? Until he asks for something, I'm stuck waiting for the other shoe to drop. Unless I kick him to the curb, which, I'll admit, I'm reluctant to do for all the reasons I listed, and for some I didn't—eyes and hair and general dreaminess are not valid reasons.

"I take it you're not a fan?" Tyler says.

"What?" I blink.

"This guy we're going to meet. You don't seem excited to see him."

"Ralph's fine," I assure him. "He's a good family friend."

"Then what is it?" He downshifts and rolls to a stop at a red light.

"What is what?"

"You're thinking hard about something." He reaches over and gently touches my face. "You get a small line next to your nose when you're concentrating."

I touch the spot he touched between my nose and my left cheekbone, knocking his hand in the process. I can't decide if it's adorable or alarming that he's trying to read me.

"Nothing," I say. "The Cubs' chances at making the playoffs."

The light turns green, and the R8 streaks off the line without a sound.

"I get that you don't trust me. I just wish I knew what I could say to change your mind."

Go back in time and show some interest in me before someone threw a rat in my locker.

"I am already trusting you far more than I should," I say

instead. "That's what I was thinking about—that I shouldn't be in this car right now, that I should be going to see Ralph on my own."

He's silent for a moment, turning this over. "I know it doesn't mean anything, really, but I want you to know that I trust you."

"Why?" I ask, exasperated. "You don't know anything about me."

"I don't have to. I just . . . feel like I can trust you." He seems uncertain, like he's afraid he's not explaining it right, or afraid of my reaction, maybe. He steals a glance at me.

"Well, it's easy to trust the victim," I say. "But thank you. I guess."

He smiles, relieved. "Is there something you can tell me while I'm still in the process of proving myself?"

"That depends. What do you want to know?" I say.

"More about you. Where do you come from? Why does everyone think you're a thief?"

I laugh. "I prefer the term *fixer*. And I come from all over. We moved a lot when I was younger."

"So you're not a Chicago native," he says. "That explains a lot."

"Does it?" I raise my eyebrow at him. He doesn't see it, because I can only raise my right eyebrow. It's a failing. I'm working on it.

"You're different. Somehow less breakable."

I'm surprised and kind of pleased by the observation. It's an odd compliment, perhaps, but I'll take it.

"Takes more than wind to knock me over, I suppose."

"It feels sometimes like the people who grow up here take the wind for granted." He frowns.

"What does that say about you?" I ask. "You're from one of the founding families, aren't you?"

He concentrates on driving instead of answering. Normally, I wouldn't care if I alienated him. He's not my mark, so I don't need to lead him around by the nose. But something in me twists a little at the thought that I may have hurt his feelings.

"I'm sorry," I say into the silence. The words feel foreign and heavy on my tongue, and I realize that I haven't apologized for anything in a long time.

"Nothing to be sorry for," he says. "You're right. I'm about as native as they get." He doesn't make it sound like a good thing. "Tell me how you got here."

"We moved from Atlanta when I was eight. Before that we lived in Tucson. Before that, Seattle, San Diego, Denver, and, randomly, Mount Vernon, a tiny town in Maine."

"Was your dad in the military or something?"

"No." And before he can ask me anything else, I move the topic to safer waters. "My mom left us after Atlanta. Just didn't come back one day. And my dad decided to settle down for a while so I could go to a good school."

I could tell him more. I could tell him that my dad actually settled down to teach me the family business, that he wanted me to go to a good school so I could learn to fit in with the haves as well as the have-nots. Instead I focus on the unimportant. It's all about distraction, sleight of hand. Don't look at this; look at this shiny thing I have over here.

"I'm sorry," he says. "I didn't know about your mom."

"Nothing to be sorry for." I echo his words back to him with a smile.

Before he can ask any more potentially incriminating questions, we pull into a parking space outside Ralph's shop. I don't wait for Tyler, though he's only a step or two behind me. Chimes tinkle merrily as I push open the door.

Now, you've probably made some assumptions about Ralph. You're probably thinking potbellied, balding man in his fifties, perpetually holding an unlit cigar, shirt collar open at the neck to reveal an abundance of chest hair and a penchant for gold chains. You're also probably thinking his establishment is a seedy bar stinking of booze, broads, and billiards. At the very least, you're probably imagining a cigar shop or liquor store with a fine layer of filth along the floorboards. Maybe even an accountant's office, if you're versed in the profession.

But none of these things could be further from the truth. Well, the balding thing is accurate, actually. In all other respects, though, Ralph is not at all what you'd picture a bookie to look like. He's a short Korean man in his midsixties. He's affable and slightly shy, bighearted and super smart. He works numbers the way my dad works marks.

His shop is a musty Asian oddities and antiques store on the eastern edge of Chinatown. As Tyler and I walk through the maze of shelves and displays filled with segmented metal koi, intricately knotted red silk cords, and kimono-inspired pajamas, I remember the first time my dad brought me here.

He'd met Ralph at a backroom poker game and had formed an instant kinship with him—strangers in a strange land, I suppose, with Ralph trying to make it as an unaffiliated bookie (meaning no mob ties) and my dad trying to make it as a small-time con rather than a high-stakes grifter.

Anyway, he'd placed a few bets with Ralph and he'd just scored a take big enough to pay him back, so he brought me to be his "wingman" for the transaction. I was nine at the time. I still cared about being my dad's wingman.

I remember studying the shelves, fascinated by everything. There was a tiny Chinese tea set painted with pale pink lilies that I practically drooled on, I wanted it so badly. I remember hearing the mixture of my dad conversing with Ralph and the tinny flute music drifting through the room and feeling oddly at peace, despite the fresh scar of my mother having disappeared without a word.

After we'd chatted with Ralph and he'd given me the tea set for free (yes, I still have it—or did before our apartment was looted), we were on our way out and I was dragging my feet because I didn't want to leave the unexpected comfort of Ralph's shop. My dad must have sensed my mood and the reason behind it, because he stopped and knelt in front of me, taking my little hands in his rough ones.

"I know I'm not your mom. I'm not a natural at this like she was," he said, his eyes the most honest I'd ever seen them. "But just hang in there with me, okay? I'll do right by you."

I remember nodding and feeling like my footing was suddenly even more precarious.

"We'll get through it together—you, me, and sixty-three."

Then he stood and patted my head, pulling me to his side for a quick squeeze. And much more than confessions of parental ineptitude, this familiar catchphrase of my father's eased my anxiety. I have no idea what it means, but he's said it enough that it's become a part of our lexicon.

"Hey." Tyler's voice brings me back to the present. "Are you okay?"

His eyes show concern, though his hands are stuffed in his pockets. Maybe he's afraid of breaking something. I set down the chopsticks I didn't realize I'd been examining during my trip down flashback lane.

"Yeah," I say, and set my path for the most direct route to the back of the store. Tyler follows, sticking close, a sort of golden-retriever presence just off to my right.

"Julep, how lucky to see you today."

Ralph steps out from behind his cash register and gives me a firm but fast hug. He looks nothing but happy to see me, which likely means he doesn't know anything about my father being missing. But then, I didn't really expect him to know. I came because if anyone would know about my dad's "field of miracles," it'd be Ralph.

"And who is new boy?"

"Ralph, this is Tyler. Tyler, Ralph—an old family friend."

"Very handsome. Is he clever as Sam?"

"I'm sure he's very clever," I say smoothly.

"Sam is building World Wild Web page for me still, yes?"

"Yes," I say. I can feel Tyler smirking. "It's World Wide Web, Ralph."

He dismisses my correction with a slightly arthritic wave. "I don't care what its name. I just need page." He looks shiftily at Tyler. "For the store."

"It should be done any day now. There's some complication with the . . . um, shopping-cart function. But Sam's got it well in hand. He'll come show you how to use it when it's ready."

"Enough shop talk," Ralph says, gesturing for us to sit down in the two silk-upholstered chairs. He pulls a battered folding chair from behind the register and joins us. Then he hands us paper cups containing lukewarm water from the water cooler and jasmine tea bags.

"How your father? I not seen him long time," Ralph says.

"Actually, that's why I'm here. He's gone."

"You mean, on trip?"

"As in, someone trashed our apartment—"

"What?" Tyler says, eyes wide. "When?"

"I'll fill you in later," I say to him, and then turn back to Ralph. "Someone was looking for him, or for something he had. I can't reach him, and he hasn't been back in two days. I was hoping . . . I was hoping you could tell me something."

Ralph mumbles something in Korean, then, "I told him not to do it."

My pulse races. Could Ralph know everything? Could it be that easy?

"Not to do what, Ralph?"

Ralph gives me a look that's half shame, half pity. "He told me not to tell you." I open my mouth to protest, but Ralph continues. "I don't know much. But I tell you what I know. Bad business."

A chill settles into my blood. For Ralph, "bad business" is code for the mob.

There are two things you need to know about the mob. The first is that mobsters hate con men. Con men tend to be loners. Mobsters tend to, well, you know, mob. Con men often infringe on a mob's self-appointed territory, and they don't really share very well. Of course, neither does the mob, so you can see the conundrum.

The second thing to know about the mob is that they have a tendency to eliminate the competition in a rather permanent way. If you get mixed up with the mob, it's like betting against a casino—sooner or later, the house wins.

My dad didn't deal with the mob, and not just because the mob wouldn't deal with him. He was first and foremost a businessman. A little on the shady side, but he knew a bad bet when he saw one, and he wasn't addicted enough to the game to make stupid mistakes. In fact, the only good thing about working for the mob was—

"How much?" I ask.

"What's going on?" Tyler jumps in. "You look like you've seen a ghost. What did I miss?"

"How much did he owe you, Ralph?" My tone is chillier than a beach bunny at the South Pole. I've never been mad at Ralph before for my dad's gambling habit, mostly because Ralph was never a brute about it, but also because it's not Ralph's fault. But if he strong-armed my dad into paying a debt . . .

"No, no. He not owe me anything. He not place bet in months."

My jaw drops. "But . . . that doesn't make sense."

"What doesn't make sense?" Tyler insists. "Can one of you please tell me what's going on?"

"Ralph is my dad's bookie, as well as his friend. I didn't tell you before because it could be dangerous for Ralph if too many of the wrong sort of people know."

"The wrong sort of people?" Tyler repeats, his expression incredulous. I can't tell if he's amused or if I've offended him.

"You know," I hedge. "Upstanding sorts. People on the Pollyanna side of the law."

He shakes his head at me, a mixture of wonder and consternation on his face.

I take a breath. I didn't want him to know all this—but then why did I bring him with me to see Ralph in the first place? His knowing became inevitable the moment I got into his car.

"Ralph thinks my dad's disappearance has to do with a job he was pulling for the mob."

"What do you mean? Why would he be working for the mob? What does your dad do?" Tyler says.

"People think I'm a thief," I remind him, leaving it to him to connect the dots.

Turning back to Ralph, I ask, "What else do you know? Do you know which mob?"

"Which mob?" Tyler says, his voice sounding strangled. "You mean there's more than one?"

I sigh. "This is not the time for Organized Crime 101. But yes. Usually grouped by nationality."

"I don't know, Julep," Ralph answers. "I only know he looking for the final score."

"This isn't like my dad at all. The final score? He got out of the big con years ago. Are you sure, Ralph?"

Ralph nods, his small frame drooping a little in his chair. Weathered and sad, he's never looked more like a shriveled apricot than he does in this moment. I want to hug him, so I hug myself.

"Do you know what the job was?"

Ralph says, "Forgery, I think."

"Any idea what they wanted him to work up?" Even knowing what my dad was faking might help.

Ralph shakes his head. "That all I know, *jang mi*."

"I think he might have left something at the racetrack for me to find," I say, taking a different tack. "Do you know where he might hide something? A room? An outbuilding?"

He shakes his head again, and I place my hand over his.

"Thanks anyway, Ralph. If you find my dad before I do, give him hell and then call me, okay?"

Ralph returns my weak smile and gives my hand a light squeeze. I set my cup on the small table separating my chair from Tyler's, tea untouched.

Tyler sets his tea down as well, taking his cue from me. Ralph gets to his feet with a little hop-shuffle and scuttles around behind his register. He comes back with a shoe box full of freshly baked Korean cookies and hands me the box with fatherly pats and admonitions to stay out of trouble. He even shakes Tyler's hand.

Then he escorts us halfway to the door before turning back to his books, mumbling again. This time it catches my attention.

"What was that?" I say, stopping in my tracks.

"What?" he asks.

"What did you just say?"

"Nothing. Some nonsense your dad say before he left last time."

"What was it?"

"Eh . . . you." Ralph points at me absently, as if thinking hard to get it right. "Me." He points at himself. "And sixty-three."

THE FIELD OF MIRACLES

The next day, Sam and I ditch school and head out to the racetrack. The weather's fairly balmy for so late in the year, which is a relief. Whatever it is we're looking for could be outside as easily as inside.

"Will you knock that off?" Sam says as I slide the window down and then back up again. It's partly for the novelty of being able to decide whether the window is open or shut. My main mode of transportation being the "L," I don't often get the choice. But it's also because it annoys him. I never said I was a good person. I open the window an inch and leave it there. Sam sighs.

"Have you thought about the fact that neither of us is twenty-one years old?" he says. Before I can respond, he continues. "What am I saying? Of course you have."

I hand him the fake driver's license I crafted for him last night.

"On the house, courtesy of Julep's Department of Motor Vehicles."

"Might as well get the practice in," he says, taking the glossy card. "I hear the real DMV hires a lot of rehabilitated cons." He glances at his new license. "Sam L. Jackson? I thought the first rule of forgery was to avoid names people will recognize."

"It is," I say. "I just couldn't resist. Besides, there's a good chance we won't need it."

"Which means there's a good chance we will."

I called Sam after Tyler's and my conversation with Ralph and told him about the mob. He was as floored as I was, but it didn't seem to occur to him to back slowly away. When I then followed up with the comment that I was prepared to go this one alone, he said I was stupid and to call him back when I'd borrowed a brain. I was happy with this response, since I'd already made him the ID.

"Do you have any idea where to start looking?" he asks.

"I'm pretty sure it has something to do with sixty-three."

"Why sixty-three?"

"It's something my dad used to say. He said it to Ralph the last time Ralph saw him, so I'm betting it's somehow related."

"You're betting?" Doubt shades his question.

"It's an educated guess."

Sam mumbles something about grifters with egos bigger than a battlestar.

"I could call Tyler and have him meet us there."

"I think we have it covered," Sam says, scowling.

I smirk at him from the passenger's seat. I have no idea why Tyler bothers him so much. It's not like we haven't worked with other people before. Once, for school spirit week, we worked with the entire JV lacrosse team.

Lucky for us and our newly minted IDs, the racetrack is actually family friendly, for the most part. The only areas off-limits to minors are the cordoned-off gaming rooms with Keno, slot machines, and smoking sections. The rest of the spacious center is open to all.

The first thing you notice when you walk into the main area are the rows and rows of posh desk cubbies complete with leather chairs, reminiscent of study carrels in a library. The rows are situated in front of a bank of twenty or so large flat-screen TVs hanging from the ceiling.

Small brass lamps light each of the miniature desks with a soft golden glow, and matching brass plates affixed to the sides of the cubbies display progressing numbers. My heart rate picks up for point-nine seconds, until I realize the numbers are all in the triple digits. There's a 163, a 263, and so on, but no plain old 63.

Sam must notice the same thing, because he asks, "Where are the tens?"

"He wouldn't have made it that easy."

"Easy?" Sam gives me a look like I've been mainlining Looney Tunes. "Easy like leaving a cryptic note that leads to nowhere? Easy like getting involved with you-know-what in the first place?"

"If I'm right and he's leading me to something, he'd make it as hard as he could in case someone else was on the same trail. Come on, Sam. You know my dad."

Sam swipes his fingers across his phone at tachyon speed.

"We could check the banks of electronic betting machines. They might be numbered. Also, Trackjunkie953 suggests looking for numbers in the box seats."

"Where are they?" I ask.

If you're worried that Sam's Web connections could give us away to the mob, don't be. Sam knows what he's doing. It would take an act of god or government to find him when he decides to cover his tracks. Besides, the mob isn't known for their technological prowess. They're more into the blunt-instrument approach.

"Upstairs, west side," he says, turning the phone lengthwise to orient the map to our location. "Looks like we can take these stairs."

The premier box seats are located in the center of the building for the best view, of course. Next to the entrance is a giant bronze plaque with a list of names of all the donor families responsible for the latest racecourse renovation. Richland and Stratton are both on there, along with several other recognizable surnames from St. Aggie's. If I needed any more proof that I'm attending the most elite school in Chicago, well, now I have it.

Sam and I comb the empty rows, looking for sixty-threes of any kind. No luck. The seats are labeled with letter-number combinations, with nothing above the number forty.

"At this point, I'd be satisfied with a sixty-three spelled out in M&M's." I smack the back of one of the seats in frustration.

I remember my dad bringing me here once when I was little. I remember the sounds most: people shouting at the horses as they hurtled around the track, the trumpet as it announced the start of each race, the loudspeaker calling for last bets. We weren't sitting in the box seats, though. We were sitting in the stands. I remember crawling over the benches, collecting discarded bet receipts among the sticky patches of spilled soda and cigarette butts.

"Bet receipts?" I say. "Do bet receipts have numbers on them?"

"I'm sure they have lots of numbers on them," he says. "But most of them aren't fixed numbers. They change based on the race and the horse you bet on."

He's right, of course. But something about the idea is nagging at me.

I sidle past Sam and slip a couple of bucks into a betting machine. Rows of colorful buttons pop up on the screen. First, I need to pick a track. I'm about to select the Hawthorne Raceway when my hand stops in midair.

"Sam, the tracks are numbered."

There are thirteen racetracks from all over the country to choose from. Each track has a corresponding number, but they're not in numerical order. They're random, at least to my untrained eye. But there is a sixty-three.

"Churchill Downs," I say. "So, what? Are we supposed to go there?"

Sam inhales sharply as his fingers fly over his phone. "The over-twenty-one rooms have names. I thought I saw . . . There it is! Churchill Downs."

I grab the phone out of his hands so I can read the tiny lettering for myself.

"Sam, you're a genius!" I say, kissing the phone, which of course makes it go all wonky. I hand it back to Sam, who gives me a strange look. "Whatever. Just get us there."

I follow him back down the stairs and around the corner, then suddenly remember that we need to act our parts to get in the door.

I grab the back of Sam's hoodie. "Hold it," I say, breathy from excitement. "We need to be college students, remember? We need to dial it down."

"Right," he says, collecting himself with a roll of his shoulders.

I straighten Sam's Columbia College hoodie I had one of my previous clients "borrow" from one of his older brothers. Then I further muss my messy ponytail and check my eyeliner and too-bright lipstick in my trusty pocket mirror. I take off my jacket and loop it over my arm, tugging down my spaghetti-strap tank top to reveal more of my minimal cleavage, complete with a convincing tattoo of a butterfly.

"Let's go," I say, taking Sam's arm like the fawning girlfriend I am.

Strolling into the over-twenty-one area is easy. No one asks any questions, partly because we look confident and cocky, like we're challenging people to card us, and partly because it's not a big race day, so there isn't much risk of underage betting.

"Sam, look," I say, pointing at the desk cubbies, exact duplicates of the ones downstairs.

Sure enough, the brass plates are numbered, and it takes us no time to locate sixty-three. I feel under the desk and under the chair, search the shelves, and press along the back, checking for false walls. I don't even know what I'm looking for—a piece of paper, I'm guessing. But I don't find anything. I try to cuff my disappointment. Obviously, I'm not thinking of something. Sam is tapping his phone.

Then I notice the desk lamp—specifically, that one of the screws in the base is loose. I elbow Sam and hold out my hand. He sees where I'm looking and gives me his Swiss Army knife. The knife is old, so pulling out the mini-screwdriver is easy.

I shakily unscrew the rest of the base and give the knife back to Sam. I barely feel him take it from my grasp.

When I tip the lamp off its base, a folded piece of paper pops out, as if saying *It's about time, rookie!*

I snatch it up and unfold it, leaving the lamp where it lies.

MEN TURN INTO BOYS WHEN CONSUMED BY THE LAND OF TOYS.

"What's it say?" Sam asks as I sink into the green leather chair.

"It's another stupid clue," I say. "Why is he doing this? I con people; I don't *sleuth*."

Sam tinkers with the remains of the lamp.

"What's this?" he says, pulling a small silver key from the base.

I take it from him to examine it more closely. No distinguishing marks, no numbers or letters of any kind. But it is an unusual shape. The shaft is cylindrical, with two small teeth on the business end—similar to a skeleton key, though it's smaller than a house key and has an unusual art deco handle.

I have no idea what it opens. Safe-deposit box, drawer, mausoleum, windup toy . . . it could be anything. And there's nothing I can see in the note that even hints at the answer. Or even a place to start looking. Which means I'm back where I started.

"Hey, what are you doing?"

A disgruntled racetrack employee with a receding mullet tromps into my line of vision. Hairy arms fold across a barrel chest.

"Defacing private property?" I say with a sheepish grin.

"I need to see your IDs."

Clearly he's not in the mood for repartee, witty or otherwise.

Sam hands over his ID right away, though he downplays his nerves to the point of aggression. Perfect.

I make a big production of rummaging in my purse, rolling my eyes, and popping my gum, which just proves how much my character is enjoying being carded.

The bouncer pores over our IDs while I flip my hair and Sam scowls. But eventually he hands them back to us, his grip just a touch too tight to make taking them back easy.

"Well, the boss tends to frown on property damage. Out—before I call security."

No need to tell me twice. Especially if I've already got what I came for. So Sam and I are out and belted into his car in less time than it takes to fleece a celebutante.

"That was close," Sam says, pulling out onto the highway.

"Not really," I reply absently. "The IDs are solid, and taking apart a lamp isn't worth prying guards out of their cozy jockey box."

I settle into my seat, drawing the whole mess out in my mind like a blueprint. Dad missing, racetrack clue, gun, mob involvement, forgery, toy-land clue, meaningless key. Nothing seems connected. Sure, the mob might have some link to the racetrack—they often do. But without knowing which mob, I likely won't be able to figure out the racetrack connection. Still, it might be worth looking into.

And what do the races have to do with toys? Or the mob, for that matter? Could "toys" be a euphemism for guns? Drugs? Strippers? What other "toys" do mafiosi covet?

Okay, forget the clues. Maybe I'm going at this from the wrong angle.

What kind of mob business requires sustained amounts of forgery? The occasional passport can be purchased from a vendor. Hiring a full-time forger, especially for the rates I'm sure my father charged, implies a larger initiative. But what? Drugs don't require credentials. Just a customs official willing to look the other way.

Out of the contemplative silence, Sam swears softly.

"What is it?" I ask.

"Nothing. Just traffic." He nods at the GPS display in his dashboard. "If we want to get back before we're missed, we'll have to take back roads."

"You mean before *you're* missed," I say under my breath, gazing out the window.

Sam frowns but doesn't argue. "We'll find him, Julep," he says.

I bite my lip to keep my doubts from spilling out. If there's one thing a grifter knows, it's that confidence is everything. I can't afford to lose my own confidence, let alone Sam's.

Another few minutes pass in silence as we travel down a road in the middle of exactly nowhere. Trees and fields rush by in a blur of green and brown. But then a flicker of something in the side mirror grabs my attention. It's black, with two broad white stripes running down its hood.

"Sam," I say, leaning forward for a better look in the mirror.

"What?"

"We've got company."

"Probably thought he'd avoid the traffic, too."

I shake my head. "I know this car."

"What do you mean?" Sam's eyes flick up to the rearview.

"I saw it the day"—I pause to recalibrate, deciding on the fly that telling him I saw it and its owner outside my window is not in my best interest—"the day my apartment was tossed. It was parked at the Ballou."

Sam presses the gas pedal and the Volvo leaps forward a few feet. Whoever's in the muscle car behind us speeds to catch up. Actually, he's accelerating faster, pulling up closer, like he's trying to kiss our bumper.

Sam shifts from eyeing the rearview to fiddling with the GPS. Swearing again, he hits the steering wheel.

"There's nothing for miles. How'd he even know where to find us?"

"Must have followed us. Me, I mean," I say. "How do we lose him?"

"We don't. At least, not until we dump out onto a bigger road."

Our pursuer pulls out to the side and forward, coming even with Sam's rear fender, and then swerves suddenly into our lane, missing us by inches as Sam cuts the wheel to avoid the hit.

"What the hell is he doing?" Sam presses the pedal to the floor and takes a turn too fast for comfort. He shifts into fifth, splitting his attention between the asphalt ahead and the car behind. The Volvo devours the road with a whisper that is swallowed by the roar of the muscle car as it makes up the distance.

I grip the door handle in one hand and my seat belt in the other. I trust Sam not to kill us, but I can't say the same for the car behind us. What does he want?

"Sam, pull over."

"Are you out of your mind?"

"I can talk us out of this."

"No, Julep. Not even you can talk us out of this."

He downshifts to fourth to take another hairpin turn at

forty miles an hour. The Volvo rocks on its wheels, centrifugal force giving us a temporary pass.

"We can't keep racing him, Sam. Sooner or later, he'll run us—"

This time when the black car swerves at the Volvo's fender, it connects. The Volvo fishtails, its tires screeching as they lose purchase, and we skid into the passenger's-side ditch.

THE MAN IN BLACK

My muscles tense in anticipation of the impact. Sam manages to haul the wheel to the center enough to keep the car moving forward along the ditch a few yards, slowing our momentum before we come to a stop. No crash. No air bag deployment, though the seat belt has left a nice welt on the side of my neck.

And then for some reason I'm not scared anymore. I'm enraged. I fly out the door, hell-bent on chasing the Chevelle on foot if necessary. I tune out Sam's protests. I am ready to kill, or at least permanently maim.

Turns out I don't have that far to run; the Chevelle has pulled over a few yards down the road from us. The driver's-side door swings open on creaky hinges. I register the black boots and coat first as the person I caught watching me steps out of the car.

I start toward him, my fists tight and not a stitch of a plan in my head.

He tried to kill me. He tried to kill Sam.

But then I'm yanked backward by a grip on my arm strong enough to leave bruises.

"Julep, stop!" Sam yells at me. "You don't know what he wants. He could have a gun!"

"Let me go!" I tug at his hand.

"Not until you come to your senses," Sam says calmly, his lips next to my ear. "Stay still."

I shiver with anger, but I listen. He releases his grip, and I cross my arms. It's then that I notice the gun my dad gave me in Sam's other hand.

"How—?"

"Not now," he says.

"I thought you said it wasn't loaded," I say.

"He doesn't know that."

I concede the point. Sam's plan is as good a plan as any, because he's right. I can't talk our way out of this, especially without knowing the mark. If I knew something, anything, about him, I could use it to our advantage. But I've never even seen him up close, let alone heard him speak, let alone had a conversation with him. I could just as easily say the exact wrong thing as the exact right.

"That's far enough," Sam says, raising the gun. His voice is steadier than I'd have thought it would be, given the situation. "What do you want?"

The man in black stops, assessing Sam without fear. He

looks unruffled, disinterested, like standing in the sights of a loaded gun is a regular occurrence.

I strain for a closer look at his face, though he's still far enough away to make distinction difficult. *Man* is perhaps a misnomer. He can't be much older than Sam and I, if he's older at all. He's maybe nineteen at most. His hair is light enough to look almost gray at this distance, but it's actually blond, cut jaggedly just above his ears.

"If you want to live, stop looking."

My mouth drops open. "He" is definitely a "she." With an Eastern European accent. Which raises a whole slew of questions. Including *Why won't she come closer so I can punch her in the throat?* I can't believe she ran us into a ditch for this.

"That's it? That's all you have to say to me? Where is my father?"

"I deliver the message. Stay away." Her voice is a blizzard—soft, cold, deadly but dispassionate, as if she's just the messenger and the letter she's handing me is the actual threat.

She turns back to her car and I notice a gun tucked into a shoulder holster under her open coat. Her bearing, stance, and expression identify her as a professional mob enforcer, despite her age. But she hasn't drawn on us, which in itself is promising. If I can just get her to give something away.

"Wait! Just tell me who has him, who I can talk to. Please." *Tell me he's alive.*

She gives me a forbidding look over her shoulder and slips into the driver's seat. Skidding tires, a splatter of mud and gravel, and the Chevelle is gone.

Sam touches my shoulder, and I realize I've been standing staring after her for too long. I lean into him and he closes his arms around me. He doesn't say anything, because he knows there's nothing he can say that is both true and something I want to hear.

The Volvo is tilted at a significant angle and sunk in about four inches of mud. The likelihood isn't good that we'll be able to get it out ourselves.

"I'll push first," I say, and move around to the back of the car. Sam takes the driver's seat without arguing.

Ten minutes later, covered in mud, I switch places with Sam. The car only settles deeper into the ditch. We try for another five minutes before Sam gives up and joins me, climbing into the passenger's seat.

"You going to call your parents?" I ask.

"And admit we cut school? No way. Besides, my mom gets one whiff of a crazed lunatic running us off the road and some serious questions are going to get asked."

"Good point. Triple-A?"

"Then they'll find out for sure. You really want me grounded right now?"

"They'll find out when your dad sees the damage," I say.

"I'll tell him it's in the shop, making a funny noise or something, and pay for the body work with cash."

"I can pay for it," I say, hating the idea of forking over thousands of dollars I can't afford to spend but hating the idea of Sam paying even more.

"Don't be ridiculous, Julep. It's like a month's allowance for me."

"Whatever. I don't want to argue about it now. We still have to get home."

I let my head fall back against the seat and look up at the ceiling, which remains annoyingly mute on the subject of rescue.

"There's one person we can call," I say, pulling my phone out of my pocket and giving Sam a sort of guilty look.

Sam returns it with a questioning look before catching on. "Aw, come on."

"Have you got a better idea?"

Silence falls as he tries and fails to come up with an alternative solution. "Fine," he says, and I press the appropriate sequence of buttons. "But just because you trust this guy doesn't mean I do."

"Shhh." I put my phone up to my ear.

The other end of the line picks up. "Tyler?" I say, gazing out at the darkening sky. "I need your help."

"With what?" he asks. "How'd the racetrack go?"

"Well, the racetrack went fine, but we hit a snag on the way home."

"Sam's Volvo break down?" His tone is straightforward, but playful automotive mockery is implied.

"Not exactly." And what follows is a perfunctory but mostly accurate portrayal of the events of the past half hour.

When I'm finished, there's a weighty silence on the other end of the line.

"Tyler?"

"Let me talk to Sam."

I hand the phone to Sam, who heaves a sigh as he puts it up to his ear.

"Yeah?" Sam says, and then immediately yanks the phone away from his head. I can hear yelling coming from the phone, but I can't hear what's actually being said. I make a grab for it but Sam fends me off while putting it back to his ear, his jaw clenching. He doesn't say anything for a while—he just listens. At one point, he glances at me with an assessing look and mumbles something in the affirmative. Then more silent listening.

A few minutes later, he gives Tyler our location according to his GPS and the nearest mile marker and then signs off, handing me back my phone.

"What did he say?"

"His dad owns a towing company, which is not surprising since his dad owns half the city. He's sending a truck for us."

"That's good," I say, wincing at the thought of tow rates from the middle of effing nowhere. "But what was he yelling about?"

Sam slouches in his seat. "He was chewing me out for taking the back roads in the first place, with your being stalked and everything. And he's right. It was a stupid thing to do."

"Oh, come on. I'd have done the exact same thing if I'd been driving."

"Well, then he'd have yelled at you. But as it happens, I got the reaming, and rightfully so."

I pull Sam's jacket from the backseat and try to wipe some of the mud off my chest with it. My eyes catch on my dad's gun lying innocently on the dash.

"When did you take it?"

"The night you showed it to me," he says without apology.

"Why didn't you just ask me?"

"I was afraid you'd say no, that you'd be worried about me getting caught and arrested for carrying around a possibly un-registered, definitely concealed weapon."

"Oh," I say in a small voice. That hadn't even occurred to me. I pick up the gun, which feels even more like a viper now than it did the first time I held it.

"Aren't you going to ask me what I found?" He takes the gun and turns the handle toward me to give me a closer look. "I took it home thinking that if it was registered I could find out to who, and that might give us somewhere to start. Of course, it wasn't registered. But as I was cleaning it, I noticed two things."

"Which are?"

"The first is that it's been fired. Probably a lot. There's wear on the side, and the feed ramp's polished smooth from use."

"Well, peachy," I say. "But I guess that's to be expected, it being a gun and all."

Sam taps at a spot just to the left of the grip. "There's also some kind of inscription—initials, I think."

I nudge his finger out of the way.

"Not your dad's, though. Which kind of threw me."

PER A.N.M., LA MIA FATA TURCHINA

A.N.M. Alessandra Nereza Moretti.

"That's because this isn't my dad's gun," I say as the bottom drops out of my stomach. "It's my mom's."

THE DEAN

"How's the Volvo?" I ask as Sam joins me at our usual table in the dining hall. It appears he's bypassed the chicken Parm and gone straight for the Tater Tots, Jell-O, cheddar biscuits, and chocolate milk. And yet nothing's filling out that quarter-zip pullover but his shoulders. Sometimes I hate boys.

"Resting comfortably at Levi's Auto Body." Sam steals one of my fries as he sits across from me.

"And your dad?"

"Barely even looked up from his tablet long enough to acknowledge he'd heard me." Sam shrugs as if this doesn't bother him. But I've seen the way he looks at my dad—which is hilarious, because my dad is about as far from perfect as it is possible to be in the parent department. I think Sam just wants somebody to show up.

"Did Levi say how much it would set me back?" I say, taking a bolstering sip from what I'm starting to call my Barista Mike Special. It's not as bad as it sounds. Okay, it's a work in progress.

"Are we really going to do this?" he asks, putting down the Tater Tot he was about to pop in his mouth.

"We could skip to the end, where I hand you the cash," I say.

"You're impossible," he says. "Why can't you just let me—"

"That's not how this works." I cut him off because I'm as tired of this well-worn disagreement as he is. Besides, I have something else to talk about before the show starts. "So, my email's blowing up with requests for fake IDs. I need an online form where people can input the info they want to go on their IDs."

Actually, the words *blowing up* are not quite adequate to describe the response. I'm well beyond the St. Aggie's criminal element now. Even past the thrill-seeking crowd. I'm into the straight-up straitlaced population. Plus all their friends and cousins and Dobermans twice removed. Last time I checked, I had forty new emails. That's a lot of lamination. If it keeps up, I'm going to have to draft Sam into the fine art of forgery.

"Word travels fast," he says.

"Made the Kessel Run in less than ten parsecs."

Sam gives me a look of long suffering. "Twelve parsecs. The quote is 'twelve parsecs.'"

"Yeah, but word made it in ten."

Instead of a jibe at my nonexistent nerd cred, he responds with a conflicted frown and an uncertain silence.

"What's up?"

"Julep, I was wondering . . . That is, I, uh . . ."

Sam rubs his ear. He does that a lot when he's thinking through a problem. It's so quintessentially Sam that I get a certain feeling when I see him do it. It's similar to the feeling of setting up a con I can really sink my teeth into.

"Spit it out, Sam."

"Are we going to the formal or what?" he says in a rush.

"Why? Did somebody ask you?" I'm distracted by Heather as she comes storming into the cafeteria, looking for blood. "You can go if you want, Sam."

"That's not what I—"

"Shhh," I say, gesturing at Heather.

Sam sighs and turns in his chair to watch. I scan the crowd, but as predicted, none of the faculty is present. They tend to avoid the dining hall when possible.

"There's Murphy," Sam says.

Sam's worked a minor miracle on Murphy. He still looks like a nerd, but now with artfully mussed hair, new glasses just this side of hipster, and clothes that actually fit.

Murphy is lowering his tray to a table when Heather marches up to him, her face red with rage. He glances up in surprise. But before he can ask the question, she gives him a full, flat-handed slap across the cheek. The sound echoes through the dining hall and all conversation ceases at once.

Murphy looks floored for a second before he stiffens, probably adding two and two and getting the square root of Julep. He puts a hand to his reddening cheek but doesn't say anything. Heather, appearing satisfied, draws herself up to her full five-foot-nine and whirls around, stomping back out the way she came.

Sam whistles low as the whispers start. Everyone's sizing up Murphy with great interest, including Bryn Halverson.

"Well, you were right," Sam says. "Girls."

I raise my *watch yourself, Y chromosome* eyebrow at him.

"I'll never understand how reverse psychology works on them every time."

"First, it's not reverse psychology. It's straight-up female brain. Model-hot Heather cares enough about model-airplane Murphy to slap him."

"And second?"

"Second, I'm a girl. Jerk."

"You going over there?" He nods in the direction of Bryn's table.

"Got to strike while the irony's hot."

I gather up our lunch detritus and head to the tray-disposal cart, threading through the tables in as roundabout a way as possible to pass by Bryn's group. When I get a table away from them, I put the trays down and check my phone for a non-existent text message.

"I heard that he dumped Heather because her boobs are too small," says one of the cattier girls. Which amuses the heck out of me, because I never started that rumor. I love it when the pettiness of people works in my favor.

"He's gotten cuter for sure. When did that happen?" Bryn says.

Score!

"Yeah, but would you go to the formal with him?" asks another girl—Portia, I think her name is.

"Count me in," says the first girl.

Bryn shrugs. "I'm still waiting for Tyler to ask me."

Crap.

Their conversation quickly turns to inane topics like how the economic downturn might affect the availability of the newest Vera Wang collection, so I make a beeline for the tray repository and then hustle to the door, where Sam is waiting for me.

"Well?" he asks as I fall into step with him.

"There's a small hiccup," I admit. "But I think I can fix it."

"What kind of hiccup?"

"A Tyler-shaped hiccup, actually."

"Hey, Julep," Heather says. "The dean wants to see you in her office."

"What? Why?"

"She didn't tell me." Heather waves absently at a passing friend. "I almost broke a nail on those crappy Kenneth Cole glasses, I'll have you know."

"When does she want to see me?"

"Right now," Heather says, disappearing into a knot of sophomores.

"Any thoughts on what she might want?" I ask Sam as we head toward the dean's office.

"Maybe she found out about the folder."

"Doubtful. Tyler intercepted her before she searched me.

Unless she has video surveillance set up in her own office, she has no idea it's even been tampered with."

"Well, whatever she wants, be careful with your backstory. She's been suspicious since the Franklin job."

The Franklin job was a scam we pulled our first finals week at St. Agatha's. Dr. Franklin, our philosophy teacher, had given Christina LaRocca a B-minus on her oral report, and since she couldn't have the subpar grade besmirching her perfect A-plus record, I "accidentally" spilled a Coke on his laptop while conferring with him about a reading assignment. When he called the IT department, Sam, posing as an official Net-jockey, showed up and fixed both the computer and the grade. Unfortunately, we weren't aware that all repairs require an approval form, and when Dr. Franklin submitted his, IT sent up another technician. The lazy tech didn't bother reporting the anomaly, and by the time the dean learned of the discrepancy, Dr. Franklin had retired and joined a service mission in Uganda.

"She has no proof that was me," I grumble. Though I know as well as anyone that she doesn't need proof. She has something much more powerful—a hunch.

Sam splits off from me as we near the Brockman Room, St. Aggie's ostentatious tribute to past contributors to the school. I climb the heavy wooden staircase, which is the only functional element in the Brockman Room, to the administrative wing. I always feel slightly uncomfortable climbing these stairs. Nothing says *You don't belong here, Julep Dupree* like gilt-framed portraits of frowning, bearded white men. Their disapproving eyes follow me all the way up to the gallery.

The dean's office is a far cry from the Brockman Room. Where the Brockman Room is formal and brocaded to within an inch of its life, the dean's office is a mishmash of contemporary styles, from Asian influence to techno-modern and everything in between.

"Ah, Ms. Dupree," Dean Porter says with only the thinnest veneer of cordiality. "Thank you for coming. I trust you've had no further rodent incidents."

"Nope—just the one," I say, and she moves aside to admit me to her inner sanctum.

The dean gestures to the floral monstrosity on the student side of her desk, and I oblige her by sitting in it, immediately affecting a slightly guilty expression.

It's a little-known fact that innocent people always look guilty. Only the truly guilty splutter in self-righteous indignation that they have nothing to hide. Is the dean savvy enough to know this? Honestly, I don't know. I make it a habit to keep myself off the dean's radar as much as possible. Three conversations in less than a week is not a precedent I should be setting.

"You were not in class yesterday," she observes. "And before you claim to have been ill, I should tell you I noticed your friend Sam Seward was not in class, either."

I look down at my hands long enough to call up my patented watery-eyed expression of woe. "He skipped school to help me." It's true enough, and the first lesson of Lying 101 is that it's best to begin a lie with a scrap of truth—it lends an air of credibility to an otherwise false account.

"Last I checked, helping a truant friend is not a legitimate excuse for missing school." She picks up a pencil and makes a mark I'm certain means nothing on a sheet of paper on her desk. The scritching of the pencil lead on the paper is meant to unnerve me. Amateur.

"He took me to the hospital to find my dad," I say. "He was in a car accident."

"Oh, dear," the dean says with not a whit of actual sympathy. None even of pretend sympathy. She either doesn't believe me or she has no soul whatsoever.

"That's why he didn't call to report my absence."

"I see," she says, tapping the point of the pencil . . . well, pointedly. "No note?"

I stare at her, mouth agape, because—you guessed it—no note. I allow myself five full seconds to be thoroughly disgusted at my mistake. The real me would have thought of that. Who am I, and what have I done with Julep Dupree?

"I'm sorry. I—I forgot," I stammer. The stammering is not as on-purpose as I'd like it to be. "I can bring it tomorrow."

"Don't bother," she says, tossing the Scantron torture device on her desk and leaning her elbows on the surface. She interlaces her fingers and pins me to my chair with a triumphant smirk. "It will take a lot more than a note to convince me your excuse is genuine. I want to speak to your father directly."

THE FAVOR

"Okay," I say. "I'll have him call you when I get home." And before she can stick me with anything else, I get up and head to the door. "Thank you, Dean Porter, for your understanding."

I examine my latest predicament from every angle as I head in the direction of my next class. The problem, of course, is that my dad is not available to lie for me. And if the dean finds that out, I'll be out of school and in the foster system before you can say *community college*.

I remember strolling through this very quad with my father the day we toured the campus. I was in the eighth grade, and St. Aggie's was the third private school we'd toured that week. He played the role of dutiful parent well, asking all the right questions about academic programs, rate of matriculation to all the top schools, opportunities for extracurricular activities, et cetera.

But I saw his eyes casing the campus. Every hall named for a powerful family and every plaque boasting a famous historical graduate added up like points in his head against every other private school in the county. Connections are more impressive than money, he always says. Connections open doors that all the money in the world can't seep through.

After the tour, I was feeling particularly guilty. It was right after my dad came back from his two-week disappearing act, and I had already decided I wanted to give up the grift. But it's hard hiding a secret that big from your dad. I dreaded the disappointment I'd see on his face, even though my resentment over his ditching me for two weeks still stung. I didn't exactly blame him, but I didn't not blame him, either.

He must have sensed something was off, because when we stopped to inspect the ostentatious arch on the north end of the quad, he leaned back against the foot of a neoclassical Minerva statue with an earnest look replacing his usual wry expression.

"You don't have to go here if you don't want, Jules. We can pick a different place, or you can stop altogether."

"I do want to go to St. Agatha's," I said, both annoyed and gratified that he'd misread me.

"Then why the face?"

I didn't know how to say what I should have, lie or truth, so I countered with a question. "What happened to Mom, Dad? Why did she leave?"

His expression sharpened from earnest to alert. "Why do you ask?"

"I just—" *I don't want this.* "I don't want to end up alone."

"Oh, honey," he said, pulling me into a hug. "I'm sorry. I had to go and I couldn't tell you. But I won't leave you again."

"Promise?" I said.

But either he didn't hear me or he didn't want to lie, because he never responded.

"Julep!"

Tyler's voice breaks into my thoughts, and he waves to get my attention as he saunters up to me. I didn't realize class was over, but people are pouring out of doors on their way to other buildings for sixth period. I'm glad. Memory lane is all well and good, but forward-action lane is more productive. I shake off my somber mood and return his greeting with a smile.

I meet Tyler halfway and draw him in the direction of the music room. I have to pick up the funds for the IDs on my way to class, and I might as well have a handsome escort.

"So I need to ask you for a favor," I say, looping my arm through his. I tell myself it might help Murphy's case if Bryn is watching. And it might. But that's not why I do it.

"You mean besides drive you to a bookie's hideout, call you a tow truck, and help you find your father, who may or may not have been abducted by the mob?"

"Well, now that you put it that way . . . yep, I do."

"I would be happy to extend any service within my capability to my fair lady," he says with a small mock bow—midstep, no less.

"I need you to not ask Bryn Halverson to the formal."

He laughs. "Not quite what I was expecting you to ask," he admits ruefully. "Let it never be said that you're predictable."

"I've got a lot on my plate."

"I can see that."

"Well? Can you ask someone else to the dance? I need Bryn Halverson to be dateless."

He gives me an assessing look, like he's going to ask the question, but then shakes his head and smiles. I need to tell him to stop smiling. It puts me off my game.

"I don't know, Julep. It's asking kind of a lot," he drawls, leaving the sentence open-ended.

"What do you want in return?"

He considers for a moment. "Help me with my dad's campaign this weekend."

That's a surprise. "You want me to help your dad with his campaign?"

I'd been hoping Tyler was becoming more of a friend, like Sam. But then, out of left field, *bam!* I'm reminded of what I am and what I do. I know I have no right to feel manipulated. I have a skill, and I owe him one (or, actually, several). The only wonder is that he hasn't called in the debt before this.

"What's the angle?" I ask, already refining ideas for a half-workable wire game.

Tyler gives me a puzzled look for a second, and then some kind of realization flits across his face.

"Oh. Not that. I don't want you to *help* my dad's campaign.

I'm just asking you to hang out with me on Saturday while I stuff about a thousand envelopes. I volunteer for a self-study credit. I figure if he's going to make me work anyway, it might as well count for something."

I'm so surprised by this that I almost get smacked in the face by the door. Tyler catches it before it can do any damage, and the freshman on the other side apologizes profusely when she recognizes Tyler.

"I—" I give myself a mental shake. "Of course," I say. "Thanks."

He quirks an eyebrow at me. "For asking you to participate in mind-numbing busywork for three hours early on a Saturday morning?"

"For everything," I say, smiling more brilliantly than I should.

He smiles back. "You're welcome."

An indeterminate amount of time later, I return to earth, realizing I'm blocking the entrance to the building. I break eye contact and step into the hallway as if nothing happened.

I wouldn't be the first girl to be taken in by Tyler's laser charm. But only a moron would fall for the same boy everyone else is salivating over. Since I'm not even a little bit of a moron, I won't be confessing that my heart is sweating and my forehead is beating too fast anytime in the near future. Er . . . something like that.

"Anyway, I thought Saturday would be a good time to talk about the next clue." He's right behind me and speaking low to keep anyone from overhearing. The practical effect of which is his warm breath ghosting along the back of my neck. I suck in a breath.

"Yes," I say. My overstimulated brain can't come up with anything better than a simple affirmative.

"Great. I'll text you the address."

I turn to smile at him and glimpse through a nearby window a black muscle car with white racing stripes parked across the street from us. My whole body stiffens. Tyler senses my unease and looks through the window next to mine. Without a word, he heads back in the direction of the door, his expression just shy of lethal. I leap to grab his arm before he gets out of reach.

"Tyler, wait!"

"That's the car that ran you and Sam off the road, right?"

"Yes, but—"

"I'm ending this. Now."

"Don't be ridiculous. She's probably armed, and you definitely are not."

He turns his angry glare on me, and I almost step back to protect myself from the heat. But I'm no more subduable than I am predictable, so I hold my ground.

He looks as if he's about to argue with me, his temper still simmering. "Fine," he says instead, pulling his phone out of his pocket.

"What are you doing?" I ask, alarmed.

"Calling the police."

I snag the phone out of his hand. "No you are not."

"Julep." His tone radiates warning.

"We have to be smart about this, Tyler. We have the advantage."

He unclenches his jaw as the message sinks in. But he folds his arms, capturing my hand, which is still on his not-inconsiderable biceps. I mentally smack myself for making that observation. I'm no longer shocked by my reaction to Tyler, but that doesn't mean I have to indulge it.

"Besides," I say with a predatory smile, "I have this kind of fabulous idea."

I pull out my own phone and start tapping. The phone on the other end rings three times before its owner picks up and mutters a surly greeting. He's still kind of pissed at me, I'm sure, but a deal's a deal.

"Hey, Murphy," I say, cheery. "Listen, about that favor you owe me . . ."

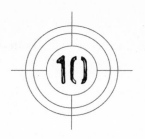

THE PHONE CALL

I click the Refresh button for the billionth time. Three more emails come in for fake IDs, adding to my steadily growing pool of reprobates. But still nothing from Murphy.

"Stop it. You're making me twitch," Sam says without even looking up from the soundboard. We're hanging out in the recording studio his parents set up for him in their ginormous basement as a Christmas present last year. He's working his magic on that phone call for the dean. I'm mostly sitting in the corner, pretending to help. He's grumpy for some reason, and I'm too frazzled to drag him out of it.

Watching the video my dad recorded at Sam's birthday while Sam extracts pieces of it to create a phone call for the dean was harder than I thought it'd be. After all, I'm getting him back. Finding his second note at the racetrack gave me a significant boost in confidence.

But still, with the autumn light fading into darkness, the nagging worry that he could be in a worse way than I've been letting myself believe is tormenting me. Mobsters may be utter morons, but they're far from cuddly. What if they have him chained up? Or worse?

I hit Refresh again to distract myself. Nothing.

"He'll send it when he has it downloaded. Give him a break." Then, in a whisper meant for himself, he adds, "Give me a break."

I hit Refresh again to spite him. He glares at me.

I set my laptop on the floor next to me, drawing my knees up as my mind returns to unwanted images of my dad in dank rooms with bare bulbs and grimy floors. My imagination adds a busted lip, a black eye, a broken arm. I squeeze my eyes shut, trying to block out the scene.

My brain is whirring so loud, I don't notice at first when Sam stops fiddling. Once I do notice, I glance up and see Sam looking at me. All the irritation has evaporated from his expression, replaced by deep concern. Poor Sam. He worries so much about me. I should say something to reassure him. But he knows me well enough to tell when I'm faking.

"We'll find him, Julep," he says, his voice not so much soothing as certain. The irony is that I'm usually the certain one. In fact, I was certain myself not ten minutes ago. But my dad's voice is echoing in my head, calling out to me to be careful of the azaleas, conversing with Sam's mom about the state of health care. Silly, inconsequential stuff to inspire such deep and abiding angst.

I sigh and try to pull myself together. "Jeez, I had no idea I had such capacity for emo."

Sam looks down at the soundboard and makes a few adjustments, then says, "Well, I think we're ready. Want to hear it?"

I get up and dust myself off, though there's more likely to be an alien spaceship in here than a speck of dust.

"Let's do it."

Sam pulls his headphone cord out of the jack and hits Play, or at least, that's what I think he does—the soundboard is indecipherable to me. My dad's voice booms out of the speakers, and Sam moves a few sliders to get the sound down to a reasonable volume.

"Good afternoon. This is Joe Dupree, Julep's dad. I approve Julep's absence from school on Thursday. She was at the hospital with me. I'm sure you understand. Thank you for marking her absence as excused."

The *excused* sounds a little more like "excuse-duh," but other than that, it's seamless.

"It's not perfect, but it should fool the dean," Sam says.

"It's wonderful, Sam," I say, squeezing his arm.

Then I hear a ping coming from my laptop. I make an unladylike dive for it, pushing the screen back as I stand, cradling the keyboard in my other arm and hoping it's not another fake-ID request.

But finally, Murphy's username—WoWarlock98—appears

in the Sender field. I click to open the message, and voilà! A high-quality, full-on face shot of my muscle-car stalker. She looks pissed, which makes me happy.

"You got it?" Sam asks, coming to look over my shoulder.

"Yep. Murphy came through."

"How'd he do it?"

I bend my head to get a closer view. Her face and shoulders are surrounded by the car's window frame. Her expression is definitely in the scowl family, but she doesn't seem to be in the act of hopping out of the car or drawing a weapon.

"I told him to use the car as an excuse to get close. He pretends to be interested in the car, taking pictures from several angles before 'accidentally' getting a shot of the driver when she rolls her window down to tell him to get lost. Brilliant, huh?"

Sam chuckles. "Now if only you'd use your powers for good instead of evil."

I forward Sam the email with the image.

"What are you going to do with her picture, anyway? It's not like we don't know what she looks like," Sam says, returning to his seat in his audio-captain's chair.

"True. What we need to know is who she is and who she's working for. And I'm not doing anything with the picture— you are." I poke him in the chest.

"Really." He leans back in his chair, lacing his fingers behind his head and rolling his eyes up to the ceiling. He sounds somewhat resigned, which is often the case when we're hip-deep in a job.

"I need you to hack the FBI facial-recognition database."

I pause, waiting for the inevitable "you must have fallen off the crazy wagon if you think I'm doing that" spluttering as his chair tips over backward, spilling him on the floor.

Instead he just sits there, staring at the ceiling.

A minute passes. Then two. I start to get nervous.

Sam is not the nonreacting sort. What is he thinking? That I'm nuts? Maybe I am nuts. Maybe I'm standing here like an idiot asking him to do the electronic equivalent of getting a strawberry-nutmeg smoothie from an ATM.

"Okay," he says.

"Okay?"

That's all he's going to say? Okay?

"Okay," he repeats.

"But—won't it be hard?"

"Sort of like trying to chip through the Hoover Dam with a toothpick."

"Oh."

He still hasn't changed position. Or looked at me, for that matter.

"But you can do it?" I ask, fiddling with the corner of the cabinet.

"I will try. I always do."

We fall into a strange silence I'm not used to hearing between us. Something's been off about Sam for the last couple of days. Probably has something to do with the mess I've gotten him in. He did get his car run off the road. And I've been so wrapped up in trying to find my dad that I've been asking a lot of Sam without giving anything back. That has to be getting old.

"I am grateful, Sam. For all your help. I know I don't say it a lot."

I feel at a loss for something to say to make him stop staring at the ceiling.

"That's all?"

I frown at him even though he's not looking at me.

You've probably guessed by now that I'm not really the touchy-feely type. I have my moments. I can emote with the best of them when the situation calls for it. But I don't tend to wear any of my weak and vulnerable bits on my sleeve. One of the ten con-man-dments: Always keep your feelings close to your vest.

"I couldn't do it without you? You're the man? What are you looking for, here?"

"Not that," Sam says. "I mean, is that all it is? Gratitude?"

"All what is? I don't know what you want me to say."

Sam looks at me then, and his gaze is the most direct and intense I've ever seen it. It lasers right through me. My insides melt a little around the beam of it, cauterizing the hole even as he creates it. He gets out of his chair and leans over me, his face inches from my nose.

"Is that all I am to you? A sidekick? A tool you can use when you need to hack into something?"

My heart stumbles over the question. Is that really what he thinks?

"You're my best friend," I say, swallowing. "You know that."

He looks disappointed in my answer, though I can't figure out why. So I try again, my voice dissolving to a whisper. "You're my rock, Sam. If anything . . . changed between us"—I can't say *if you leave me* without breaking something inside, I just can't—"I don't—I couldn't— I'd be lost."

And then, as quickly as it came, the crazy intensity leaves Sam's eyes and he slouches back against the soundboard, looking tired.

"All right," he says, rubbing his face. "Never mind. Let's just make the call."

He's typing the dean's number before I can even respond. I want to stop him, make him understand how much I value him. But my grifter Spidey sense is clamoring at me to leave it alone. At least for now. Eight years of friendship and we've never had a come-to-Jesus moment like that one. Not that we haven't argued, or he hasn't balked at some impossible task I've set for him. We're best friends; we're going to get into some disagreements.

But this was different. I've unwittingly unleashed something capable of breaking Sam's faith in me. As much as I want to resolve it, I can tell that if I keep pushing him to find out what it is, I'll just lose him faster.

Before I come to terms with this new complication, the dean's answering machine picks up the line. Sam and I calculated the best time to call the dean's office to have the greatest chance of getting her voice mail. After years of working the system, we have her routine down pat—four-thirty coffee break, in her office for another hour, rounds of the campus to make sure the buildings are empty and locked, back to her office to pack up, and then home.

The trick for us was to call when she was out of the office but before she left for home. Sounds like we've timed it perfectly. Sam begins the playback of the recording.

"Good afternoon. This is Joe Dupree, Julep's dad. I approve—"

"Hello? Hello?" the dean's voice interrupts. Sam races to stop the recording before she realizes what's happening.

Damn it. She must have been waiting by the phone to catch me out. What is up with my awful luck lately?

I give Sam a sharp nod. He punches a few buttons and inches up a slider from a different track on the soundboard. My dad's voice comes through again, this time with a good deal of static interference masking some of his words.

". . . Hello? Sorry—there seems to be some . . . on my end of the . . . wanted to confirm Julep's absence is excused as she . . . at the hospital . . ."

Then Sam disconnects the call.

"Whew," I say, clinging to the soundboard as I sink to my heels. "That was close. Glad we decided on the backup."

"Do you think she bought it?"

"Doubtful," I say. "But she got a call. She can't prove anything. I'm safe for now."

"Safe?" Sam says, sounding exasperated. "What about any of this is safe?"

I push myself to my feet and place a hand on Sam's knee. It stills under my touch.

"I have to go," I say, unsure where we stand after our earlier . . . whatever it was. "I owe you. I won't forget."

I draw the door shut behind me and wince a little as it clicks into place. Then I beat feet to the bus stop at the end of Sam's street, catch the 379, and settle into the circle of my troubling thoughts.

I change bus lines twice before giving up entirely on getting my brain in order. But it isn't till I'm on the train home to Forest Park that I realize I'm being followed.

THE NEW GUY

The thing about being tailed is that if you're a good grifter (and I'm a great grifter), then you don't have to deal with people tailing you. So I'm hardly an expert at detecting them. If I didn't have to make so many connections to get home from Sam's house, I'd never have noticed him.

That's right. Him. This time I'm sure of the gender. In fact, I even know the guy. I've only seen him a handful of times, but I'd bet my last latte it's him.

Once I caught a glimpse of the Yankees cap at the "L" station after having noticed it two bus rides back, I knew I was being followed. Then it was only a matter of creative phone-camera use to get a clear view of his face.

Disembarking didn't help me get rid of him. He's there now, four people back, his shoulders hunching his jacket collar up enough to cover the lower half of his face. Too bad for him I've already made him. The only question is, now what?

Throwing prudence out the window, I take a quick turn into an alley I sometimes use as a shortcut to get home. A few steps into the alley, I duck behind a Dumpster and wait for him. The smell of moldy cheese and rotting marinara with an overload of garlic identifies this particular Dumpster as belonging to Scalpetti's, the Italian bistro on the next block over. I'm hoping the slime on the asphalt under me is spilled olive oil, but I would *not* bet my last latte on that. Thankfully, my shadow is only a few yards behind me.

I hear his footfalls echo under the ever-present street noise. He slows when he doesn't see me. When he's about even with my hiding place, I leap out and grab his hat so he has to deal with me.

It isn't until a few seconds later that I realize I might not want him to deal with me. I've surprised him, though, which is gratifying. He whirls to face me. Then he sighs, shoulders slumping. Not the reaction of a hardened criminal bent on my destruction.

I fold my arms, the bill of his hat bumping my elbow. "The Ballou's a good ten miles from here."

"Look, it's not what you think," says not-so-much-a-barista Mike.

"Hard to believe, since what I think is that you're following me."

"Okay, it is what you think. But not for the reason you think."

I pull out my phone. I have no intention of calling the police, but he doesn't have to know that.

"You have until I finish dialing nine-one-one to tell me what the hell you think you're doing."

I touch the nine.

"I was hired to follow you, to protect you—make sure no one tries to hurt you."

I pause, thumb poised over the one.

"What?" I say.

"I'm a private investigator," he says, fishing through his pocket and handing me a card. I take it with my hat hand since I don't want him snagging my phone. It reads MIKE RAMIREZ, PI, along with a bunch of phone numbers, an address on the North Side, and the lamest tagline ever:

We put the "private" in "private investigator."

"Who hired you?" I ask, though I've already surmised the answer. I'm going to kill my dad. First a screwy scavenger hunt, and now this? If the mob hasn't already strangled him, I might.

"I have to respect client confidentiality," Mike says, having the good grace to look both embarrassed and a little afraid of me.

Client confidentiality, my eye. He might know where my dad is, or at least give me a clue that will point me in the right direction.

I touch the one.

"Wait. I'm trying to help you."

"Help me by telling me who hired you," I say, touching a third number, the Call button, and then raising the phone to my ear.

Mike rubs his head, thinking.

"Hello? Yes, I'd like to report a man following me."

"Okay! Christ! You win."

I give him an expectant look, phone still at my ear.

"Sam Seward."

I hang up on the tinny computer voice repeating "Your call cannot be completed as dialed; please check the number and dial again" and hand Mike his hat.

"That boy is so dead."

"He'll fire me if you tell him you caught me."

"That's the idea."

"You could use the help. Rumor is you're a person of interest."

"To who?" I ask. My dad may not have hired him, but he may know what I need to find out anyway: *Which mob?*

"I don't know," he says. "Just that some of the street crews are keeping an eye out. No hit order, though."

"Well, that's comforting," I say with not a little sarcasm.

"Please don't narc on me. I have the time, and you need someone watching your back."

"Yeah, like I need a hole in the head. No offense, Mike, but I can't be stumbling over a bodyguard right now."

"I really need this job. I haven't had a client in months. If I can't make this stick . . ." He spreads his hands palms-up in a helpless gesture.

Which is probably the only argument that would sway me. Well played, Barista Mike. Well played. When did I become such a freaking softy? In the absence of any convincing evidence to the contrary, I decide to blame Tyler.

I string a couple of unsavory swearwords together with Sam's name on the end and retrieve my backpack from where I dropped it.

"Come on," I say to Mike, gesturing down the alley toward a nearby diner. "Might as well fill me in. I need some caffeine, anyway."

Once we're settled into the cracked vinyl booth at the diner, I scan Mike with my patented grifter scrutiny. I don't think a PI would care one way or the other about my extracurricular activities, but one can never be too sure. Most PIs are out-of-work cops. Not all, of course. Some are fresh-faced newbies with more Philip Marlowe in their brains than sense. They wash out pretty quickly, though. It's the haunted-eyed cops who linger.

A waitress with a vintage-style updo and a bored expression comes over to our table.

"I'll have coffee," I say, ignoring the rest of the menu.

"Me too," Mike says. "Black is fine."

"Tough guy, huh?" I tease. Something about him, hulking as he is, reminds me of a puppy. A puppy in the same doghouse as me—straddling the line between honorable and shady, trying to eke out a living in a city that only respects the really rich and the really dirty.

"Nah," he says, patting his gut. "Wife has me on a diet."

"The things we do for love," I say. But when the waitress brings our cream-colored mugs, I drink my coffee black as well. I like my froofy drinks froofy and my blue-collar brew as bitter as burned oven scrapings.

"So you've been following me since that day at the Ballou?" I ask.

"Off and on. The Ballou's as close as I can get to school grounds."

"And you don't know which set of wiseguys wants me watched?"

"I'm not that connected. I don't work the syndicates, but I hear things. If I get a bead on it, I'll let you know. What do they want with a high school kid, anyway?"

I eye him without answering. What does he already know? What can I get away with not saying?

"Most kids, especially rich kids, don't get noticed by the mob. You got something they want?"

"You're looking at what I've got," I say.

"It helps me protect you if I know from what angle."

He's pushing, but he's still within the bounds of normal curiosity and professional interest, so I'm not too worried about him. I could tell him about the key and the clue, but I won't. At least, not yet. PIs are notorious busybodies. He wouldn't be able to help himself, and he'd probably trample all over my dad's trail. Besides, the guy lied to me. That kind of thing takes time to get past.

"I don't have anything that belongs to anybody but me," I say, taking another swig of coffee.

"Fine, don't tell me. But I'll probably stumble across it sooner or later. Trust me, sooner is better than later, and telling is better than waiting. If I have to stumble across it, it's usually too late to help."

"Noted," I say. Then I have a thought. "Actually, there is something you should see."

I retrieve my laptop from my bag. When it blinks on, the first thing to pop up is the picture of my stalker. I turn the screen to face Mike.

"Do you know her?" I ask, though I'm not holding out much hope for a yes.

Mike shakes his head. "Who is she?"

"She's as bad at following me as you are," I say. "But then, she's not actually trying to stay hidden."

Mike perks up. "Is she part of the family that's harassing you?"

"I don't know," I say, shutting the computer and sliding it back into my bag. "The one confrontation we had led to exactly no usable information. But it stands to reason."

Mike checks his watch and gulps his remaining coffee. "Got to check in with the wife. But I've short-rented the room down the hall from you. If you get in any trouble, scream."

"Thanks," I say, sarcasm sharpening the response.

At the door, he says, "Don't worry, kid. We'll figure it out."

After he's gone, I Google him on my phone. There's a website, nothing remarkable—a home page with a picture, some history, his specialties, and his license number. I check the IDFPR license lookup, and his license number is legit—

registered to Mike Ramirez for the last ten years. That's enough confirmation for me that he's on the level. Besides, Sam would have done his homework.

I head back to my apartment, ignoring the feeling of eyes hot on my back. It's probably my imagination, but I keep my pace brisk just in case.

When I get home, confronting the mess again nearly overwhelms me. The idea of cleaning makes me feel like I'm moving on, letting my dad go, giving up the rescue. I can't clean until he's here to help me. Besides, it's his fault there's a mess in the first place. It's only fair that he help me put Humpty back together again.

Anyway, I have too much to do to stand around like a stunned pigeon. Driver's licenses don't forge themselves. It's going to be a long night. Luckily, sleep's about as inviting these days as swimming in cement shoes.

My St. Aggie's–issue black tights make my legs itch, so they're usually the first things I take off after my shoes. But it's cold in the apartment tonight. I'm not sure if it's the temperature or the chill of the unremitting silence. Either way, the tights stay on as I sit at the kitchen table and open my computer. I pull up my half-finished history paper on the effects of American involvement on the Atlantic U-boat campaign of World War I. I generally find history entertaining, but tonight it's hard to focus.

About an hour later, I fish myself out of the Atlantic, having done my duty for god and country and Mr. Matthews. I save and close the document, only to have Stalker Girl's picture pop up. I study her malevolent expression, her unruly hair. I wonder if the ink staining the skin above her shirt collar is a gang tattoo, and if having it means she's killed someone.

Her Russian-sounding accent is telling. It may mean she works for an Eastern European gang. Or it may not. She could have contracted out to one of the other families. And even if she is connected to the Eastern Europeans, she could be working for any of a number of factions. I'm not aware enough of the organized underworld to pin her to a specific group.

Whatever her history, she knows who's after me, what they want, and where my dad is. She's the key to this whole mess.

My dad's bread crumbs will lead me to him, or to whatever it is he's hiding. If what my gut is telling me is true and he's already been taken, and if I can get my hands on the thing the bastards want, I can use it as leverage to get my dad back. But I'd be a fool to think that I'll be able to negotiate a simple trade. By then, I'll know too much, and any crime organization that knows what it's doing doesn't leave loose ends like me lying around.

That's where Stalker Girl comes in. She's my backup plan. If I can figure her out, I can get a jump on who's behind this.

Speaking of getting a jump on things, I've got about a bazillion IDs to create, a crapload more homework, and a clue to unravel.

Forging a believable driver's license is not as easy as it used to be. The advent of holograms and magnetic strips has made my job harder than it was when my dad first taught me using a typewriter and an iron. It's a more time-consuming process now, with diffractive film, online templates, and laminators. But sometimes I still use the iron for old times' sake.

After sixteen IDs, I look up from the painstaking task of clogging the diffractive sheet with varnish and roll my shoulders to get the kinks out. I glance at the clock, which is still lying on the living room floor, partially obscured by the shower curtain, and am not surprised to see that another three hours have passed. My stomach grouses, and I decide to call it quits for the night.

I root around in the cupboard for the jar of extra-crunchy peanut butter. Grabbing a spoon from behind the toaster, I dig into dinner. I'm already tired and I haven't even touched the rest of my homework. I take my peanut butter to the table and stick the spoon in my mouth while I rummage in my bag for my pre-calc book. Not there. Must be in my room.

I drag myself to my room and try not to gaze too longingly at my pillow while I rifle through the pile of stuff on my bed. I find the book, but in the process, my hand bumps the cold weight of my mom's gun. Forgetting about pre-calc, I perch on the bed amid papers, a hairbrush, textbooks, clothes, and the laminator and pull the sidearm into my lap.

For the first time in months, I intentionally call up memories of my mother. After she left us, I buried all the things I remembered about her. Other than the conversation my dad and I had at the St. Aggie's arch, we never talked about why she left. Maybe he knows more about her reasons than I thought.

She's nothing like my father and me. She's mercurial, musical. She always brought my dad to life when she was around. I remember her smell the most. Roses—her favorite.

I'm struck with the sudden urge to dig through the trunk she left behind. Maybe it will provide some sort of enlightenment. Maybe it'll still smell like her. Assuming, of course, that the crooks who tossed my apartment didn't scatter everything to the wind.

When I drag the trunk from the back of my dad's closet, it's clear that someone's been through it, but nothing appears to be missing or broken. Of course, there's nothing of any real value to steal, and not much that's really breakable. Just remnants of a life lost: discarded bits of a wardrobe suited for the wife of a high-rolling con man gambling in the big leagues of jets and caviar; a jewelry box; some old makeup; a few scribbled grocery lists; a hair dryer; some faded, unlabeled photos of people I don't recognize. No journal, no stack of letters, no explanation of who she is, why she'd have a gun, why she left.

But it does still smell like roses. So I refold, rearrange, and replace everything carefully and then seal up the trunk, the gun still on the floor next to me. Some memories are better left stacked in the back of a closet.

I should call it a night. It's still early, only eleven or so, but I'm not doing myself any favors sitting in a sea of broken things with nothing to show for my time but gritty eyes and family baggage.

I'm halfway to the bathroom when someone knocks on the door. It's a testament to my tiredness that I'm not more alarmed at the prospect of an unexpected visitor.

"Who is it?" I say, my hand paused at the chain.

"It's Tyler."

THE FILE

He's wearing jeans and a long-sleeved T-shirt, and he's holding a pizza box with the most tantalizing smell wafting from it. "I know it's late, but I— What's wrong?"

He brought me pizza.

Down the hall, Mike pokes his head out, checking on me. I wave to let him know Tyler's okay.

"Who's that?" Tyler says.

"Neighbor. Come in."

He enters, setting the pizza on the sofa, and I lock the door behind him.

"What's wrong?" he asks again. "It looks like you've been crying."

Oh, jeez. Was I?

"It's nothing." I rub self-consciously at my cheeks. "I was looking through my mom's stuff, hoping to find something useful."

"Did you?"

I shake my head. "Just a generous helping of ouch."

Tyler takes my hand and leads me to the sofa, shifting the pizza to the coffee table so we can sit. I let him pull me, mostly because I'm too tired to calculate the risk-benefit ratio but also because it feels nice. Really nice. His eyes sweep the mess without comment, but his grip on my hand tightens.

A tiny part of me is worried I'm being too open about my melodrama with him. The only person I let see me ruffled like this is Sam, and him only rarely. But that part is the girly bit of me, and is therefore suspect. I ignore it in favor of relishing the warmth of his hand around mine.

"Well, I have the perfect remedy," he says. "Close your eyes."

Out of curiosity, I humor him.

"Okay, open them."

When I do, he's making a ridiculous face—eyes crossed, head tilted forward, one finger stretching his mouth into a clownish grimace. I laugh reflexively. His face snaps back to its normal gorgeousness, his delighted smile echoing mine.

"Works on my little sister every time," he says. "Ready for another one?"

I nod and close my eyes.

"Okay, now."

This time he's sticking out his tongue and pushing his nose

up so his nostrils look huge. I laugh again, even without the element of surprise. He goes back to Tyler and takes my hand again, loosely enough that I don't feel trapped.

"You have a good laugh," he says. "You should use it more often."

I study him in the comfortable silence that falls between us. I can't for the life of me figure out why it's so easy being open with him. And for once, I don't care that I can't figure it out. Because here he is, at eleven on a school night, trying to cheer me up, of all the useless, adorable things. My guard crumbles to dust, and I grip his hand actively instead of letting him cradle mine.

"What are you thinking?" he asks, his fingers soft against my palm.

Guard or no guard, I'm not ready to tell him what I'm feeling. I have my limits.

"I'm wondering where your parents think you are right now," I say. "Even seniors have curfews, right?"

"No one in my family sleeps. My dad is always out at state functions, and when my mom isn't with him, she's catching up on current events and drafting speeches. Even my sister stays up till two or three reading or doing homework. I told my mom I was helping a friend."

"A friend?" I say.

"A good friend," he says, squeezing my hand.

"Oh," I say. And then, because it's true, and because I don't have anything more intelligent to add, I say, "I'm going to die of starvation if I don't get a slice of pizza in the next five seconds."

"Well then." He hands me the biggest slice and settles back into the sofa.

I take a giant bite of pepperoni deliciousness, and say, with a drop of hot oil dribbling down my chin, "Aren't you going to have some?"

"Nah. I'd rather watch you."

I swallow and take a smaller bite this time. After finishing the slice, I wipe my chin on a napkin. I'd lean back, but the cushion that is normally here was too destroyed to keep. Seeing my dilemma, Tyler scoots closer to the other end of the couch so I can share his cushion without sacrificing my personal space.

"Such a gentleman," I say, and move a few inches in his direction.

"It's how my mama raised me."

I sigh and lean back against his cushion. "I wish I could forget about all this for one night." Once I realize what I've said, I stammer, "I—I don't, I mean, I know my dad's in trouble—"

Tyler pulls me into a comforting half hug. "There's nothing wrong with being tired. If he wanted you to find him right away, he'd have left better clues. You're doing great, Julep."

I shift in his hold and lean my head on his shoulder. I don't bother to argue. I know what I'm doing and, more important, what I'm not doing. I'm my father's wingman. I should be with him.

"You've earned a break," Tyler says into my hair.

And whether or not I agree that I've earned it, I decide to go with it.

"Tyler?"

"Yes?"

"Can you do some more faces?"

$$\bullet \quad \bullet \quad \bullet$$

The next day at school is utterly wretched. Having stayed up till four in the morning with Tyler, I feel like my head is a drum kit and some no-talent hack is going to town on it. Days like this are what keep the sunglasses industry booming.

I take another envelope from my bag and slip it through a locker vent.

With Tyler's help, I managed to fill all the ID orders last night. It was fun, actually, teaching someone else how to craft a decent forgery—once I got past my initial hang-ups about giving away family trade secrets. We laughed a lot, smearing each other with liquid latex. And any time the conversation strayed to my dad, Tyler would make a ridiculous face to derail it.

Go ahead, judge me. For being weak, for caving to my adolescent urges, for leading an innocent lamb down the path of wickedness. You're right about all of it. But the truth is, something shifted last night. I'm sure I'll have regrets, but even if I wanted to, I can't go back now and undo it. And I don't. Want to, that is.

"You look happy," Sam says as he comes up to me. I look up from the next envelope. "Yikes, and hungover."

I glare at him, but I fear the effect is lost through the sunglasses. "I'm not hungover. Just blitzed from staying up all night."

"Want me to help deliver?"

"I don't want to risk you getting pinched for it. I'm almost done, anyway."

I move down the hall toward the next locker, Sam following.

"I started working on the picture project you asked me about yesterday," he says.

I steer us past a group of kids huddled around a phone, watching clips of the latest celebrity wardrobe malfunction. "Already? What about the history assignment?"

"Did *you* do the history assignment?"

"As a matter of fact, I did. And I'm a degenerate. What's your excuse?"

"I'm a degenerate's yes-man."

"Touché."

"Anyway, I haven't managed to crack the firewall yet, but I poked around and may have found a partial back door. It will require building a batch file, which will take some time, but—"

"You do realize that I only got about a third of that, right? In Julep, please."

"I've got a lead."

"Fantastic," I say, smiling as much as my aching head will let me. "How about the form?"

"Already up and running on the usual IP."

"Keep this up and I might nominate you for best minion of the year." I punch him lightly on the arm. "I'll send out a follow-up email."

"You sure you want to encourage people? You seem pretty overloaded."

"I'm still short on cash, Sam." I don't bring up the Volvo, but it hangs in the air between us.

The bell rings.

"One more thing," Sam says. "I translated the inscription on the nine-millimeter. 'For A.N.M., my blue fairy.' Any idea what it means?"

"Beyond the literal, no. I've never heard of anyone calling my mom a blue fairy. My dad never did. And even if he did, I can't imagine how it would get me any closer to finding him."

I realize belatedly that I should keep my voice down. People are clogging the hallway in their rush to get to their lockers and then to class before the second bell rings. The dean is making her rounds as well, stopping occasionally to issue reprimands to those students not subtle enough in their uniform alterations.

"You'd better get going," I say.

"See you at lunch," he says, and takes off in the opposite direction.

I weave around students, ducking the dean's watchful eye by slipping into classrooms whenever her gaze sweeps in my direction. By hopping from room to room and using other students as shields, I manage to steal past her without incident.

The rest of the day passes quickly as I deal with the administrative side of my one-person forgery ring. If orders keep pouring in at this rate, I'm going to have to start a sweatshop. Or at least hire a delivery service.

I catch glimpses of Tyler in the halls. He doesn't look any the worse for wear after our night of lawbreaking abandon.

Lucky jerk. But he always has a smile for me when we pass each other, so I can't be too irritated with him.

After my last class, I head to the Ballou to catch up on something I've been meaning to do but haven't had time for.

When I walk in, Mike winks at me and heads to the bar to make me a drink. Maybe having a bodyguard playing a barista has its perks. I wave and take a seat in the corner with my back to the wall. If the dean catches me, she can't technically do anything about it since the Ballou isn't on school property. But if you're going to be absorbed in illicit activity, you might as well position yourself so that no one can sneak up behind you.

Once I'm settled—coat draped over my chair and phone checked—I pull out the unlabeled manila folder Heather handed me in the music room the other day.

"A little light reading?" Mike says when he sets my triple-caramel macchiato down at my elbow.

"Depends on what's inside," I say. "Could be dark, foreboding, and dangerous. But only to me."

"Your student file?"

"How'd you guess?" I ask, smiling.

He flips the hand towel he's holding over his shoulder. "I got into my fair share of scrapes when I was in school."

"See, that just makes me like you more," I say.

He laughs. "I'll let you get back to it. But don't take it too seriously. Whatever's in there isn't going to kill you."

"Yeah," I say. "I have other avenues for that."

He returns to the bar to take another customer's order as I

open the folder and start reading. The first few pages are no surprise—statistical data, transcript, class registration receipts. Then there are a few incident reports—the rat, an IT account of the damage done to Dr. Franklin's computer, some scraps of circumstantial evidence for other jobs I pulled last year, and even a couple of references to incidents that had nothing to do with me.

But then it gets weird.

There are full-length dossiers on each of my parents. My dad's is considerably shorter than my mom's, and there's not much in it that I didn't already know. Apparently he did a three-week stint in the air force that I knew nothing about and had a girlfriend in Vienna before he met my mom. But everything else I pretty much know.

My mom's record, though, is considerably more extensive. There's an entire family tree, linking her to all sorts of people I've never heard of. A copy of her birth certificate states that she was born in New York, when I know for a fact that she was born in Oklahoma. Or do I? Who is this person staring back at me with an older version of my chin?

I close the folder, feeling a little sick. It's not like I thought I knew everything there was to know about my mother, but this indicates a huge, gaping chasm between the mother who used to braid my hair and sign my fake-illness excuse notes and the woman she actually is.

"Hey, kid," Mike says. "Your drink's getting cold."

I lean on the table, trying to regain my equilibrium. What is the dean doing with all this information? What does any of it have to do with my internment at St. Aggie's? The answer is nothing. So why is she digging into my history? Even taking into account how much she hates me, it doesn't track that she'd want all this background on me.

"Kid, are you all right?" Mike says.

"Do you know who my mom is?" I ask him on a whim.

"No," he says. "Should I?"

"I wouldn't think so. But then, I don't know her, either, and you would think I should, right?"

"What do you mean?"

I stuff the folder back into my bag, waffling between keeping it and burning it. "I wish I knew."

"Does it have to do with whoever's hassling you?"

"No," I say without thinking. Then, "Maybe. I don't know."

"If you find out it does, you better tell me," he says.

"I will. Thanks, Mike."

Murphy opens the Ballou door then and, catching sight of me, comes to join us.

"Hey, Julep—got a sec?"

Mike bows out of the conversation and Murphy pulls up a chair.

"The makeover isn't cutting it. Bryn's not going to say yes because I got a new pair of glasses. What's my next move?"

"Chill, Murph. We've got this." I confess I'm having a hard time getting worked up over Murphy's love life when my own life is such a mess. But a paycheck is a paycheck.

"The dance is only a week away. If she says no on Tuesday, I'm sunk."

"That works to your benefit. She's still dateless, and a girl like Bryn doesn't go stag."

"There's got to be something else I can do."

"There is," I say, putting my hand over his to stop his finger from tapping. Boys are so jittery. "Two somethings, actually: the buildup and the proposal."

"Buildup?"

"Write down all the things you like about her—the real her, and don't say algebra—and give it to Sam. He'll work up something fancy out of it, and then you'll fill her locker with flowers on Monday, secret-admirer-style. She'll be obsessing all night over who it could be. Curiosity is what we're going for here. If she's curious enough, she'll say yes, no matter what her prior perceptions of you are."

"Thanks for that, I guess," Murphy says. "But how do I—?"

I anticipate his question and hand him a folded half-circle piece of aluminum I cut out of a soda can at lunch.

"What's this?"

"It's what you'll use to pick her locker lock. Wrap it around the bar and slide it down into the lock. Pull up on the bar, and you're in."

Murphy eyes the aluminum scrap doubtfully. "Why am I the one planting the flowers when you're less likely to mess it up?"

"Because if you're the one caught rose-handed, it'll actually increase your chances of getting the girl. If it's me or Sam, you're finished before you've even asked."

Murphy nods. "And the proposal?"

"We'll do something understated, classic—like lighting up

the quad or hijacking the intercom system. Maybe something with a glitter cannon."

The look on Murphy's face is priceless. He's such an easy mark it's almost not even fun. Almost.

"Maybe not the glitter cannon," I amend as the door to the Ballou opens, admitting Bryn and a few members of her entourage. Murphy, whose back is to the door, responds before I can warn him.

"Don't push it," he says. "Just make sure Br—"

I have to shut Murphy up before he spoils the whole con. So I grab him by the button-down and haul him half over the table for a crushing kiss. I hear several shocked gasps from the other end of the room.

Good enough. I gently push the speechless Murphy back into his chair in time to see Bryn and her friends giving us strange looks and a wide berth. It's not ideal, him being seen with me. People know what I do, so Bryn could potentially put two and two together. But the kiss might throw enough of a curveball to keep her guessing.

Unfortunately, Bryn and her friends weren't the only spectators. Tyler also picked that moment to walk through the door. But instead of the reproving glance and hasty retreat you'd expect, he smiles at me and shakes his head. He does leave, but he winks at me as he closes the door behind him.

"Are you crazy?" Murphy hisses at me, wiping his mouth.

"Of course," I say, smiling.

THE RED, WHITE, AND BLUE

This is what campaign offices look like?

I check the address Tyler texted me, and then look up again at the swanky house, complete with cupola and circle drive. I guess I expected more of a grassroots, seedy-shopping-plaza kind of office. Or at least something downtown, near the federal building.

This place is deep in the heart of the Gold Coast Historic District and looks like it was built at least a hundred years ago. And there's topiary. Honest-to-St.-Francis topiary. What this says about the senator's campaign, I don't know, but it says something.

There's a doorbell pull rather than a button, and the din it makes when I tug it sounds vaguely cathedral. A uniformed maid opens the door for me, and after I state my business, she escorts me to a large library in the back of the building.

Calling it a library is a bit generous, in that the room doesn't appear to have the function of a library. There are books arranged neatly in ornately carved built-ins all along the walls, but they seem dormant, as if their purpose is to suggest a library's atmosphere rather than to impart any real knowledge. There's a table in the center with chairs that match the shelves surrounding it, and a pair of tufted leather armchairs conspire over cognac near the brick fireplace on the other end of the room.

"Hey," Tyler says from behind me.

"Your dad's offices are pretty classy. I'd hate to see where the other guy is working."

Tyler smiles. "These aren't my dad's offices; it's our house."

"Oh," I say, feeling dumb. "That explains the topiary."

"Nothing explains the topiary," Tyler says. "Come on. I've set up shop in my room. It's slightly less ostentatious than this."

I smile and follow him to the kitchen and then up the back stairs to the third floor. He leads me down a few halls to what I assume is the apartment over the garage. It's enormous, easily as large as the library, with its own bathroom, sitting area, video room, and office. My entire apartment could fit in his closet.

Sadly—to me, at least—it also looks staged, like a fancy new home with fake family pictures and paraphernalia to make house-hunters connect more with the room. This puts a crimp in my ability to read him, his wishes and flaws, his history.

But maybe I can read something from the utter lack of him in this room. Judging from the library, this is a house built to maintain an impression. Maybe Tyler is part of that facade. I know how I'd feel about that, but I still can't read Tyler's feelings about it. He doesn't seem either proud or embarrassed as I walk into his room—just unaffected, as if I've been here dozens of times already.

He leaves the door open behind us, which might mean nothing or might mean everything. I can't tell much until we start talking. If he talks too loudly or watches the door, I'll know it's not safe to speak freely. If he acts like his normal Tyler self, then leaving the door open is either his way of circumventing any boy-girl weirdness or it doesn't mean anything at all. Knowing boys, it's probably the latter.

He's laid out some stacks of printouts and a couple of boxes of envelopes on the artificially distressed trunk that serves as the coffee table. At the far end of the table is a post office–issue mail-carrier bin.

"So I should probably warn you that I'm a paper-cut weenie," I say.

"No problem. I have Band-Aids. Besides, your main objective today is keeping me company. I'll do the heavy lifting—or folding, in this case. You can do the stuffing."

We sit on the floor between the coffee table and the couch. He folds the pages and hands the packet to me, and I stuff it as best I can into the slightly-too-small number-ten envelopes.

For an hour or so, Tyler and I chat easily about nothing and everything—school, the dean, even some old cons I pulled in middle school while I was learning the ropes from my dad. I fill him in on the odd information in my student file, Sam's attempts at infiltrating the FBI database, my backlog of fake ID orders. In return, Tyler tells me all about the drama going down in the drama club, which I had no idea he belonged to.

"I can't get over you being in drama," I say. "Sports don't take up every spare minute of your time?"

He gives me a sardonic look. "I'm more than just a pretty face, you know. 'If you prick us, do we not bleed?'"

Tyler's voice is light and easy, which ups the odds that I don't need to worry about malefactors listening in. He's laughing in that genuine way that warms me down to my toes. He's too easy to believe in. So much so that I even tell him about my name.

"You mean Julep's not your real name?" he says in mock surprise.

I shoot a rubber band at him. "Do you want to hear this story or not?"

"Definitely." He takes a break from folding to give me his undivided attention.

"I was pulling my first solo con. I hadn't told my dad about it, because I wanted to surprise him."

"How old were you?" he asks.

"Ten."

"What could you possibly pull off as a ten-year-old?"

"Honestly, pretty much anything. The con is about the outcome, not the method."

"How so?"

"There are as many ways to pull off a single job as there are people. If you can work with what you've got, whether that's age or good looks or a sports car or whatever, you can get the Golden Fleece. The trick is to know your assets, and then form the con around them."

"Okay, I'm with you. So what happened when you were ten?"

"I conned my way into my dad's favorite bar, sat on the stool next to his, and successfully ordered and was served my first mint julep. My dad had no idea it was me until I told him."

"When you were ten?" he asks, stunned. "How?"

"I disguised myself as a little person of the male persuasion."

"And that worked?"

"Of course," I say, my mind drifting to my dad's equally astonished expression, which morphed quickly into excitement and pride. I'd glowed under the praise, and, okay, the glowing might have had something to do with the alcohol as well. That night, my dad gave me my first lock-picking practice set and my grifter name as a congratulations gift.

"What are you thinking?" Tyler asks. "You seem a million miles away."

"About my dad," I say, smiling an apology.

Tyler reaches for my hand and my heart rate increases by a few beats per minute at his touch. He leans closer to me and my nerves tingle.

"He's out there, Julep. You'll find him," he says, his voice low and earnest. Almost word for word what Sam said, but just as empty a promise. I can feel waterworks welling behind my eyes and start desperately thinking of baseball to keep the pipes from leaking.

Lucky for me, Tyler's dad picks that moment to pop in.

The senator is tall, with big hands. Not freakishly big, just capable big. Tyler gets his eyes, and the cutthroat charisma behind them, from his dad. The auburn hair is similar as well, though the senator's is shot through with the perfect amount of distinguished silver.

The two are clearly cut from the same Star-Spangled Banner. Which is why I'm a bit puzzled by the slight hardening in Tyler's eyes when they touch on his father. I didn't realize how much I'd assumed Tyler leads a charmed life, but now I wonder if that's really the case. I suppose it could be your average parent angst, but the brittleness in Tyler's smile seems more disdainful than resentful.

Then the senator turns the full wattage on me. "You must be the inimitable Julep," he says, and I don't notice that my hand is in his until I feel him shaking it. Firm grip, by the way. "I've heard so much about you."

"Really?" I say, raising an eyebrow at Tyler. "I can't imagine there's much to say."

"You're too modest, my dear." Ugh. Politicians. I'm pretty sure their gearshifts are stuck in patronizing. "In my experience, the most exaggerated accounts are usually the most accurate."

"I'm still too young to vote, Senator," I say, returning his smile and retracting my hand.

"Not too young to help the campaign, though, I see."

Smooth.

"Did you want something, Dad?"

"I wanted to see how your project was coming," he says.

"I'm handling it."

"When do you think it will be done?"

"When it's done," Tyler says, steel in his voice. "It takes time."

The senator narrows his eyes but doesn't comment on Tyler's tone, and I have to wonder what they're talking about. The mailing is almost ready, and yet the temperature in the room has gone decidedly arctic.

Then the senator's smile is back and his eyes twinkle at me as he says, "Well, it is very nice to meet you, Ms. Dupree. If you'll excuse me?"

I wait a full thirty seconds after he's left before saying anything.

"What was that about?"

Tyler looks down at the envelope he's holding.

"Nothing."

When I continue to stare at him, he sighs and looks up.

"He . . . interferes a lot. Drives me crazy."

"It's the parenting prerogative, I guess. Or at least, they think it is." I lean back against the chair. "My dad's doing his best to keep me from going to college."

Tyler laughs. "Seriously? Why?"

"He thinks college is a scam. Actually, he wanted me out of school a couple of years ago. He thinks the foundation is all you need, and then you can research the rest as necessary." I put on my best Dad expression, affecting his voice as closely as I can. "'The only chemistry you need to know, Julep, is the chemistry between people.'"

I expect Tyler to smile at my silly impression, but he doesn't. Maybe he senses the guilt behind the teasing.

"It's an old argument," I continue.

Tyler squeezes my hand, which he has somehow managed to regain possession of.

"Anyway, my dad thinks school is a waste of time, especially for me."

"And you don't agree."

"No, actually, I do agree. For what my dad wants me to be, I need college like a fish needs a 401(k). Grifters only go into debt if they have vices." *Like gambling,* I think but don't say. "But . . ."

"But?"

"I don't want to be a con artist anymore. I don't want a life where I'm constantly running and hiding. I love my dad. I just don't want to be him."

"Then what do you want?"

"I'm tired of talking about myself," I say instead of answering. "What do *you* want?"

Tyler shrugs. "No idea," he says, grinning. "I want to know what I want. How about that?"

I smile back. Nice to know I'm not the only one with issues.

"My dad insists I go to Harvard. That's where he went, and his father before him, and his father before him. We're a legacy family with a couple of buildings bearing our name. So of course there's nowhere else I can even consider."

"I can relate to that," I say. "What is it about dads that makes them want a Mini-Me?"

"I don't think all dads are that way."

A companionable silence falls for a couple of minutes as we finish stuffing the envelopes.

"I want to go to Yale," I say as I finish the last envelope on my stack. Here I go again, revealing too much.

"Why?" he asks.

I could tell him that when my dad came back after his two-week disappearance, I lost all desire for the life of a grifter. And that in a moment of existential crisis, I happened upon a rerun of *Gilmore Girls* where Rory was deciding between Harvard and Yale, an old dream and a new one. And that by the end of the episode I latched on to a new dream I could live with. I could tell Tyler that I stole Yale from a TV show. Instead, I tell him something more true.

"I want to be a real person—to be me. I know it sounds strange, but I don't actually know who that is anymore. When you can be anybody, you become nobody. Does that make sense?"

He looks uncertain, so I try a slightly different angle.

"I guess I want to be ordinary," I say, though that doesn't feel quite right. "Actually, I want to be extraordinary. But in an ordinary way. Which is why I want to go to Yale. I want to be normal, but I want to be the best at it."

Tyler smiles. "Well, I can't imagine you as ordinary. But extraordinary's not a stretch at all."

I straighten my stack of envelopes unnecessarily to distract him from my pleased expression.

"So what is your real name, then?" he asks. "Wouldn't going by your real name help you figure out who you are again?"

"Yes, but not yet. I have to stick with Julep until she gets me where I'm going."

"You're seriously not going to tell me your real name?"

"No one knows it but me and my dad," I say. "Well, and my mom. Wherever she is." My teasing smile fades when I think about the gun. Tyler's thoughts must be flowing along the same lines, because his smile dims as well.

"So you're sure it's your mom's gun?"

"I didn't even know my mom had a gun. My dad obviously redacted a lot. I've always assumed my mom left because she was sick of the con thing. Now, after seeing all the crap about her in my student file, I'm not so sure."

"What do you think his leaving you the gun means?"

"Haven't the foggiest," I say. "It could have something to do with the clues he's leaving me. Or it could be something of my mom's he wanted me to have. Or it could be him telling me to be careful, that I need to protect myself. Who knows?"

"Why didn't he just leave you a note and a map?"

"Because any idiot could read a note and follow a map."

"So what about the clue you found at the racetrack?"

I pull the folded note out of my jeans pocket and hand it to him.

" 'Men turn into boys when consumed by the Land of Toys.' "

"Any thoughts, guesses, wild speculations?" I ask.

He shakes his head and hands back the scrap of paper. "No, but I'm sure you'll figure it out. Did you say there was a key, too?"

I tug the chain I threaded it onto for safekeeping out from under my sweater and pull it over my head.

He snatches it out of my hand, staring at it in shock.

"I know this key," he says.

THE STRAND

"Why are we doing this, again?"

Sam and I stare up the broad stone steps to the heavy, barred door guarding the entrance to the Strand, the private club that belongs to the key dangling around my neck. The flat gray edifice dominates the block, as if the arrogance of its wealthy members has seeped into its stones. I'm not at all surprised that the senator is on the executive board. The building itself screams *privilege*.

"Because the lock my dad's key goes to is in there." I adjust my wig. Damn thing itches like a mofo.

"I mean, why can't Tyler walk you in?"

Tyler asked the same thing, actually, after he tracked down his father's version of the key to show me. The senator's key has the same art deco–style head as the key Sam found in the lamp at the racetrack. It's the same size and is made of the same material. It has to be from the same source as the senator's, and the senator's is from the locker room of the Strand.

Tyler and I argued about my involving him in this next part of the game. He wanted to infiltrate the club with me, even helped me devise how to do it. But this isn't the place for him.

"Plausible deniability. I'm not sure what we'll have to do when we get in there. I don't want Tyler going down for this."

"How noble of you," Sam says. "You don't mind us going down for it, though?"

"I don't mind Chester and Dwayne going down for it, no," I say, flicking his recently forged badge. "Besides, we're professionals. Tyler's a rookie. Odds are in our favor."

Sam smiles at that. Good to see his smile again. It's seemed rarer the last few days.

We continue around the side of the building to the service entrance. I pull at the sleeve of his tan coveralls, which happen to match mine, which I happen to have had Tyler commandeer from the garage chain his father owns. Lucky connection, that.

"There's the truck," I say, rolling my shoulders forward in a slouch and indicating the step van just ahead of us with my freshly goateed chin.

Sam and I stroll up to the back of the van. It's already half empty, but there are still enough boxes for Sam and me to each grab a couple and haul them in through the service entrance.

"God, what's in these?" Sam asks, wrinkling his nose.

"Cod, I think," I say. "Close, though."

"I'd laugh, but I'd have to breathe, and that's not something I really want to do right now."

The hallway from the door to the kitchen is surprisingly narrow and low-ceilinged. But it's good cover. No one watching the route. The only danger is running into the real delivery guys coming back for another load.

And of course, as soon as I think that, Joe and Blow come around the corner. Sam hesitates for a step, but I nudge him from behind with my box. He can't help it. It's an ingrained response to hesitate when you're afraid you're going to get caught. But that's exactly when you get caught. Never hesitate.

Sam shifts his box slightly higher on his shoulder to hide his face. I follow his example. And sure enough, neither of them looks at us, probably assuming we're Strand employees helping bring in the goods. In any case, we walk right past them and into the kitchen. We drop off the boxes under the watchful eye of the sous-chef, who probably thinks we're with the guys who just left.

We exit through a side door into the main dining room. Ducking into the men's room, we stow our coveralls under the sink behind an overflowing trash can.

It drives me crazy when people on TV throw away perfectly good disguises after swapping into their next character. What if the job goes south and you need to get invisible fast? You could've had that fabulous masquerade-mask outfit you came in wearing, but instead you stuffed it in the fireplace when you shed it for your cat-burglar outfit. Amateurs.

I straighten my black bow tie with a white-gloved hand.

The wig still itches like crazy, but it's one of my most convincing disguises. Messy, a touch too long for a manly cut, and an unflattering shade of orange.

There's a method to my madness, as always. It's stupid hair. People look away from stupid hair faster than they do from nice hair. Hair that's too nice is an attraction. It's important not to get carried away, though. Nasty hair attracts even more attention than nice hair.

Sam has switched out his newsboy cap for a pair of wire-rimmed glasses. His dusky skin tone is pretty distinctive, but he's practiced enough now in deception that a shift of his shoulders and a change in his bearing are enough to convince even me he's a different person. I look away to hide a smirk.

"What's so funny?" he asks.

"Nothing," I say, the smirk widening into a grin.

"I don't have to put up with this abuse," he says as he follows me into the restaurant. "I have better things to do."

"Like hanging out with that girl you've been pining over?"

I'm making it up, of course. I have no idea if he's pining over a girl or not. But sometimes the best way to get information is to pretend you already have it.

Sam tries and fails to cover his shocked expression, and I realize that I'm right. He *is* pining over a girl. Interesting. I make a mental note to torture her name out of him later.

"Where are we going, smart-ass?"

"This way," I say, pointing to another door at the far end of the dining room.

The place is like a maze. It's a giant, square building in Old

Town, which means it's been renovated umpteen times over the years. Most notably during the Prohibition era, when every property owned, operated, or occupied by the male half of the population was supplemented with a network of hidey-holes to shield the demon liquor and its associated vices.

But it's an opulent maze. The dark wood paneling isn't reserved for service hallways—it flows throughout the place, making the doorway lintels, the window frames, and the wainscoting seem heavy and overbearing. The vermilion wallpaper, the ornate crown molding, and the bulky baseboards add to the anchored feeling. The rooms, like the service hallway, are smaller than you'd expect, which lends credibility to my suspicion that there are rooms we're not seeing.

Tyler sketched a map of the place to the best of his knowledge. He knows the location and layout of the locker room with some certainty. He's less sure about the rest of the building, especially the upper floors, since they're reserved for clandestine conference rooms and special overnight guests. But Sam and I can fake it if we need to. In any case, the locker room is our starting point.

The waiter disguises were the best I could come up with on short notice with no way to conduct my usual analysis of the place. Towel boys would probably have been a better choice for the locker-room search, but I have no idea how long the search will take or if we will need to move on to a different room. Waiters seemed like the inmates with the most mobility, considering the high probability of the facility offering room service to its elite overnighters.

Sam pushes open the door into the main lobby. A thick Oriental rug worth more than my entire tuition at St. Aggie's muffles our footsteps as we cross the room. We detour around the claw-footed table with the boulder-sized lily-and-orchid flower arrangement on it and stride purposefully toward the glass doors leading to the gym area.

As I tug the chrome handle to open the door, a rush of humid air immediately heightens the itchiness of my wig. Must be the right place. The wood floor continues into the foyer of the gym area, but it's the only interior element shared by the rest of the building. The gym sports a more contemporary design, with modern furniture, unadorned walls, and the occasional bamboo-infested water feature.

Five banks of lockers with mahogany benches between them fill the main space of the locker room. Larger lockers line the walls, leaving space for the room's corners and about three feet of wall from the tops of the lockers to the ceiling. The door on the opposite side of the locker room must lead to the showers and toilets. The side door, judging by the occasional sounds of grunts and ball-wall impacts, must lead to the various sport courts and equipment rooms. Maybe to a sauna and pool as well. Sam darts to each door to check for incoming patrons.

"We're clear for now," he says, taking off the glasses and stuffing them in his vest pocket.

I take out the key and pull the chain I've fastened it to over my head. There's no number on the key, so we're going to have to try each locker. I start at the nearest bank of lockers and work my way around in a serpentine pattern while Sam plays lookout.

"Good thing we came on a Sunday. A lot of them are probably golfing," Sam says, mostly to break the silence, I think. Talking makes the time pass faster for him when he's nervous.

"Not great weather for golfing," I say, thinking about the brisk autumn wind pushing against us as we walked to the Strand.

"There are indoor driving ranges. Business is better over golf. Squash leaves you too breathless to bullshit."

I laugh, even as the key fails to open the fifteenth locker.

It's not the next locker or the next, and both Sam and I are starting to get antsy. We can only count on an empty locker room for so long.

"This isn't working," I say as I round the edge of the third bank of lockers. "We don't have time to try every one."

"Is there a sixty-three?" Sam asks.

"No," I say. "They're labeled with letters."

"How many letters?" Sam says, perking up.

"Three."

"Is there a pattern?" Sam abandons his post to come look over my shoulder. His presence is solid and warm behind me.

"No." I slam my hand into the offending locker. "Makes no sense at all."

"They're initials." He reaches past my shoulder to run a finger over the metal plate with the engraved letters.

I let my head fall against the locker, closing my eyes. Of course.

"You're brilliant, Sam."

"That's why you keep me around," he says, bumping my shoulder. "But which initials are we looking for?"

"My dad's, maybe?"

But a quick search of the room reveals no JAD in the lot.

"What about your initials?" Sam suggests.

There is a locker with my initials, but the key I have doesn't open it.

"Maybe it's like the gun. Your mom's initials?"

Another quick search, for both her married and maiden names, but no dice.

"What now?" Sam asks.

I shake my head, thinking. "Land of Toys" . . . Not ringing any bells. And I'm pretty sure that "Land of Toys" refers to the club itself, anyway.

On a whim, I search the lockers again, this time for my real initials, though with a good bit of doubt. My dad hasn't called me by my birth name since he gave me my grifter name. My mom named me, and I think the name reminds him of her.

And bingo. A wall locker near the corner of the room bears the initials of my given name.

As soon as I insert the key, I know it's the right locker. I know even before I turn the key and hear the fateful click. The door swings open. My heartbeat ratchets up about twenty notches and Sam leaps a bench to back me up. No dead rats this time, though.

It's so much worse than that. The locker is empty.

THE STASH

"You have got to be kidding me," I say.

Sam doesn't say anything, which confirms that we're screwed. Dead end, possibly literally for my dad.

"He must not have meant the physical locker," I say, scrambling. "Maybe the key means something else." My eyes feel dry and irritated, like I've somehow gotten dust in them. "We have to get out of here. If we get caught—"

"Julep, look!" Sam points at the wall behind the bank of lockers. A slight vertical crack has appeared in the otherwise seamless paint. He moves past me to the wall, running his fingers along the opening between the back of the lockers and the wall, widening it.

"It's a door," I say in the Captain Obvious way that only true astonishment can evoke.

"I thought the dimensions of this room looked off," Sam says with not a small amount of glee. "I noticed as we were coming in from the lobby."

Sam pulls harder at the bank of lockers to expose the remaining hole. Flecks of green paint fall on us, dusting our uniforms. But the door mechanism is well oiled and silent, and the newer floor tile leaves the bottom of the panel of lockers free to swing open where a rug would impede it.

Once Sam pries the door open far enough, I peek inside. It's as black and silent as a crypt. A triangle of light from the locker room spills onto a stained cement floor.

"He must have rigged the locking mechanism to release the catch on the other side of the door," Sam says, examining the hidden hinges.

"How did he even know it was here?" I say, nearly lost in the sea of questions this new discovery has dumped on me. How long has he had this locker? How did he reserve it without a membership? Why go to all this trouble? A stunt like this would have taken extensive planning.

I'm pulling my head out to tell Sam what I'm thinking when I feel his hand on my back, shoving me through the doorway and pushing the bank of lockers closed behind me. I open my mouth to protest, but instead I hear a voice chastising him for shirking his duties and ordering him to deliver a tray of shrimp and sesame sticks with apricot dipping sauce to the third-floor conference room. I hear Sam's muttered "Yes, sir" and then his footsteps as he leaves the room.

I lean back against the now firmly shut panel of lockers. There's enough give in the hinges that I think I can get myself out. The oppressive darkness and stale air constrict my lungs for a few seconds until I manage to get hold of my imagination. Yes, it's pitch-black. No, there are no monsters.

I pull off my gloves and wave my hand in the air, trying to determine the dimensions of the room. My knuckles smack against what feels like a slim wooden post. I grab the post and pull myself closer to it. I wave my other hand out from the wooden construct to find what else is in here, and my fingers brush a thread dangling from the ceiling.

A ray of hope sparks in my brain as I give the thread an experimental tug. There's a promising click, but no light filters through the room. I hear the tiny buzz of antiquated electricity, though, so I wait a few seconds. My patience is rewarded as a dim orange glow begins to emanate from overhead, lighting a small circle of the room around me. It's weak and nearly useless, but any light is better than the oppressive unknown of a moment ago.

The wooden structure I'm holding on to is a spindly, empty shelf for wine bottles. Other than the shelf, the dust, and the long-dead secrets, the roughly eight-by-ten space is filled with a whole lot of nothing. Again I'm at a loss as to what my dad could possibly have meant for me to find, until I realize the string I'm holding is tied to something.

I pull the string up, catching the torpedo-shaped object in my hand. It's a toy airplane. I can't be sure my dad was the one who left it, but since it's the only thing in the room not coated with decades of dust, it stands to reason it hasn't been here long.

I tuck it in my waiter's vest pocket and turn back to the door, more than ready to be out of the room, out of the con, and out of the building. And to find Sam. I press my shoulder to the door and it swings open with only a moderate amount of effort. I can only hope no patron has wandered into the locker room while I've been mucking about in the dark.

"Who the devil are you?" asks someone from the other side.

I quickly don my gloves and pop out of the room to face a pudgy businessman wearing a towel.

"I apologize for startling you, sir." I search for a plausible explanation for my out-of-wall appearance, but there's really no need to lie about it. "I stumbled upon this secret Prohibition-era storeroom, and I need to report it to my supervisor."

"Really?" The businessman's demeanor shifts from annoyed to intrigued in nothing flat. A discovered secret trumps an errant employee any day. I think he's almost forgotten he's in nothing but a towel as he crowds closer to me to get a look.

"It's right through here," I say, gesturing him behind the bank of lockers with a sweep of my hand as I back up and head out of the room. He's too fascinated by the secret room to notice my departure. Now, where did that flunky send Sam? Third-floor conference room?

I dart to the left staircase as soon as I hit the entryway, but my luck has apparently run out. Instead of Sam coming down the stairs, I run nearly headlong into Mrs. Stratton, of all people—Heather's mom, who incidentally knows me as Jena Scott, attorney-at-law. There's a good chance she won't recognize me, but I don't like to take those kinds of chances. I duck my head and melt against the wall, an overdone show of deference, but one that will likely keep her from looking too closely at my face.

"I beg your pardon," she says with a huff as her heels tromp down a stair or two past me.

I've barely breathed a sigh of relief when she stops and turns. She climbs back up to my level and gives me a searching look.

"Do I know you?" she demands.

A lesser con artist would shake her head in a mute appeal for the woman to wave off the nagging feeling of recognition and go. But my father taught me better than that.

"Yes, ma'am," I say, adding a slight Boston accent to my voice that Ms. Scott lacked. "I had the pleasure of serving you on one of your previous visits to the club."

Is it a risk? Of course; this could be her first time at the Strand. But the bigger risk is answering counter to her instincts. That kind of thing is memorable. And since Mrs. Stratton is the kind of person who is obsessed with appearances, the kind of person who only notices people she wants to notice her, waitstaff would be all but invisible to her. It's a risk, but a calculated one. Like every other con.

She *hmms* and continues down the stairs, casting a final "You are covered in dust" over her shoulder. I have to find Sam and get out before any more "luck" comes my way.

I'm up and down the stairs and hallways a half dozen times before I finally track him down. He's in a sitting room in the presidential suite, laying out a tea service.

"Your newness is no excuse for your deplorable tray preparation," I hear the manager berating him. "Your doily is hanging half off the tray, your cups are right side up instead of lying on their sides, your teaspoons are in a jumbled pile, and you call that a fan of napkins? Disgraceful."

"Excuse me, sir," I interrupt, clinging to the door as if I'm intimidated by the manager.

"Fantastic," the manager says, throwing his hands in the air. "Charles sends me another trainee when I need to have this service set in ten minutes."

"Actually, sir, Charles asked me to bring Dwayne back to the kitchen."

The manager makes a disgusted noise and waves us away. "Fine, fine. It would be faster if I did it myself."

Sam backs away a few steps before turning and making a beeline for the door.

"What took you so long?" he says as we jog down the stairs.

"Mrs. Stratton," I mumble.

"What?"

"Never mind. We have to get out of here."

I put a gloved hand on his elbow and herd him down the nearest stairwell. Trooping down stairs takes more time than I'd like, but I feel safer in the boxed-in switchbacks of a stairwell than I do in the open lobby. Disguises are great, but avoiding contact altogether is better.

"Did you find it?"

"I think so, but—"

Before I can finish, we burst through the basement door and run into the sous-chef we met earlier, standing next to a pair of security guards.

"That's them," says the sous-chef, pointing at us.

THE MERRY CHASE

I barrel backward into Sam, who is still holding the door to the stairwell open. Sometimes bluffing your way out is not an option. The trick is to know when it's time to turn tail and run. Like now, for instance.

Sam instinctively pulls the door shut and grabs the crash bar, holding it in the locked position against the pulling and pounding from the other side.

"Grabbing your belt," I say as I whip off his belt and then my own. I loop the first belt around the metal stair railing behind me, threading the end through the metal clasp and pulling it tight. Then I loop the other belt around the crash bar and pull it tight. The belts almost reach each other, but not quite. There's about six inches between them.

"I can't hold it much longer." Sweat stands out on Sam's

forehead as he strains against the bucking door. He puts a foot against the wall for more leverage.

I drop to my knees and pull my shoelace free. Fastest costume change in the West. I thread the lace through the belt-buckle holes on each belt and double-knot the excess.

"Let's go!" I'm bounding up the stairs even as I say it.

Sam runs after me, not bothering to look back to see if the belts are holding the crash bar.

I swing out of the stairwell onto the third floor and race to the nearest unlocked door, which turns out to be a supply closet packed to the gills with towels, toilet paper, cleaning carts, and other hotel paraphernalia. Sam squishes in behind me and closes the door.

We're pressed up against each other so close I can hear his blood racing and feel his breath on my cheek.

"Why'd we run?" he pants. "We could have let ourselves get caught. What's the big deal if we get kicked out?"

"We have a spotless record—never been caught. I'd rather not start getting sloppy now," I say, thinking about how long his parents would let him continue associating with me once I let him get pinched for doing anything even marginally illicit.

"Well, what now?"

We can't go back for the delivery-guy outfits, since the sous-chef saw us in those as well. I pull off my wig and goatee, which are useless now, damn it. Good wigs are not cheap.

It is simply time for Plan B, as my father would say. But I hate having to go with Plan B. Plan B is invariably not as strong as Plan A. Obviously, or it would be Plan A.

165

"I have an idea." I speed-dial Mike's number.

When he picks up, I say, "How fast can you run?"

Three minutes later, I hang up with Mike and start strip-ping. Sam clears his throat and shifts uncomfortably. I'm hop-ing he doesn't think to ask who I called.

"Take off your vest," I say as I squirm against him, trying to get my pants off.

"This is not exactly what I—"

"Stuff a sock in it, Sam. We don't have time to coddle your delicate sensibilities. Ditch the vest."

"Taking off my vest isn't going to make up for my being the only ethnically ambiguous guy in a sea of white people."

"Which is why you're going to hide in the supply cart." I finally get down to my bra and underwear and start unfasten-ing his vest for him.

"No one will fall for that." His voice catches a little. I don't blame him—the thought of riding around in a cart, helpless in securing his own escape . . . must be maddening.

I tug the vest off him and toss it into the nearest cart.

"Gloves, too," I say. "If you do have to make a run for it, I don't want you looking like a waiter. You might be able to lose them in a crowd in a white shirt and black pants."

"I don't think you'll blend into a crowd very well in your underwear," he says.

"O ye of little faith," I say, and tug the nearest maid's dress from a clothes rack on the other side of the door. It's a stretch, since there are two carts between me and the dress. I pull it on and repin my hair.

"How do I look?"

Sam's face is unreadable. "Like a million bucks," he says.

"I was going more for minimum wage."

"That, too," he says, his voice husky.

A walkie crackles out in the hall as one of the security guards approaches.

"Quick," I say, pulling the cart's curtain aside. It's empty. Thank goodness for lazy maids.

Sam dives into place, folding his lanky frame into the cramped quarters.

"Next time I get the dress," Sam whispers.

I shush him and drop the curtain. Then I back out the way we came in, pulling the cart with me, and barely miss bumping into the guard.

"Sorry," I mutter, assuming my most oppressed working-class expression.

"Have you seen two waiters come by?"

I shake my head and push my cart to the first door I see. I pretend to pull a key card out of my pocket, but the security guard has already moved down the hall and turned the corner.

"Are we there yet?" Sam asks.

I kick the frame of the cart to shut him up and move as leisurely as I can to the elevator.

The smooth jazz in the elevator makes me think of those scenes in comic caper movies where the hero enters some sort of wormhole of calm in the chaos of the chase. Like the juxtaposition is necessary to give the viewer a greater sense of impending doom. The elevator is our waiting-room scene, I guess. It would be amusing except that I have to worry about Mike.

Sam still doesn't know that I know about Mike. I don't like lying to Sam, and I like letting Sam get away with being such a henpecking nursemaid even less. In any case, I can't have Sam figuring out that I know about Mike and am using him for my own ends at Sam's expense. Ugh—another reason I'm not a fan of this whole arrangement. Still, we're in trouble, and Mike is in a position to help.

When we finally get to the bathroom where we left the coveralls, Mike is already there. He opens his mouth to greet me, but I put my finger to my lips and shake my head sternly. He clamps his mouth shut with no further urging.

I drag Sam's coveralls out from where we stashed them and hand them to Mike.

"Put this on," I say as I rustle around in the cart for my wig and goatee. The goatee might not stick anymore, but it isn't really necessary, anyway. If all goes according to plan, the guards will only see Mike's rapidly retreating back.

He shoots me a questioning look. I point at the cart and mouth *Sam*.

Mike's eyes widen, but he stays silent as he steps into the coveralls and zips up. They barely fit. Mike's shoulders and chest are wider than Sam's, so the suit is stretched tight. But Sam's taller than Mike, who is closer to my height, so there's a lot of extra fabric down around Mike's boots. Oh, well. Doesn't have to be perfect.

Mike puts the wig on and attempts to add the goatee. It

doesn't look that trustworthy, but again, it's not really important. I might be fooled from a distance into thinking Mike is me if I'd only seen me for a split second, the way the guards did.

"Here's the plan," I say in a hurried whisper. "You get the guards' attention and run out the front while we sneak out the back."

He nods and leaves the bathroom. I wait until I hear him shout in "surprise" at being discovered. Then I wheel Sam out the door and down the narrow hall we came through a couple of hours ago.

My pulse quickens as I turn the corner and see the light from the alley framing the door to the outside. We're almost there, almost there, almost there. . . .

"Hold it!"

THE MOLOTOV

I stop, catching my breath, as the sous-chef comes trotting after us.

"Where do you think you're going?" he says, his expression angry.

"To take out the trash," I say, taking a chance.

"You're not supposed to take the cart out of the building. Didn't Sally train you on the proper protocol?"

"I'm sorry," I say, thinking fast. "It's heavy, and I'm afraid I'll strain my back. Which means I'd have to file a workers' compensation claim. And I'd hate to have to fill out the forms."

The sous-chef blanches a little at that. I gambled that he'd be held responsible for an injury happening on his shift, and I won. Mark one for the grifter.

"All right, but bring it back in immediately. Have one of the staff help you lift the bin."

"Yes, sir," I say, and duck my head.

He spins even as I say it and marches back down the hall. Infuriating busybody. Not for the first time, I feel a stab of guilt-tempered gratitude that grifting lets me avoid working for jerks like him.

I push the cart out the door and into the alley. As I suspected, once the "intruder" was sighted, the back door was left completely unguarded.

I love it when things go according to plan.

"All right, Sam. Come on out."

Sam spills from the side of the cart onto the concrete. He pushes himself up by his shirt-covered forearms, clearly trying to avoid dirtying his hands on the questionable alley floor. I can't say I blame him; I've been through a lot of alleys in my time, and I wouldn't want to touch them, either, though I still have to roll my eyes at his squeamishness. Rich people. So predictable.

"Who were you talking to? Who met us in the bathroom?"

"Never mind that now," I say, and show him the airplane I found in the secret room.

He takes it and turns it over in his hands. "Why an airplane?"

"I haven't a clue."

He chuckles. "Which is funny, because that's what it's supposed to be."

I grumble under my breath.

"What's this?" Sam asks. He shows me the side of the airplane, where its tiny door-hatch has cracked open.

I snatch the plane back from him and pry the door open a little farther, peering into the barrel of the fuselage. There's something stuffed inside. I wedge two of my fingers through the door, trying to get the paper out.

"It's too small."

"Let me see," Sam says, and I hand it back to him. He turns the plane upside down and every which way before handing it back to me. "We'll have to find a pair tweezers."

Once we're safely back in my apartment, Sam heads to the table with the airplane while I rummage around the bathroom until I find the tweezers in a black pouch my dad keeps his shaving stuff in. I feel a twinge of renewed worry. The longer it takes me to find him, the greater the sting when I think of him or see something that reminds me of him.

I hustle back to Sam and hand him the tweezers. Sam opens the door and carefully extracts the paper.

THERE IS NO ESCAPE FROM THE DOGFISH.

"What the hell's a dogfish? What does it have to do with an airplane? What does either have to do with the mob?" I toss the paper on the kitchen table in frustration.

Sam gives me a sympathetic look but no answers. Maybe Ralph can help me again. I'd rather keep him out of it if I can. He's not big enough to be on the mob's radar yet, but if he starts getting in their way, he stands to lose a lot more than his business. Turf is sacred to the mob. Almost as sacred as family.

But going back to Ralph is the only thing I can think of, and I'm getting tired of thinking. I rub my eyes and check my watch. Eight p.m. Ralph should be closing up the storefront.

I look up to find Sam typing away on his laptop, which I didn't even notice him getting out.

"What are you doing?"

"The FBI database. I think I'm almost there. I had to send the director an email from a dummy account with some sleeper code that executes from the email itself."

"A virus?"

"More like a back door into the system. It sets me up with a username and a password from inside their firewall—as if I'm hooked directly into the system."

"I didn't think that was possible."

Sam smiles. "It is if you're me."

"Well, I'm off to Ralph's," I say, standing up. Then I look down at the maid's dress I'm still wearing. "After a quick change."

"Can I watch?" Sam smiles wickedly.

I smack the back of his head as I pass by.

I'm dressed in my usual jeans, T-shirt, hoodie, and jacket in two minutes flat. Sam has already packed his gear.

"Want company?" he asks.

Since I'm guessing I'll already have company, I shake my head.

"No thanks. It's better if I talk to Ralph alone this time."

"All right," he says, his reluctance showing in his hesitation.

"Don't worry so much, Sam," I say, giving him a lopsided smile as I sling my bag over my shoulder. "I can get myself out of anything I can get myself into."

"Speaking of," Sam says as we walk out the door and down the stairs, "you dodged my question earlier about who was in that bathroom."

I've taught him too well. "A friend who owed me a favor. You don't know him."

"How is it possible you know someone I don't?"

"I could have a life outside St. Agatha's."

"Do you?"

"Well, not as such," I admit. "He's a friend of my dad's who owes him a favor." Now why didn't I think of that before? Lying to Sam always throws me off my game.

"You're changing your story," Sam says, suspicious.

"Fine," I grumble. "He's a cop who almost busted me on that Skinner job."

"What?" Sam nearly stumbles on the last few steps in his shock. "When? For which part?"

"Remember when I was late coming back from tagging that water tower?"

"You said that was because you almost got caught by the facilities bureau."

"I fibbed." Actually, I did almost get nabbed by the facilities bureau—specifically, a ranger in a park-issued pickup truck.

"Why?"

"I didn't want you to worry."

"Well, I'm worried now," he says, glaring at me. "Don't do that again. Just tell me the truth."

And now I feel like dirt.

"Okay," I say in a small voice, duly chastised.

"Why does he owe you a favor?" he asks as he holds the front door open for me.

"I gave him a tip on a big-deal case."

"What are you talking about? You don't work with the police. Ever. It's con artist rule, like, three-eighty-four."

"I know, I know," I say. "Forget about it, okay? Go home."

Sam sighs, opening the door to his car. "Can I at least give you a ride to Ralph's?"

"And have you grill me for the next ten minutes? I think I'll pass."

Sam shakes his head and slides into the driver's seat. Seconds later, he's pulled into traffic and out of sight.

"Did you tell him you know about me?" Mike asks as he comes up behind me. He hands me the neatly folded coveralls.

I shake my head, guilt gnawing at my insides. "You didn't have to fold them."

Mike shrugs. "A PI can't be neat?"

I don't comment as I stuff the coveralls into my bag.

"He suspicious?" Mike asks as we start walking.

"Yes and no," I say. "He's suspicious of me, not you."

"Well, it's something, I guess. Where are we going?"

"Ralph's," I say. I don't say "my dad's bookie," because if Mike's any good at his job, he already knows.

"You think he can help?"

"I don't know," I say.

"What were you doing at that club, anyway?"

I deliberate for a moment before handing over the clue. There's no real point keeping it from him. And since I crossed the line in asking him to help us get out of the Strand, I might as well go all in.

"What the hell's a dogfish?" Mike asked, looking at the paper.

"That's what I said," I say. "I'm hoping Ralph knows something about it."

"What is this all about?"

"How much have you heard?" I ask.

"Not much—only that you're a person of interest."

"Come on, Mike," I say, calling his bluff. "You're an investigator. You haven't heard anything else since we talked?"

Mike looks wary. He's hiding something.

"I may have heard something about a forgery job that went south."

"My dad," I say, stuffing my hands in my pockets and picking up my pace. "He's missing, but he's left me a scavenger hunt to help me find something. And now you know all I know."

"The club was one of the clues?"

"Yep."

"What about the girl in the photo?"

"Still no idea, but Sam's working on it. He's trying to hack into the FBI facial-recognition database to see if he can get a hit on her."

Mike looks impressed. "He can do that?"

"We'll find out," I say.

A short "L" ride and a few blocks later, we're standing outside Ralph's shop. It's dark, as I expected it would be this late at night. But Ralph often works on his bookie business in the back after he closes the store. The back door that opens into the alley (yes, another alley—spies have cocktail parties, I get alleys) is located in Ralph's office. All after-hours business takes place through the back door.

I use Ralph's signature knock, which he taught me himself. I wait a few seconds, but there's no response. I try the knock again, and wait again. Still nothing. I give Mike a worried look and he pulls out a gun.

I start to say that I don't think the gun is necessary, but I stop myself. The way this whole situation is going, it very well could be.

Now, what to do about the door? There's not even a handle on the outside. It's always locked, so it opens from the inside only. I take out a hairpin and approach the dead bolt. But as I touch the hairpin to the keyhole, I notice that the door is not latched. Mike takes one look at my face and shoulders me aside. He's first through the door, gun up at eye level.

"Clear!" he says from inside the darkened room.

I'm scared of what I'll find. But it turns out there's nothing more than a dark and empty office. I should be relieved, I guess, but I'm not. Ralph's not where he's supposed to be. And grifters are trained to be highly suspicious when things are not as they should be.

Mike and I search Ralph's office for hints to his whereabouts littered among the stacks of folded paper lanterns, silk parasols, and boxes of plastic-wrapped kimonos that crinkle when I sift through them. But there's nothing. No hint that the mob has abducted Ralph, either. Nothing is tossed, ripped, or wrecked, or seems in any other way to have been searched.

Mike is over at the industrial table Ralph keeps his computer on, its plastic casing yellowing as the years pass and Ralph misses another chance to upgrade. The CPU is a giant box dwarfed in size only by the ancient box monitor, complete with green POS screen.

"Anything?" I ask.

"I can't even work this thing. It's some random database program from the seventies or something. I've never seen anything like it."

I sigh and scratch my head. "There probably isn't any kind of word-processing program or connection to the Internet. Computers aren't Ralph's style."

Mike hits the Escape key a few times to exit out of whatever it was he was attempting to do.

"I didn't find anything, either," I say, frowning in concern. Maybe Ralph really is taking the night off. But better to be safe than sorry. "Let's check the front. If we don't find anything there, we can go."

Mike trails after me through the entrance to the store, around the sales counter, and in among the shelves of trinkets and tourist trash. I look around for anything out of place. After about ten minutes of wandering around, I finally come to the conclusion that my dad's disappearance is starting to make me see intrigue where there is none.

"I don't think—"

But I never get to finish the thought, because three shadowy figures jog past the shop and a flaming fireball comes crashing through the window.

THE RESCUE

"Mike!"

Mike flies into action before the Molotov cocktail even hits the floor. No, literally, he flies. I've never seen a person who isn't in the NBA jump like that. He tackles me out of the way of the flaming bottle.

Unfortunately, he doesn't have the luxury of pointing us at a nice, cushy couch or pile of pillows. Instead he plows us right into a shelf full of glass and pewter figurines of dragons and potbellied Buddhas. My ear strikes the edge of one of the shelves, and it smarts like you would not believe.

But worse than that, the entire case, which is hardly stable at the best of times, comes toppling over, crashing its entire weight on top of Mike, who is still on top of me. The impact is deafening, outpacing the sound of the firebomb as it crashes on the floor barely two feet from us.

Mike takes the worst of it, his head ricocheting off the concrete floor only to smack into a steel crossbar. The heat is intense as the gasoline flares into a bonfire, flames licking up the rack of brightly colored silk shirts. I'm dazed by the sound, the pain, and the heat.

"Mike," I say, trying to gather my wits. "Mike."

But Mike isn't answering. I shift myself out from under him, desperate to get us out of the burning shop.

"Mike!" I shake him, shove the case of now destroyed figurines off him, and turn him over. His eyes are closed, but his chest is moving. He's breathing. Warm, sticky blood seeps from the back of his head, pooling on the floor. I check myself for blood, but other than his, the only blood on me is from a few minor scratches from the shards of broken glass glittering like diamonds in the firelight.

The smoke is starting to affect me now. I'm coughing and my eyes are watering. It's hard for me to draw a breath. The fire has spread from the rack of shirts to the wall of paper cranes, cutting us off from escape out the closer front door. Which means I have to somehow drag Mike's two-hundred-some pounds across the floor and out the back door before the fire spreads to us.

I suffer through another fit of coughing, trying my best to protect my nose and mouth from the smoke. I'm starting to get disoriented and nauseated, and I realize that it's now or never.

I loop my hands under Mike's shoulders and start pulling him by his armpits, my knees pressing into the concrete as I drag him an inch or two away from the fire that is creeping ever closer to his boots. My eyes are running by this point, though whether from smoke or from sheer terror and hopelessness, I can't be sure.

Then, with a rush of cold air, someone is next to me, pulling me back, wrapping me in a cool coat. Whoever it is hands me a cloth to hold up to my face to block the worst of the smoke. I cough into it like my lungs are going to leap from my chest, and it comes away covered in black.

I'm bewildered by the chaos, so much so that it takes me a moment to recognize the muscle-car mob enforcer as she gently pushes me to the side. I try to protest, but instead of forming words, I find myself racked with another bout of coughing.

She ignores me and pulls Mike up to a sitting position. Kneeling next to him, she pulls his arm around her and positions his hip over her shoulder. She shoves herself up, lifting his hefty frame entirely free of the floor, and nods to me.

I scramble much less gracefully to my feet, the coat keeping the worst of the smoke away from my head and face. I stumble after her as she makes a beeline for the back of the shop. She rounds the sales counter and disappears into Ralph's office.

For a heart-pounding second, I am terrified that she's left me alone in a burning building—that she was only a figment of my panicked imagination. I hurry around the corner, clipping my elbow and running right into her. I mumble a quick sorry, to which she grunts a response and moves to the back door.

I should be more concerned. Some tiny part of my brain is screaming at me that I'm escaping the fire only to wind up back in the frying pan. But I can't seem to put a plan together for once we're out in the alley. What if the shadowy figures who lobbed the Molotov in the first place are simply waiting out back with cudgels and cement shoes?

Still, I can't help feeling grateful to our rescuer for saving us. Whatever else she has planned for us, death by fire has to be worse.

I shudder as I pass through the back door and into the crisp, ice-cold air of the alley. I cough and hack and wipe off black stuff, and all the while I'm breathing in the sweetest, most delicious scent of gradually decaying garbage and rat excrement. I've never been so happy to see an alley in all the days of my life.

"Move. You are still in danger."

I know there are a million reasons why I shouldn't. I stand there in uncharacteristic indecision. Can I trust her with my life? With Mike's? He certainly didn't sign up for this, no matter how much Sam is paying him.

She stands there, too, waiting for me to come to the only conclusion I can. I don't know what's out there, except that whatever it is has no compunction about killing me to get what it wants. I have no choice.

As soon as she sees my decision written on my face, she turns and carries Mike through the alley to her waiting Chevelle.

I watch, mute and helpless with nerves, as she opens the passenger's-side door.

"Get in," she says. "Quickly."

I slide into the backseat just before she pushes the seat back and dumps Mike's bulk into the front. She rounds the car in seconds, pulling the key from her pocket and shoving it into the ignition even as she's shutting her door. With a short squeal of tires, she accelerates away from the curb.

"We have to take him to the hospital," I choke out, my voice a thick rasp. I use Mike's headrest to pull myself forward in my seat.

She nods sharply and checks her mirrors.

"Is someone following us?"

"*Nyet*," she says softly.

"What?"

"No. But we are lucky. We have little time."

"Little time for what? Why are you doing this?"

She brakes hard and swerves into traffic on the boulevard. A brief wave of relief washes over me as I realize she really is taking us to the hospital.

"I told you to stay away, stop looking. Now you see what happens."

"Did you do this? Why bother to destroy Ralph's shop if you were going to rescue me?" I demand.

She swears softly in another language. "No! I'm trying to help you."

Now, that is just crap. Crap, crap, crap, and I am not buying it.

"You ran us off the road!"

"It was the only chance I could have to talk to you without discovery."

"What are you talking about?"

"I work for those who are trying to hurt you—"

"Well, that much is obvious."

"Let me finish!" She flicks an angry glare at me through her rearview mirror. "I work for them, but what they are doing is wrong. I worked— I knew your father," she finishes softly.

"Knew?" I say, my throat tight with more than smoke.

"Yes," she says.

We pass a few blocks in silence, her focus on the road, mine on my lap. Tears stream down my face. It will take the smoke a long time to leak out of my eyes completely. A long time.

Thinking of smoke, I make a quick call to the police station about Ralph's shop. The fire station has probably been alerted already by Ralph's alarm-system company, but I want to be sure someone starts looking for Ralph.

I turn off the phone and sink into the enforcer's coat, her smell starting to make its way through the brimstone—spicy, like clove cigarettes. I close my eyes and try to unhear her use of the past tense. Why would my dad have bothered to set up the clues if there was no one left to find?

I open my eyes again and see her watching me, with concern, in the rearview. Concern and regret. I imagine it's not an expression her face wears very often.

Her tank top leaves a lot of skin bare, or rather not bare. Her arms and back are covered with intricate tattoos. The ink peeking out along her shoulder blades suggests the gothic ceiling of a cathedral. Her outstretched arms feature long pinion feathers ending in manacles at both wrists. I have no idea what it means, but it looks painful. The meaning, I mean. The meaning looks painful.

"Who is doing this? Who do you work for?" I ask, quiet but resolved.

"It is best you do not know. I promised him I would keep you out of it. Whatever it takes."

"Telling me that will only make me look harder."

She clenches her jaw. "Your father said you were stubborn."

"He did, did he?" I am not amused. "Well, I'll find out eventually, and better to be in on it with me than against me and in the dark about my plans." Okay, I am not at all convinced I will find out on my own, but she doesn't have to know that.

She gives me a sour look. "I can be stubborn, too," she says.

And that is all she's going to say on the subject. It's obvious in the way she tightens her jaw, turns her steely stare back to the road, and squares her shoulders against my glare. We are at an impasse.

"What if I make a bargain with you for the information?"

She quirks her eyebrow at me in the mirror; she's listening.

"I need to find the people who took my dad. In exchange, I'll keep you out of it when I go to the cops."

She shakes her head. "You cannot make any bargain that I will agree to for what you are asking. I already risk much by sticking my neck on the line as much as I have. You are not only endangering yourself. You are threatening—"

She shuts her jaw with a click, clearly having said too much.

"What? You?"

I know that isn't it, though. I'm baiting her to see if I can rile her into telling me.

"You're asking the wrong question."

"Come again?"

"Haven't you wondered at all why your father came to grief with the people we worked for?"

I open my mouth to retort that of course I have, but stop myself when I realize that I really haven't. I've wondered at times if the clues were leading me to an object rather than to my dad. But I've never once asked myself how he angered the mob in the first place. He knows how the mob operates. He'd never be stupid enough to steal from them. And what's more, he doesn't have to. So why would he allow himself to get on their bad side? What could possibly be worth it?

She sees the chagrin on my face.

"You cannot understand what you are interfering with. Back off or you will ruin everything."

"I'm supposed to trust you?"

"I saved your life."

Well, she has a point there.

She pulls into the circular drive at the entrance to the emergency room and gets out of the car. She comes around the back to our side. When she opens the passenger's-side door, she has to stoop to catch Mike as he rolls, unconscious, toward the ground. She eases him out onto the concrete and a passing orderly comes to take our information. I climb out of the backseat, careful not to step on Mike's still form.

The orderly leaves and comes back with a few nurses and a gurney. One of the nurses takes me aside to question me. His hurried questions touch on all kinds of topics I'm uncomfortable talking about, like who, what, where, when, and how. Actually, the when I'm okay with. Everything else hits too close to home. But I give what information I can, pulling the coat tighter around me against the night chill, which is becoming less welcome by the second.

Finally, the nurses wheel him into the emergency room, leaving me and my rescuer standing in the too-bright lighting of the ER entrance. I turn to her, sliding the jacket off my shoulders to hand it back.

"Keep it," she says, seeming entirely unaffected by the wind. "They will find me out sooner or later. It might as well be my coat that gives me away."

"I don't need your coat," I say, even as I slide my arms into the sleeves.

"Maybe not, but you do need my advice," she says, stepping too far into my personal-space bubble. "Do yourself and your friends a favor—stay away from this. I promise your father will be avenged."

"I don't believe you."

She seems to take offense, her eyes narrowing, as if I am saying she can't do what she claims. I hold up my hand to fend off her protest.

"I mean I don't believe he is dead."

She sighs and puts her hand out toward me as if she means to touch my arm, to offer comfort. But instead she lets her hand fall awkwardly to her side.

"I'm sorry, *milaya*. I would not be the one to tell you this, if I c-could . . . ," she stammers, her English breaking up. "He is dead. I saw him die."

THE FALLOUT

Sitting in the waiting room of a hospital is the least grifter-like experience I can think of. It involves waiting, for one thing. A lot of senseless, boring, ineffectual waiting. You have no control over the outcome. You have no control over when the outcome is even going to take place. You have even less control over the three-year-olds crying miserably in their mothers' arms over ear infections, sick bellies, and sprained ankles.

Quite frankly, sitting in the waiting room of the ER is what I imagine the ninth circle of hell to be like. And yet, here I am, waiting to hear the doctor's opinion about Mike's condition. I've been here at least three hours. You'd think the doctors would have made it to him by now. The waiting room isn't that full. But no. Still waiting.

It's after midnight, and I've just been told my dad is dead.

My dad is dead. The words themselves sound utterly ridiculous. Like they have no meaning whatsoever. It's only a sentence. A grouping of words without depth, without truth. You'd think if my dad were truly dead, I'd feel something when someone said it. Like a knife cutting something loose. Like a grenade going off in my stomach. Like a block of wood in my throat.

People have been staring at me since I sat down. I must look a complete wreck, with my hair wild and singed, soot all over, and wearing a long black jacket that clearly doesn't belong to me. The stares seem unfriendly and judgmental, as if I've done something wrong in all this. As if they know that I let my dad die.

I could call Sam. But it's after midnight, and I'm in the ER. He would flip out. His parents would have a freaking cow. And I can't deal with that right now. I want him here, but I can't deal with the fallout.

I pull the coat tighter around me and wonder about Ralph for the first time in three hours. How could I have forgotten him? I sniff mightily, trying to rein in the saline.

I only have the number for his shop. I call Information in the vague hope of tracking him down, but Information is ironically lacking in the information department. Ralph must be listed under his Korean name, which I don't know.

I hang up and cradle the phone, trying to come up with a new plan. I need to make sure Mike is okay. I need to find Ralph and make sure he's okay. I can't fail them like I keep failing my dad.

Part of me still clings to the hope that he's okay. Even if the enforcer is telling the truth, she can only report what she saw. Which could be anything my dad wanted them to see. People fake their deaths all the time, and my dad isn't people. He's a mastermind.

But part of me is savvy enough to acknowledge that it's much less likely that he's alive somewhere, waiting for the heat to die down. He's brilliant, but he isn't immortal or infallible, and he definitely isn't bulletproof.

A third part of me suggests the possibility that he is alive somewhere but has no intention of coming back for me. And that thought kills me, because I have no one else, not really. No one who owes me a favor. No one who cares enough about me to wonder where I am. It's the cost of being a con artist. If you fake connections long enough, you end up friendless and alone.

And then the phone beeps. It's a text from Tyler.

R U OK?

I'm so not okay. Beyond the concept of "not okay." So I call him, despite the fact that it's late and I'm teetering on the edge of hysteria.

"Julep?"

The sound of his voice on the other end of the line breaks me. I think I say something along the lines of, "The hospital is awful and Mike won't wake up and nobody loves me." Maybe I don't say "nobody loves me," but I can't swear to it.

"I'll be there in fifteen minutes," Tyler says.

Fifteen minutes to the second later, which I know because I'm watching the clock, Tyler strides in, finds me curled into a ball of abject misery on one of the hard waiting-room chairs, and rushes over.

"What happened?" he asks, kneeling in front of me.

"I—" Where do I start? "I went to Ralph's. I took Mike. There was an explosion—"

"Who's Mike?"

"Mike's the— He's a—" I make a frustrated sound as I rub my eyes, trying to think through the fog of exhaustion and smoke inhalation. Too many damn secrets. "It's complicated."

"He's what?"

"He's a friend. That's all."

"Why is that complicated?" he asks.

"Don't tell Sam about him."

"I don't exactly make a habit of telling Sam anything. Julep, what's going on?"

"Nothing. He's just helping me figure out this mess with my dad."

"What does that have to do with Sam?" He sits in the chair next to me without breaking eye contact. "If he's anti-Mike, then I probably am, too. We don't agree on a lot, but I trust him when it comes to you."

I shake my head. "It's not like that. Mike's not bad, he just—" I can't think of anything right now that won't eventually lead to Mike getting fired. I should just come clean, confront Sam, especially now that Mike's probably out of the Julep picture anyway. But I should talk to Sam first, so I say again, "It's complicated."

Tyler frowns at me but lets it go.

"Why were you even out so late? Are you trying to get yourself killed?"

"I went to ask Ralph about the clue."

The clue. I completely forgot about it. I check my hoodie pocket, afraid I lost it in the craziness. But no, its comforting pointiness is still there.

"What clue?" Tyler's hand tightens on mine.

"The clue I found at the Strand."

"Can I see it?"

I take it out and hand it to him. After reading the clue, I tucked the paper back inside the plane for safekeeping. Not that I need it, really, since I have the words memorized.

"A toy airplane?" he says, puzzled, as he turns the plane over. "What did Ralph say?"

"He wasn't there." I leave out the part that he could be dead.

"What happened then?"

He hands me back the plane and leans closer, tracing the tiny cuts and bruises on my face with gentle fingers. And it feels so perfect that I don't answer right away. Instead, I rest my head on his shoulder and close my eyes.

In seconds, I'm out cold. I have no notion of how much time has passed when I feel Tyler nudging me awake.

"Julep," he says softly against my hair. "The doctor wants to talk to you."

I blink up at a cheery-looking Indian man who can't possibly be old enough to have a medical license. But then, who am I to judge?

"Miss? I wanted to update you on your uncle's condition."

"How is he?" I ask, straightening in my chair. My little white lie surprises Tyler, but he doesn't butt in.

"He'll be all right. He woke for a few minutes and answered some questions. But he fell asleep again and is resting comfortably."

"Oh, thank god," I say. "Can I see him?" I start to push myself out of the chair, but Tyler's grip on me tightens.

"I'm sorry, but I think it is better for him to rest now. His wife just returned our call, and she should be here in a few minutes." He pats me awkwardly on the shoulder.

I'd like to stay and see his wife—and apologize—but I know that I'm the last person she needs to deal with right now.

"I'll take you home," Tyler says, pulling me to my feet and partly supporting my weight until I feel steady enough to stand on my own. Smoke inhalation is a bitch—don't let anyone tell you any differently.

Fifteen minutes in the car seem to fly by. Tyler, gentleman that he is, doesn't push me. He waits for me to be ready to talk. And I try to, a few times. But I never get beyond the intention to do so. What would I say?

He parks in front of a fire hydrant so he can get as close to my building's front door as possible. I want to argue, to say that I can walk a block or two. But the truth is that I don't think I can.

And once I open the door to my apartment and see the

tumbled mess of all my dad's things, I don't have it in me to cross the threshold.

"I can't."

"What?"

"I can't do it. I can't go in there."

"But, Julep—"

"It's all right, you can go. There's a motel down the street."

"Don't be ridiculous. I'm not leaving you here this upset."

"I'm not upset," I say, though I'm hardly convincing, so I end up sounding like a fool as well as a liar.

Only when he pulls me into his chest and I am bound by his arms do I notice that I'm shaking.

After a few minutes, he says, "Where can I take you?"

"I don't have any place. I don't have anyone."

"You have me," he says, and my heart feels a little less like a prisoner of war.

He closes the door to my apartment and walks me back to his car. After we're seated and buckled, he pulls into traffic.

"We can go anywhere you want," he says gently. "Just tell me where."

I told him I don't have anywhere to go, and I wasn't lying. But I can at least give a condition.

"Take me someplace they can't find me. At least not tonight," I say.

Tyler stiffens. "'They' who?"

"The people who killed my—" I can't say it. "Who tried to kill me tonight."

"What?" Tyler asks with a calmness that suggests icebergs in quiet seas.

"At Ralph's."

"I think it's time you tell me what happened," he says, his knuckles white where his fingers grip the steering wheel.

So I do. I tell him everything—even about the girl in the muscle car rescuing us, and what she said about my dad. It almost chokes me, but I tell him everything.

And once it's out there, my shivering stops, as if holding it all in had been like closing the vent on a pressure cooker. But it's also irrevocable, like a tanker spill. The oil is out, and no amount of baby-seal rescuers armed with vats of liquid detergent is going to put it back in the ship.

I'm almost frightened to look at Tyler to gauge his reaction. If he has any sense at all, he'll drop me off at the nearest bus stop and keep going.

A tense undercurrent that hadn't been present in our drive to my apartment is making my skin itch. This time, I might have finally pushed him past the level of crazy a privileged teenage boy is willing to put up with.

And as if to confirm my assessment, he pulls onto the shoulder and puts the car in park. It's after two a.m. now, but there's still traffic.

"What—?"

"Stop looking at me like that," he says, turning to face me in the small confines of the car.

"Like what?"

"Like I'm going to jump out and run screaming down the side of the road."

"I am not look—"

"Yes, you are. Have I ever done anything to make you think I would just abandon you at the first sign of trouble?"

"Well, no, but—"

"But what?"

I straighten in my seat. "But why *aren't* you jumping out and running away? This is hardly just a sign of trouble, and it's not the first, either. I'm dealing with death here. Any sane person would be miles from me by now. So why aren't you gone already? What's in this for you?"

He leans back against his door, gazing at me, turning something over in his mind. I can see him struggling with whatever it is. But struggling how? Struggling to put it into words? Struggling to figure out what to tell and what to conceal? And does it really matter? Nothing he says changes the fact that every minute he's with me, he's in danger.

"You're likely the best grifter in Chicago. Do you really not know?"

I don't answer. I'm not letting him deflect me this time. I need him, yes. Somehow he wormed his way in and made himself essential. Because of that, I've been ignoring his reasons for doing so. But it's past time to lay our cards on the table. And since he's the one who opened Pandora's box, he can go first. So I wait him out, arms crossed.

"You told me the other day that you want to know who

you are, that you don't feel like a real person. But the truth is, you're the most real person I've ever met. You see beneath all the glamour to who people really are, what they really want. That layer people wear to show who they wish they were—you don't have that. Sure, you can put on and take off any of those layers like clothes. But they don't define you. The only thing you are is you."

I'm stunned into silence, my carefully marshaled arguments flying right out of my head. I want to tell him he's nuts. But at the same time, something deep in me resonates with his words. I feel like a struck bell, pure, full, and vibrating.

I clear my throat, my head buzzing. "Even if that's true, it doesn't explain why you're still here, given everything. Why you still care."

"That same day, when you asked me what I want, I told you that I want to know what I want. Remember?" He takes my hand, rubbing the back of it gently with his thumb. "When I'm with you, I know what I want."

My breath catches at the expression in his eyes. I have no answer to that.

His grip tightens. "But you always have one foot out the door, like if you don't let yourself need anyone, you'll be safe. Not only is that not possible, it's damned annoying. Just once, Julep, ask for help."

"I ask for help," I say.

"I'm not talking about calling in favors. Favors are payment for services rendered. I'm talking about depending on someone, trusting someone to hold you up when you can't do it yourself. Do you think you could do that? Just once in your life, let someone else watch the world while you sleep?"

I don't realize my jaw is hanging open until I click it shut. "I . . . I don't know."

"Try."

"Okay," I say. And because he seems to be waiting for more, I add, "I'll try."

He smiles briefly. "That's all I wanted to hear."

Then he drops my hand to shift gears and pulls the car into traffic. Once we've reached cruising speed, he reclaims my hand. The silence between us is friendly again, the air clear.

The idea of someone else taking charge is so foreign to me that I don't think I can wrap my mind around it. It's a terrifying thought to not be in control, but at this moment, it also sounds like a death-row reprieve.

"Thank you, Tyler," I say. "Really, for everything."

"I didn't do it for thanks," he says. "I did it because I care about you."

"Oh," I say, looking at the door handle.

And that's how, without my even noticing, the first boy to ever make my heart race, to ever make me think I could have a normal life *now*, in *high school*, not in some random future dream, but *now*—that's how the first boy I ever wanted to kiss takes me home to meet his mother.

THE SOCIAL WORKER

"Seriously, Tyler," I hiss in a panic as he parks the car next to his mom's BMW. "Don't make me do this, not looking like this."

"Remember what I just said about asking for help?" he says in a half-exasperated, half-amused tone. "This is what help looks like."

I hide my face in the enforcer's coat. "She's Sarah Richland. She's not someone whose house you show up at in the middle of the night looking like the creature from the black lagoon and smelling like a smokestack."

"She's my mother. And you look fine."

"Don't wake her up," I say. "I can sleep wrapped in a bed-sheet."

Tyler laughs. "As tempting as that is, I think you'll be more comfortable in actual clothes. Besides, I don't have to wake her up. No one actually sleeps in my house, remember?"

I put off moving until Tyler comes around to my door and opens it. I give him the Julep stink-eye. "This isn't the best way to encourage me to ask for help." But I get out anyway and follow him through the side door to the Richland mansion.

"Elle, will you go get my mom, please?" Tyler asks a maid making tea in the kitchen.

"Wow, you weren't kidding about no one sleeping around here," I comment when the maid leaves with the tea tray.

By the time we reach the living room, I've divested myself of the enforcer's coat and my own ruined jacket and hoodie. My shirt mostly survived, but it smells as bad as the rest of me. I try to do something with my hair, but I give it up as a lost cause when I hear someone clearing her throat behind me. I swivel slowly and see Mrs. Richland standing at the bottom of the stairs wearing an ivory silk pajama set, her disapproving glare putting me instantly on edge.

"Mom," Tyler says, taking me by the elbow, "this is Julep. She needs help."

"I—yes, I'm sorry to intrude. But it's very nice to meet you." I don't try to offer my hand. It's disgusting, for one thing. For another, she doesn't seem too terribly impressed by me.

"The feeling is mutual, to be sure," she says in a tone that makes it clear the opposite is actually true. "What assistance do you need?"

The woman adds new dimension to the term *ice queen*. I

open my mouth to say that this may not have been the best idea, but Tyler speaks first.

"She needs a shower, and something to sleep in. I've invited her to stay the night. In the guest room."

Mrs. Richland presses her lips together, no doubt to hold back what she thinks of this idea. But she nods and sends Elle for some spare clothes before going back upstairs.

Elle returns with a robe, slippers, and a gorgeous satin nightgown. I'm already self-conscious about it, and I haven't even tried it on yet. And self-consciousness is not a thing I feel often.

I follow Tyler up the stairs to the second floor. He heads in the opposite direction of his room and guides me to a spacious guest room in a darkened wing of the house. The room has its own bathroom, complete with a shower, into which I disappear without further persuasion.

As good as the water feels, I don't linger long. I'm tired down to my bones, and hungry enough to eat the slippers. I don't hold out much hope for food, but the bed is waiting for me with its plush down-filled comforter and three-thousand-thread-count sheets. Lonely and bereft, I'll likely have trouble sleeping, but even the idea of lying down is almost enough to make me weep.

When I emerge, satin nightgown swishing against my skin, Tyler is sitting on the chaise fiddling with his phone, a tray of biscotti, cheese, and tea on the end table at his elbow.

"Is that for me?" I ask, eyeing the tray with, I'll admit, a little drool at the corner of my mouth. I may or may not have licked my lips.

Tyler doesn't answer right away, so I start to worry it isn't for me, but when I tear my gaze away from the tray to confirm with him, he's staring at me.

"What?"

Then I remember that I'm practically naked and I back-pedal into the bathroom for the robe. When I come out of the bathroom the second time, we both apologize at the same time, and then laugh uneasily.

"Better?"

"Much," I say, and dig into the food.

He watches me scarf down cheese and biscotti, getting crumbs all over the fluffy white robe lapels. I feel bad brushing them to the carpet, so I ignore them. I'll wait till he leaves.

When I've polished off all the food and tea, he takes my hand and pulls me to the bed. "Time to sleep," he says. "It's a school night."

"Oh, man. It's Monday again, isn't it? Dang it, Monday— why you got to be all up in my grill?" My snark is somewhat checked by my enormous yawn. With Tyler here, my loneliness is at an all-time low. If only I could shrink him and carry him around in my pocket.

I lie down, robe and all, on top of the comforter. Tyler covers me with a throw he pulls from the chaise and then stretches out next to me, facing me, a respectful foot or so between us.

"How are you feeling?" he says, and he doesn't mean the

bed or the food. He means everything else, and he knows I know it.

"Awful," I say honestly.

"What can I do?"

"You've already done so much."

"Ask me."

I know what he wants to hear, what I want to say. If I'm brave enough.

"Please stay with me," I whisper past the fear in my throat.

"Okay," he says, taking my hand and holding it to his chest.

I fall asleep minutes later to the beat of his heart.

When I wake up, the birds are chirping, sunlight is streaming through the curtains, and Tyler is gone.

I sit up, still covered in the blanket, feeling a Tyler-shaped emptiness that refuses to be ignored.

He left. After that big speech about depending on others—on him, in fact—he up and leaves at first light. Or earlier; maybe he only waited long enough for me to fall asleep. Though even that is a kindness, and I shouldn't begrudge him wanting to sleep in his own bed.

I swing my legs over the edge of the mattress. Well, *swing* is generous. More like painfully inch my sore muscles over the edge as I stretch to get the kink out of my neck. I hear a pop and some tension releases. After what I put my legs through last night, I can hardly blame them for being sore.

I'm about to stand when I hear someone tromping up the stairs.

"I don't care what meeting he's in—give him the message,"

Tyler says as he opens the door and smiles at me, a cup of something cappuccino-ish in one hand and his phone in the other. "Thank you," he says, and hangs up. He passes me the coffee and swings my book bag to the floor.

"It's official," I say as I take a sip. "You're my hero."

"If you like that, you'll love what else I brought," he says, unlatching the bag and pulling out my school uniform.

"How'd you get this?" I ask.

"You didn't lock your place when we left last night," he says. "I woke up early and went to get it. I figured you wouldn't want to go to school looking like you'd survived a fire."

I could kiss him, I'm so happy. He even brought my toothbrush.

"I thought you left," I say.

"I did," he says, as if pointing out the obvious. "And then I came back."

"Thank you," I say.

"Thank me by believing that I'll come back," he says, sitting down next to me on the bed.

I lean into him and, finally, the last remaining resistance gives way. I believe him. He's real. And I can feel myself attaching to him like a barnacle to the bottom of a barge.

He leans into me, too, and before I know what is happening, his lips are on mine, stealing my breath.

The kiss starts soft and sweet, tentative, asking for a leap of faith. I have little experience with kissing, which only adds to the strange liquid heat in my arteries. I imagine myself glowing with the radiation as he deepens the kiss, folding his arms around me and drawing me closer. I'm barely conscious of anything but all the places where his body touches mine. All the places my skin is on fire.

Countless minutes later, he pulls back, a satisfied smirk on his face. I try not to look as flustered as I feel. But the kiss was nice. I liked it. A lot. So I lean closer to him, tangling my fingers in his hair, and kiss *him* this time, taking control.

Even more minutes later, I pull back, breaking the kiss abruptly.

"What time is it?"

He's still smiling as he checks his watch. "Twenty till eight."

"Crap! If I'm late again, the dean will have me drawn and quartered."

"Need me to run interference?"

"No, I just need to get my butt to school."

I snatch up my bag and race to the bathroom. But before shutting the door, I change tack and pounce on Tyler again. One more kiss for the road.

• • •

As I race to get ready, the sun is shining through the stained-glass window of the bathroom with the promise of a new day. I'm almost a new person. Yesterday was rough; I'm not going to lie. And I'm still desperately worried about my dad, Mike, Ralph, and even my stalker, oddly enough.

But with the day already off to an amazing start, I can't help but take a sunnier view on my circumstances. For example, the more I think about it, the more possible it seems that my dad is still alive. He'd never get himself into a situation he didn't have eight contingency plans for. As for Mike and Ralph, the doctor said Mike would be fine, and I'll find Ralph. I feel like I can do anything today.

And then there's Tyler. . . .

"You almost done in there?" he asks, knocking on the door as I finish running a brush through my hair.

I toss the brush on the counter and then open the door and fling myself at him, attacking him with another dizzying, oxygen-depriving kiss. Now that I've started, I can't seem to stop.

But then the downstairs clock strikes the hour, and I forcibly detach myself from him.

"Let's go," I say, pulling him by the hand and grabbing my bag on my way out of the room.

Mrs. Richland is sitting in her morning room, sorting through papers stacked neatly on an antique rolltop desk. I stop long enough to give her my heartfelt thanks. She responds with a noncommittal noise of acknowledgment and an imperious look, but the chagrin I should feel rolls right off me. I'm having a good day.

When we get to St. Aggie's, Tyler opens the door for me and offers a hand to help me out of the car. The rest of the students in the parking lot stare at us, mouths literally hanging open. All the better—once word gets back to Bryn, Murphy's chances of getting a yes will increase exponentially.

I give Tyler's hand a squeeze as we separate, each of us going to our respective buildings. As he pulls away, my heart aches a little in a very cliché, very nice sort of way. I really could get used to this. And that should worry me more than it does.

"Julep!" Sam says, coming up behind me.

I turn to him and smile, but his expression morphs to horrified when he sees my face.

"Jesus, Julep, what happened?" he asks as he takes a step closer than he usually would.

He moves my hair aside to examine a gash on my forehead that's longer than the others. I pull back, uncomfortable. Just because I'm getting all handsy with Tyler doesn't mean I don't require a certain amount of personal space.

"Molotov cocktail through a shop window," I say. "Nothing I couldn't handle."

"Oh my god, are you okay?"

I take a deep breath, not really wanting to relive the whole thing now that I've regained a hopeful perspective.

"I am now," I say. "Can you keep your voice down?"

"I will if you tell me what happened."

So I give him the brief history of a girl and a fire—leaving out Mike, of course, and the sleeping-next-to-Tyler part.

"She rescued you?" he asks, sounding as incredulous as I felt at the time.

"I know. Weird."

"Did she say why?"

"Just that she knew my dad and promised him that she'd look after me."

"That makes no sense," he says, pulling some printouts from his bag.

"I know," I say. "She said something about the people she works for doing something bad—"

"No kidding," Sam says, handing me the paper.

On top is a mug shot of the enforcer, looking a little younger than she does now and thoroughly sullen. Her tattoo is different from when the mug shot was taken; it covers more of her skin now, and has more detail. The name next to the photo is Danijela "Dani" Ivanov.

"You did it," I say, impressed. "I mean, I knew you would eventually. But wow, that was fast. The botched-files idea worked out?"

"Batch files, and no," he admits. "But I found another way in. It was hard. And incredibly dangerous."

"Right," I say, scanning every inch of the profile.

"Look at her known associates," Sam says, pointing to a spot lower down in the dossier.

Jackpot.

"Sam, you're a miracle worker," I say, hugging him. "What would I do without you?"

Sam clears his throat. "Run around in circles like a chicken with its head cut off?"

I give him a withering look.

"So what are you going to do now? I'm almost afraid to ask."

I start to say something pithy about paying her a visit, but then change my mind about telling him.

"I'm going to go to class," I say instead. Then I bump his shoulder with mine. "Later, skater." Printouts in hand, I head to homeroom, skirting an early-morning tai chi class doing forms on the lawn, and push through the double doors.

"Ms. Dupree," the dean says, popping out from behind a trophy case.

I nearly shriek. Okay, maybe I shriek. But only a tiny shriek. I blame the golden glow of Tyler's kisses and Sam's discoveries for my not seeing her coming. In any case, the dean has a brown woman in tow. I say "brown" because she is thoroughly brown—brown hair, brown eyes, brown skin, brown knit skirt. The only color other than brown on her entire body is her reddish-brown lipstick.

"I'm glad we caught you," the dean continues with a self-satisfied smirk. "This is Miriam Fairchild, a social worker."

Fan-freaking-tastic. A social worker.

"So nice to meet you," I say, playing my part while surreptitiously tucking the printouts into my bag. "Welcome to St. Agatha's. I'm sure Dean Porter has a lot to show you, so I'll be off to class."

"Oh, she's here to speak to *you*, dear," the dean says. I grit my teeth. I highly doubt the dean has used the word *dear* to refer to a student even once before in her lifetime.

"What about?" I ask suspiciously, dropping the act.

"Let's go back to my office, so we can talk privately."

Somehow they know. Involving the state means that the dean has certain knowledge of my parent-free status. She could have swung by my apartment, I suppose, but it isn't likely. The only logical explanation is that somebody's tipped her off.

"I—"

"Dean Porter!" Heather says. She's breathing hard, having had to run to reach us. "I have a message for you!"

The dean frowns at her. "Can't it wait?"

"It's Ms. Fairchild's car. Someone's towing it."

"What?" the social worker says. "Why?"

"I don't know," Heather says. "The tow company wanted me to notify you. I thought it was important enough to—"

Before she can finish, Ms. Fairchild takes off for the faculty parking lot, her long bohemian skirt flapping in her wake.

"Wait!" the dean shouts, running after her.

I turn to Heather with a raised eyebrow. "Tow company?"

Heather shrugs. "It's the fastest thing we could come up with. Sam's idea, actually, though Tyler made the call."

"Her car is actually getting towed?" I say, incredulous. "How did the truck get here so fast?"

"I don't know. But Sam had Murphy dig up a couple of traffic cones and some No Parking signs from security to make it seem more legit."

"Well, thanks," I say. "I owe you—all of you."

But I feel considerably less relieved than I should. How many people are in on the secret now? Tyler, Mike, Sam? Murphy and Heather might even know. Any one of them could have told the dean.

"Thank us later," she says, grabbing my arm and moving in the opposite direction of the dean and the social worker. "We've got bigger problems."

"Bigger problems?" Oh, god. What now?

"They're trying to cancel the dance."

We're halfway down the hall when Murphy catches up to us. "Did you tell her?"

"I was getting to it," Heather says.

"The dance is a bigger problem than a social worker?"

"It is to us," Murphy says. "I'm asking Bryn tomorrow. I'm not giving up on that because some stupid pipe burst."

I sigh. "All right, back up. Start from the beginning."

"The water main beneath the library burst. The lower east hall is a stinky swamp, and the basement of the library is a swimming pool."

"But the dance isn't in the library; it's in the gym."

"President Rasmussen says the foundation is questionable and the whole east building is off-limits, including the gym. The registrar is about to burst a blood vessel because all the student files are in there and we're supposed to be starting registration for next sem—"

"Why don't they move the dance off campus?"

"The dance is this weekend. We'd never be able to find an empty space big enough that quickly, not this time of year, even if we could convince our parents to help the school foot the bill."

"This really isn't my wheelhouse, guys. I'm not an organizer."

"You're our fixer," Heather says, as if it were obvious. "You fix things."

"I can't, all right?" I open the door leading to the chapel. "I've got too much on my plate as it is."

"You've got to do something, Julep," Murphy says, his new

specs giving him an air of intelligent authority where his old ones made him look bug-eyed.

The mere thought of adding "locate a dance venue" to my list is giving me hives. New positive attitude notwithstanding, I'm not Wonder Woman. I can't do everything. And if I take on yet another responsibility, one of my others will slip. Which ball do I feel comfortable dropping at this point? School? Rent? My dad?

I start walking with purpose toward the student parking lot I came in from, which is thankfully hidden from view of the faculty parking lot as long as I go the long way, through the chapel. Murphy and Heather have to rush to keep up.

"I need a count of people attending," I say. "I'll get you a building. That's it. The rest is up to you."

Heather squeals and hugs me. "Try to find something that fits the 'Swing in Space' theme."

"Yeah, yeah," I say, extricating myself so I can continue to my goal of stealing a car. "Just keep me posted about the social worker."

"On it," Heather says as I start checking wheel wells and bumpers for magnetic key boxes. "What are you doing?"

"Getting a ride."

Murphy hands me his keys. "Just take my car."

"Oh." Duh. "Thanks, Murphy. I'll try not to total it."

"Is there a possibility of you totaling it?" he asks, turning pale.

"Of course," I say, clicking the button to make the car beep.

The lights on a Kia Sedona minivan flash off to my left. I cast a disparaging look at Murphy. "Really?"

"What? It has a good safety rating."

I refrain from commenting as I slide into the driver's seat and dump my backpack and Sam's printouts on the passenger's side.

"Where are you going?"

I start the car and rev the engine.

"I've got to see a criminal about a fish."

THE RACKET

When I hit 55, I head south.

Known associates: Nikolai Petrov, suspected leader of Ukrainian organized crime syndicate.

Last known address: S Madison St.

I can't do anything about Petrov without further information, but I know exactly who to shake down for that. I was too distracted by nearly getting blown up to put any real pressure on my rescuer. But even with the right leverage, she'd be a tough nut to crack. Far easier to spy on her to get what I need.

I take the IL-83 exit and make a left toward the canal. Scrub bushes and warehouses squat along the road. I pull over in front of a likely-looking building—dilapidated enough to avoid too much notice, but without the air of abandonment of potential raver hangouts.

I do a quick equipment check: minivan, AV gear, book bag full of sooty clothes, and . . . maybe? I root around in the bag and pull out the wadded-up coveralls. Tyler didn't take them out.

Tyler. I probably should have told him where I was going. Not even twenty-four hours and I'm already forgetting my promise to stop excluding him.

I reach for my phone.

"Julep, where are you?" Tyler asks after the first ring.

"The warehouse district along the canal," I say. "I'm going to . . . um, do a little reconnaissance."

"Without backup," he says.

"I keep forgetting about the backup."

"The backup is the most important part."

"Sorry?" I'm pretty sure that shouldn't be a question. I try again. "I'm only doing a quick look-see. No confrontation involved."

"That isn't exactly comforting."

"I'll keep you on the line. You'll hear everything."

He's silent for a second. "Not good enough," he says at last. "Wait for me. I'm on my way now."

"Is Sam with you?"

"No. Should he be?"

"No, it's fine. Nothing's going to happen. I just want to find out what they're up to. If I know the game, I can manipulate the players."

"Fine," he says. "But you'd better wait for me, or there will be consequences."

"You make that sound like a bad thing."

I hang up and sit still for a whole minute before I get out of Murphy's van and into the coveralls. Not much I can do with my hair other than pull it back into a low, careless ponytail, but my plastic frames add a layer of protection. I know I should wait for Tyler. I just have this mental block when it comes to letting others take the lead.

I grab some incomprehensible tool that looks vaguely diagnostic from the back of the minivan and take on a hunched-shoulder, slightly twitchy affect as I lock the minivan's door. I scuttle across the road to the nearest fuse box and duck my head behind it, pretending to assess something.

In the first warehouse, rows of metal shelves are stacked to the rafters with unmarked crates. Anything could be in those crates—guns, drugs, Cuban cigars, or even legitimate inventory like paper or dish detergent. Crime bosses often own aboveboard businesses as fronts for their sleazier trades.

Two workers in hardhats jockey forklifts through the stacks, moving crates from one place to another. So far, neither of them has noticed me. But as long as they're sitting on the goods, I'm not going to be able to investigate.

I "check the meter" at the next warehouse over and spot the Chevelle parked behind the building. I shuffle to the junction box, which happens to be under a window directly behind the car. I peek through the glass long enough to see Dani arguing with a too-thin woman with a bad dye job. The woman rolls her eyes at Dani, but the gesture is undercut by a fear of Dani that's so obvious I can see it from all the way over here.

Most of what she's saying is in Ukrainian, but I pick up an English word or two. One of those words is *let's*, followed by *go*.

I abandon Murphy's tool on top of the junction box and scurry around the back of the car, away from the door leading into the warehouse. No sooner do I duck around the side of the building than I hear the door swing open, and two sets of footfalls head toward the Chevelle. Seconds later, the Chevelle growls to life, nearly stopping my heart, and then fades away into the distance.

Not wanting to push my luck too far, I continue on to the bay doors near the front of the building. With a little wriggling, I squeeze under the crack at the bottom.

The lighting is almost nonexistent, which is fine by me. It's light enough that I can see crumpled balls of paper skirting the edges of the concrete floor like urban tumbleweed. Bits of broken glass and years of grit and gristle line the fissures in the floor. In short, it's seen better days. And probably a few homeless people with oil-drum fires.

I slink over to the wall and sketch a quick perimeter. Nothing jumps out at me. It's a big, empty room with a wooden staircase lining one wall. In fact, the staircase is the only thing that looks like it's seen any recent traffic.

Now I really should wait for Tyler. I have no idea what's up there, and I'll have no one guarding the only escape route should anything go pear-shaped. But no matter how reasonable waiting sounds, my feet aren't listening.

I'm not sure what I expect to find when I get to the next level. Probably everything worth narcing on is in the other warehouse. But then why were Dani and Bad Dye Job hanging out in this warehouse? My gut says I need to see what's up there, even though it's churning with dread at the same time.

When I get to the second story, I peer cautiously through the metal railing. Blacked-out windows make the lighting on the second level even dimmer than on the first, and it takes my eyes a minute to adjust. But they eventually do, and I'm puzzled at first by the rows and rows of mismatched sheets strung up on lines crisscrossing the space. No one is immediately visible, so I take a few steps into the passage, which is lined on either side by dingy fabric.

As I creep past the third sheet, I hear a woman's soft cry behind it. A murmur meant to comfort spills over the whimpering, shushing it back into silence.

My fingers pull the sheet back a half inch, enough to see without being seen. Enough to glimpse a young girl no older than I am with her arms around another girl, a little older but more damaged. There's a bed. A metal frame with a mattress and a threadbare blanket. A metal handcuff, one end cuffed to the bedframe, dangles to the floor. I can't tear my eyes away from it. I can't accept what it implies, but I can't deny it, either.

Then the girl who's not weeping starts to raise her head.

I snap out of my trance just in time to let the sheet fall back. If any of them raises an alarm, I'm as good as dead. But I can't leave. Not until I'm sure.

I sneak to another row and twitch back a sheet. Another girl staring through a streaked black window. The third space I check is empty, but I can hear a girl in the space next to it mumbling to herself in Ukrainian. I'm pretty sure she's praying. She sounds like she can't be older than twelve or thirteen.

I back up, slowly at first, but my pace quickens into stumbling as I move in the direction of the stairs. I count the rows of curtains. There must be nearly a hundred makeshift cells. I try to be silent, but in my desperation to get away, a few shuffling sounds escape. I know I'm not being careful about hiding my presence, but I'm barely keeping my panic in check.

I almost make it to the stairs before an iron arm circles my waist and a hand clamps over my mouth.

22

THE ENFORCER

I struggle against my captor, all higher-level reasoning obliterated by the single terrified thought that I'm going to be sold into slavery as well. But whoever has me is stronger and pulls me into another unoccupied sheet-walled room just opposite the stairs.

"Be still," Dani hisses in my ear, and my overwrought brain is torn between relief and rage. She keeps me muffled and restrained, even when I stop struggling.

Then I see Bad Dye Job's head appear as she climbs the stairs. Dani pulls me back farther into the shadows. The other woman would have caught me for sure if Dani hadn't grabbed me.

Dani lets me go but imprisons my wrist. When Bad Dye Job is far enough past us to risk it, Dani manhandles me to the stairs, nudging me none too gently ahead of her. I can tell how furious she is with every movement. But her anger is nothing compared to mine.

She pushes me through a side door that opens between a fire escape and an HVAC unit. The hum coming from the equipment obscures sound from inside the building, so it will probably do the same for us. And as it happens, I have a lot to say.

"What the hell do you think you're doing?" I shove her, wishing I could Tase her instead. Rescue or no rescue, she's a reprehensible person for being involved in this.

"What the hell do you think *you* are doing? Why should I bother pulling you out of fires if you insist on running right back in?"

"They're kids! They're just—"

The anger on Dani's face freezes into a stony mask, but she doesn't deny anything or defend herself.

"Tell me my father wasn't involved," I say, more plea than demand.

Dani sighs. "You are not supposed to be here. You are not supposed to know any of this. Why do you not listen?"

"Why would I listen to you? You say you saw my father die and did nothing to stop it. You work for a monster who holds girls hostage, girls younger than you, and from your own country. Would you listen to you if you were me?"

She looks hurt but doesn't flinch. "You think you know everything? You know nothing."

"Then tell me. What is Petrov doing with them?"

"Go home. Now. Before anyone sees you."

"I'm not leaving without answers. Or would you rather I go back in there and lead them all out?"

"And take them where?" she says, her anger returning. "They wouldn't follow you, anyway. They'd turn on you and give you to Petrov in pieces."

"Are you saying they want to be here?"

"No," she says, followed by a string of what are probably expletives in her native language. "But this is complicated. If they involve the authorities, they'll be deported, maybe imprisoned."

"It has to be better than being used as, what? Sweatshop workers? Sex slaves?"

Dani's piercing look confirms my worst fears.

"Many of them are running from lives worse than this," she says. "And those who aren't have been told their families will suffer if they try to escape. The threat is real, and they know it."

"I have to do something," I say. "I can't leave them here."

"Anything you do would only make matters worse."

"Just tell me if my father was involved," I say. "You owe me that much."

"Owe you?" Her ice-blue eyes narrow.

"You said you owe my father. If he really is dead, then that debt goes to me. Tell me what I want to know."

To her credit, she never drops eye contact, which is how I can see her emotions as she considers my demand.

"No. When he took the job, he did not know why Petrov wanted the documents."

I close my eyes, relieved.

"He found out," she continues. "I don't know how. I did not tell him. And somehow he figured out I was not as loyal as the others. What they were doing, it did not feel . . ." She leaves her thought unfinished.

"I believe the word you're searching for is *right*. Or maybe *ethical*, or *remotely morally defensible*."

"Lower your voice. Tanya will hear." Her gaze darts inside. I try and fail to break the grip she still has on my wrist. She doesn't let me go until she's certain no one's coming. I yank my arm out of her reach when she finally releases me.

"Why didn't he call the cops when he found out what Petrov was doing?"

Dani gives me a you-know-better look, and she's right. I do. My dad couldn't turn to the police without implicating himself, not without evidence to bargain with.

"Petrov has connections. There's nowhere your father could have reported it that it wouldn't have been covered up. Even if these women"—Dani gestures toward the building—"had been recovered—deported, imprisoned, or set free—Petrov would never have seen a jail cell. Your father wanted to end it. And he wanted to protect you."

I don't want to believe the situation is as hopeless as it seems. But knowing now what my father knew, it's clear why Petrov wanted him dead, and why he now wants me dead on the chance I'll figure it out.

The collar of Dani's new coat flips up in the wind. "Your father must have found evidence against Petrov. It must be how they discovered his betrayal."

I lower my head, not wanting to hear.

Dani shrugs deeper into her coat. "I didn't know. I was on an errand. I was . . ."

"You were what?"

"I was watching you. For your father."

I shiver. It's cold, and this conversation is getting too surreal for me.

"I returned just as Petrov raised the gun. I was too far away to interfere."

I fight the lump in my throat. I can't let myself feel anything right now.

"Your father was right about me," she says, taking a step closer. "I have my own passage to pay. But that payment will not include harming the innocent."

Her expression is contrite. She wants me to understand. And I'm wishing desperately right now that I didn't, because I want to be angry with her, to blame her for what's happening to my family. But would I have done so differently in her place? Am I doing so differently now? I'm just as much a criminal as she is.

"I've been watching over you for months," she says, running a loose twist of my hair through her fingers. "I will not stop until Petrov is no more a threat. Go home. Forget about this. Live your life on your terms, or your father will have died for nothing."

"If you've been watching me for months, then you know I can't do that."

Dani shakes her head, smiling a little. "Yes. But I had to try.

Your continuing to throw yourself at the enemy makes my job harder."

"Then you're not going to be happy with what I'm about to do next." But before I have the chance to explain, I hear Tyler's shiny sports car pull up.

"Wait for me?" I say to her. "I'll only be a minute."

"Hurry. We risk too much as it is."

I jog up to Tyler's car. He gets out and clear of the door just in time for me to throw myself into his arms.

"What is it? What happened?"

I shudder, taking off my glasses and digging the heel of my hand into my temple. Tyler pulls me behind the minivan, out of view of the building.

"Tell me." His expression is concerned, earnest. And I want so much for him to be able to fix it. But even his connections aren't going to get those hostages out of there.

"I know what they're doing. The mob—they're smuggling people into the country as slaves."

His face pales. "Are you sure?" he asks, looking sick.

"I wish I weren't."

"I had no idea," he says, almost to himself.

"We have to get out of here." I cross my arms to ward off the chill in my blood. "Dani could come back anytime."

"Dani?" He sounds distracted, like he's listening to me with only part of his brain.

"My stalker. Sam found out who she is. She's an enforcer for the Ukrainian mob. The one my dad was working for."

He's silent, staring at the ground, unseeing. His distress

seems worse than mine, but then I've had longer to absorb the new information.

"We have to get out of here." I grab his hand and pull him toward his car.

"We have to help them," he says, resisting me. "We can't leave them there."

Having just said the same thing myself, I have a difficult time switching to the opposite argument. I don't want to be on Dani's side on this, but it is what it is.

"We can't help them now," I tell him. "If we tried, they'd rat us out."

He pulls his arm away. "How can you be so heartless? Some things are worth getting caught."

Okay, that hurt.

"I'm not being heartless, I'm being realistic. We can't rescue them—not without help," I say.

He straightens. "What do you need me to do?"

But before I can answer, his phone beeps.

He unlocks the phone and checks the notifications. "Damn it. I'm supposed to be on the field in five minutes."

Saved by the beep. And here I thought I was going to have to convince him.

"This weekend's the championship, isn't it? You have to go," I say.

"They'll just have to play without me. I'm not leaving—"

"It's fine, Tyler. In fact, it's exactly what I need you to do. Pretend everything's normal. The less attention we draw right now, the better."

"What about you?" he asks. "You can't go back to school with the dean gunning for you."

The dean. I'd forgotten about that completely.

"I'm going home," I lie again, taking a deep breath. Okay, so I suck at backup.

"No way. Not alone. You didn't see your face when you tried to walk in there last night. And anyway, what if someone sees you?"

"I have to figure out the last clue. I need to find whatever it is my dad's hidden."

"You think he's really dead?"

"I don't know anymore," I say, trying not to think about it. "I was sure he wasn't, and then I was sure he was, and then this morning I thought he wasn't. But I really have no idea. In any case, it doesn't change my next move."

"I don't want you to get hurt," he says, pulling me close. His coat is rough under my cheek.

"I don't want me to get hurt, either," I say.

"How do you know you'll find anything that will lead you to the next clue?"

"I don't," I admit. "But with Ralph gone, the only tie I have to my father is his stuff. If there isn't something there to guide me, then we're screwed."

I pull away from Tyler, pushing him more gently in the direction of his car. "We have to get out of here before someone recognizes us."

"Call me if you find something," he says.

"I won't forget this time," I promise.

I get in the van and turn it on, watching as his taillights disappear around the corner. Then I kill the ignition, get out, and head back to where Dani is waiting.

The look she gives me when I reach her is unreadable. Not because there isn't something there, but because there's too much, and it's all contradictory.

"Ready?" I ask.

"For what?"

"To take me to Petrov."

THE DOGFISH

"I can't believe I am doing this."

The front seat of the Chevelle is much more comfortable than the back. The faux-fur seat cover feels like a warm hug and smells like Dani, which despite our conflicted relationship is oddly comforting.

"I should be taking you home. Or to a mental hospital. Only a crazy person would confront Petrov."

"I'm not confronting him. I have a proposition for him. One that will actually make me safer."

"How do you know he won't kill you where you stand?"

"Because I'll convince him that he needs my brain intact. Which means no more hit attempts for you to protect me from."

She mutters under her breath, then repeats, "I can't believe I am doing this."

She turns the Chevelle onto a road I recognize, and before I can fully grasp the significance, the stone edifice of the Strand appears. Petrov is a member of the Strand? Was that why my dad hid the second clue here?

"You seem surprised," Dani says as she squeezes the Chevelle into a spot a few blocks down and around a corner. "Do you know this place?"

"I guess not," I say.

"If I bring you to him, he will suspect me," Dani says. "I will be useless to you if my loyalty is compromised."

"I know," I say. "Which is why you're staying here."

"But how will you get in?"

"This time," I say, unzipping the coveralls and working them off, "I'll walk through the front door." My school uniform is beyond wrinkled, but I'm not trying to be anybody other than myself, so I don't really care.

"Tread carefully, *milaya*," she says. "He has weaknesses, but mercy isn't one of them. If you injure his pride, he will kill you."

Peachy. "Thanks for the tip," I say. She seems to be strangling the steering wheel, so I put my hand on one of hers. "I won't give him any reason to hurt me," I say earnestly.

She nods and exhales. I get out of the car and shut the door behind me before she can change her mind.

When I walk in, the foyer is exactly as I remember it. The staff hasn't even changed the flowers. I send a silent thank-you to my dad, wherever he is, that I've already had the opportunity to case the building. If I need to get away, I'll have an easier time, having escaped once before.

A suited man appears like magic from a side room. "Ms. Dupree, if you'll follow me?"

"Neat trick," I say. "How'd you know who I am?"

"We keep an eye out for visitors," he says, indicating a security camera hanging from the ceiling. "And you've been on our radar for some time."

I fall into step behind him. He leads me up the marble stairs where I met Mrs. Stratton yesterday, and then down a corridor on the second floor to a door at the end of the hall. He opens the door for me, and I pass him with polite thanks into a conference room with floor-to-ceiling views of the darkening city.

Seven men in business attire sit around the conference table in the middle of the room. They must be in the middle of some kind of meeting. Probably about me. The thought makes me smile. I don't see anyone I recognize, but that doesn't mean they aren't city bigwigs. I'll certainly recognize them now if I ever see their faces again. Which doesn't bode well for me, actually. They wouldn't want to be publicly associated with Petrov. So why are they letting me see them?

I pick out Petrov almost immediately. He's the only one in the room who actually looks like a predator.

"May I offer you a seat, my dear?" he asks, indicating one of several empty chairs. His English is accented but smoother than Dani's.

His double-breasted Armani with pinstripes suggests a man

who lets others dictate his taste. But I'd be an idiot to underestimate him. He may be shortish, slender, and the wrong side of forty, but he's all gristle and bone and pointed black goatee. A career villain. He makes Mike and Dani and me look like altar boys.

"I see you've found me out. How clever of you," he says, steepling his hands. There's a gold ring on his right hand, a snake wrapped around his finger and biting its own tail. It's old gold, matte like brushed nickel instead of shiny like chrome. I expected him to be more of a shiny-gold kind of guy.

"Let's skip the posturing, shall we?" I say, putting my offense on the field. "I know what you're doing, you know what I'm doing. Nothing here is a secret." I include the silent members of our party in my glare.

"Very well," Petrov says, clearly humoring me. "What did you have in mind?"

"I have no interest in anything but keeping myself and my friends alive," I say. "I think my dad acted unwisely going up against you. I am not him."

He nods, indicating that I can continue.

"I'm sure by now you've figured out that he had something on you, and that I might be able to find it."

"I had heard something like that, yes."

One of the men, sweaty and looking green around the gills, opens his mouth to speak, but is summarily silenced by a glare from Petrov.

"I'll give it to you as soon as I find it. No cops. But you have to back off and let me find it. All this trying-to-kill-me stuff is distracting."

Petrov laughs. "You amuse me, Ms. Dupree," he says. "Lucky for you, I'm feeling rather magnanimous this evening."

"You need the evidence destroyed before anyone else stumbles across it, and you need me to find it, if you want to have it fast."

His smile sours a little. Stick successfully applied; now it's time for the carrot.

"Consider me sufficiently motivated to find it. Spare your foot soldiers some trouble. It'll go faster if you let me do my job."

"Fair enough," he says, though he's looking less magnanimous around the edges. "But I'm sure you can understand that I have difficulty trusting you, considering the circumstances. If I don't properly 'motivate' you, how am I to know you won't go running to the authorities once you find it?"

"I'd give you my word, but I'm a grifter, so clearly that doesn't count for much. But then, I'm a grifter—I have a lot to hide myself. The last thing I want is to draw unwanted attention."

"Your father used much the same argument when I hired him."

Crap. Of course he did.

"It's not only the attention," I say. "It's my friends. You almost killed Mike with that Molotov. I don't want anyone else getting hurt."

"I hope you'll excuse my skepticism, but these are not

sentiments typical of a grifter." He leans back in his chair, studying me. "I have yet to meet a con artist who thought more of others than of himself."

"I am also thinking of myself," I say. "I don't want to die. I want to get out. Out of Chicago, out of the game. I want a normal life." I'm kind of surprised that I'm confessing this to him. But he'll hear the sincerity in my voice. Just like the dean.

He considers this for several moments while the men around us sit stoically, waiting for Petrov to make his decision.

"All right," he says. "You have one week."

My initial relief at this pronouncement is usurped by the anxiety of a ticking clock. "I can't guarantee I can find it by then."

"One week," he repeats. Then he presses the call button on the conference phone in front of him. "Marcus, please escort our guest out."

The suit who led me here opens the door and comes to stand behind my chair.

"One week or what?" I ask.

Petrov smiles at me, and it chills me to my core. "One week."

• • •

Dani is leaning against the passenger's-side door of the Chevelle. When she sees me, she straightens at once, looking relieved. She opens the door and I slide in.

"What now?" she asks as she starts the car.

"I bought us a week."

"That's it?"

"That's more than we had yesterday," I say, leaning against the door. I could sleep for that entire week.

"What will you do next?"

I sigh and my breath mists the window. "Get Murphy's van. Go home."

"Is that wise?" she asks.

"It is now that I've negotiated a truce. And anyway, I need to dig through my dad's stuff."

We drive the rest of the way in silence. I tell myself it's because Dani is not a talker, but I suspect she's actually trying to give me some space to rest. I hate being this vulnerable in front of her, but I'm so tired. She has to shake me awake when we get back to the warehouse. It can't be later than five o'clock, and I feel like I've already lived five lifetimes.

I pick up the coveralls and fish out Murphy's keys. I trade the Chevelle for Murphy's van and shove the key in the ignition. Dani appears at my window and knocks on the glass with my glasses. I slide down the window.

"How do I get ahold of you if I need you?" I ask, taking the glasses.

"When you need me, I will know," she says, shrugging against the wind and heading back to the warehouse.

• • •

When I get home, I toss Murphy's keys on the counter. Sadly, no magic cleaning gnomes came in while I was gone.

I put a few of our pictures back on the wall, looking behind them for my father's neat script. I go through all the cupboards in the kitchen, remembering my first frantic search for clues. I didn't find anything then but the envelope at the bottom of the trash.

I give up on the kitchen and move to my room. But nothing seems new or unusual.

I push into my dad's room, ignoring for the moment the memories that assault me. I have too much at stake now, too many people depending on me.

I riffle through his papers and sift through his closet, searching behind my mom's trunk for hollow places, secret doors. I pile his clothes in the corner, shaking them out for any loose clues. Finally, I gather the framed snapshots of us on various outings that are littered all over the floor and set them back on his dresser.

The third picture catches my eye, because it's of me and him standing in front of an airplane grounded on a concrete pad in a park not far from here. Meigs Field.

"People don't generally believe themselves to be evil. Just strong," I remember him saying. *"And they think that the world owes them something."*

My dad leads me through the trees, pointing out the abandoned hangar from when Meigs Field was a real airport. He tells me the story of an old governor tearing up the runway in the middle of the night to head off a stalemate with the populace.

"Power is like the fish that swallows Geppetto. People become trapped by it. They're afraid that without it, they'll drown in the sea of mediocrity with the rest of us."

"Do you want power?"

"Nah, I've got my salvation right here," he says, squeezing my shoulder.

I snap back to the present, clutching the photo and the memory. I need to calm down. I need to think. I need a copy of *Pinocchio*.

I scramble for my laptop. I key in "Pinocchio text" and get a page of hits. The first few are ebooks. I skip those and go directly to the full text. Clicking the link, I type "dogfish" in the search field and hit Enter.

Can you guess who that monster was? It was no other than the huge Dogfish. . . .

I pick up my phone. I need to check on Mike, alert Tyler, bring Sam up to speed, circle the wagons. But before I can do all that, there's a vital call I need to make.

"Hello, Heather? I know where we're going to have the dance."

THE PINCH

It turns out that finding a costume for a dance with a theme as wacky as "Swing in Space" is as simple as digging through my mom's trunk again. The empire-waist, spaghetti-strap dress I liberate from the dark recesses of painful-memory storage is just free-flowing enough to let me paw through overhead bins and under landing gear with equal impunity.

That's right. Landing gear. Because if I've deciphered my dad's clue correctly, the next stop on this crazy train is Meigs Field—home to grounded metal birds and busted campaign promises. And what better way to search the as yet undedicated shiny new airplane hangar than by camouflaging my snooping with balloons and streamers and hormone-addled adolescents?

I can't take much credit for getting the dance relocated,

though. After looping in Heather and Murphy, I asked Tyler for his dad's help with the city. The rest pretty much happened by itself, and in the space of four days, no less. I can't help but be impressed. And relieved. I only have three more days to get to the end of my dad's trail of clues.

I'm adding one final layer of hair glue to the liberty-spike bun I spent an hour molding into place as my concession to the space-age aspect of the theme, when someone knocks on my apartment door.

I open it to see Tyler in his own 1920s-meets-*Jetsons* outfit—a tailored zoot suit, pinstriped fedora, and rocket ship–print suspenders peeking out from beneath his jacket. He looks like Abercrombie's attempt at a John Dillinger photo shoot.

"Hey," I say, smiling.

"I— You look—" He seems lost for words.

"Thanks," I say, feeling strangely shy. "You too."

He hands me a pale pink chrysanthemum corsage I didn't notice he was holding. I can't account for the weird glowy feeling I get looking at it. I slip it on my wrist and bring it up to my nose before noticing how completely cliché I'm acting.

"Let's get going. Can't have the decorating committee finding the clue before we do," I say as I step out into the hall and shut the door.

"Don't you need a coat?"

I hold up the gold scarf I'm using as a wrap. "I thought I'd give freezing to death a try. Cut out the middle man."

"That's not really funny," Tyler says, offering me his arm like a gentleman.

We start down the grubby apartment stairs, me carefully holding my skirt out of the dust and grime.

"It's kind of funny," I say.

Once we're in the car and driving toward the dance, he moves his hand from the gearshift to mine, threading our fingers together.

"How are you?" he asks.

"Fine," I say, though I suppose that's more lie than truth. I haven't slept much since I discovered the captives in the warehouse. I keep seeing my dad being tossed into the canal, keep hearing the whoosh of fire and the tinkling of broken glass, the Ukrainian murmurs of cold comfort. I keep wondering if there's some way I can fix it all faster, better.

"Requests for IDs are still coming in thick and fast," I add, since *fine* by itself is generally a conversation killer, and I don't want him thinking I don't appreciate his asking.

"Need more help tonight?"

My stomach flutters and I roll my eyes at myself. It's not as if Tyler didn't come over the last four nights to help me with the orders I already have. Going to a dance together doesn't mean that anything beyond laminating is going to be happening tonight.

I answer in the affirmative anyway, for all the obvious reasons. Not that I have time for making IDs or any other extracurricular activities. Petrov's clock is ticking, and my time is running out.

We pull into the gravel lot serving as the temporary parking area for the airplane hangar, and I have to hand it to the Friends of Meigs Field—they lobbied hard to get their airport back from the powers that be. The sleek, state-of-the-art facility is a testament to the influence little people can have if they never give up. Too bad I have to break in and rip the place apart to find the next clue.

We're here early to help with the setup so I can get my hands on the clue as soon as possible. The doors are wide open, letting in the last glow of the dying autumn sun.

"Any idea what we're looking for?" Tyler asks as we dodge one of Heather's minions clacking by, swathed in layers of cream chiffon and blue crepe paper.

"Sadly, no."

"How about a place to start?"

I shake my head. "I'll have to see what I see once we get in there. I'm hoping it will be obvious."

It's strange how naturally Tyler seems to be falling into the slot Sam usually fills. Sam has been avoiding me lately, and I'm not sure why. I try to tell myself that he's just dating someone new. But I don't really know that for sure. He didn't outright confirm my guess that day at the Strand. And even if he is dating someone, why keep it a secret? We always tell each other everything. Besides, I'll find out tonight, anyway. He has to bring her to the dance, right?

"Julep!"

As if my thinking about him has somehow teleported him here, Sam hurries to catch up to us, Haley Jacobs on his arm.

Haley's dress is a modern ode to the flapper dress, short enough to reveal almost as much thigh as calf, and her swoopy Gaga heels are a marvel of modern physics. Even so, she only comes up to Sam's chin. And she's obviously freezing her assets off.

"Found anything yet?"

"We just got here," I say, catching Sam's eye and throwing a pointed look at Haley. She'd better not know anything. I can't afford another loose end right now.

"Can we get inside?" Haley asks, hugging herself and tip-tapping to the door without us.

"That's who you've been mooning over?" I say under my breath to Sam.

Sam gives me a look like I'm the village idiot.

"What?"

Tyler heads to the entrance with me in tow and Sam trailing behind. We pass an odd couple of gabby socialite and sulky pocket protector setting up the ticket table just inside the door. Heather's army of sophisticates-in-training are stringing fishing-wire sparkle stars from plane wings, clusters of balloons from propellers, Christmas lights along the walls, and giant papier-mâché planetoids from the rafters. Meanwhile, Murphy's crew is stringing cables of a different sort, setting the stage for the jazz-punk band Heather procured to fit the theme.

Once we're inside, Heather wastes no time putting us to work. She assigns Tyler and Sam to the crew assembling tables and chairs. She sends Haley to the photo booth. Then she turns to me with a smirk.

"Why don't you put some of that hot air to good use?" she says, handing me a balloon.

"You do realize you owe me," I say, but I take the balloon anyway.

"Not as much as Murphy does."

I follow her gaze to where Bryn is loitering at the stage, waiting for Murphy to finish testing the sound system. She sparkles in her sequined sheath, a peacock-feathered headband around her pin curls. She also looks bemused, as if she still can't quite believe what she's doing. But then, we didn't give her much choice. We went all in with the proposal: her name spelled in LED candles and twinkle lights in the quad between classes, Murphy holding more of the purple-tipped white roses he'd planted in her locker. We flattered her pride while under-cutting every other option for a date. She had to say yes.

After blowing up three balloons, I abandon the decorating committee and start snooping. The first cabinet I come to is locked, so I take out one of my hairpins and the clip from a pen I stashed in my bra for this exact purpose. Grifter tip number 587: professional lock-picking tools are good for practice but are a dead giveaway if you get caught.

As I suspected, the cabinet is full of random plane para-phernalia. No ledger, no SD card, no prepaid mobile phone, nothing. So I move to the next cabinet, and the next.

I've been searching fruitlessly for fifteen minutes when Sam comes to find me.

"Dance is about to start," he says. "Any luck?"

I shake my head, feeling defeated.

He nudges my chin up so I'll meet his eyes. "You'll find it."

"I only have three days left." My voice wobbles, but I don't try to hide it. Not from Sam.

"All the more reason to take a breath. Come dance with me."

I laugh. "Seriously? You want me to dance right now? Besides, shouldn't you be tending to Haley?" Just the sound of her name reminds me of all the "us" I seem to be losing. "What happened to us, Sam?"

Sam takes my hand and pulls me to the almost empty dance floor. The band, mistaking us for a couple, begins a sweet, sultry version of "Stardust." I should feel uncomfortable, and I do, but not for the right reasons. I should be worried that I'm wasting the little time I have left. I should be worried about all the people depending on me. Instead, I'm worried about what Sam is going to say.

He knows me better than I know myself. Is there something I've missed? Something I've done to break us? I start marshaling my arguments, because I can't let Sam leave me. Even Tyler couldn't fill the gaping hole a missing Sam would leave in my chest.

Sam moves me across the floor with considerable skill, spinning and dipping me in time with the music. He's showing off and shutting me up at the same time. I can't help but smile. He may not be an obedient minion, but he can be devious when he wants to be.

For the final chorus, he slows us to the gentle sway of the other dancers who have joined us during the course of the song.

"I forgot you knew how to dance," I say.

"I learned from the best," he says softly, sadly. He's thinking of my dad, and I feel sympathy for his loss for the first time.

"Listen, Sam—"

"No," he says, pulling me closer. "It's your turn to listen."

Then, before I know what is happening, he leans down and kisses me. Molecules split apart and reconnect, whole galaxies rearrange themselves, and everything finally falls into place.

"Holy crap," I whisper. I am such an imbecile. I stare at him, not having any idea what to say. Thoughts of Tyler crowd my discombobulated brain. "Sam."

"I love you, Julep," he says. "I always have."

The music is loud enough that I can barely hear him. But I know what he's saying. A thousand memories bubble up, a thousand glances, a thousand touches, a thousand words. He's been telling me all this time, but I haven't listened. I haven't wanted to listen. I didn't want to know.

"Sam, I . . ." What can I say to my best friend to keep him? Either way, I lose him. "I don't know what to say."

His face falls, but he never gets a chance to respond.

"Samuel Elliot Velasco Seward?"

The couples nearest to us pull back to reveal Mike, who's wearing a suit and a grim expression. Sam looks a question at Mike, and there's not a single spark of recognition on his face. My blood freezes.

He's never seen Mike before in his life.

"Yes?" Sam says.

"Mike, what's going on?" I say.

Mike flicks me an apologetic glance, but he doesn't answer. Instead, he pulls a wallet out of his pocket and flips it open, showing us a golden badge with an eagle crest.

"Sam Seward, you're under arrest."

25

THE MESSAGE

I stand gaping at Mike for a moment like the mark on the wrong side of a con, almost unable to process the sting of his betrayal. I thought Mike was on the level, that we were made from the same hardscrabble material, that we understood each other. The sob story about needing the paycheck—he'd known from the beginning exactly how to play me. Tears of humiliation push at my eyelids, but I'll be damned if I let them fall.

With effort, I pull myself together, clamping my hand over Sam's with the force I wish I could use on Mike's throat. Throwing a pointed glare at Mike, I haul Sam off the dance floor and head to the parking lot. I won't let him be humiliated, too. I won't let Mike cuff him in front of all his friends and enemies. In my peripheral vision, I see Tyler edging over to meet us.

Once we're outside, Mike stops us long enough to read Sam his rights. Sam won't look at him, or at me for that matter.

"What's going on?" Tyler asks as he jogs up to us.

". . . anything you say or do may be used against you . . ."

"This backstabbing Benedict Arnold is arresting Sam."

". . . you cannot afford an attorney, one will be appointed . . ."

"What?" Tyler says. "Why?"

I can't answer Tyler without getting Sam into more trouble than he's already in.

". . . you understand these rights as I have explained them to you?"

Sam nods as Mike opens the back door of a dark SUV with heavily tinted windows.

"Where are you taking him?" I demand. "You have no right to do this."

"MCC," Mike says, his face expressionless. "And yes, I do."

"Don't say a word, Sam—not a single word. I'll come get you."

I watch as the SUV pulls away with my best friend trapped inside it.

"I have to go," I say to Tyler. "I have to get him out."

"I'll drive."

I don't even put up a fight. I take shameless advantage of Tyler's generous heart and let him drive me, despite everything that happened between Sam and me not ten minutes ago. The boy is either a saint or a sucker for punishment.

Unfortunately for Tyler, I spend the fifteen-minute drive to downtown silently fuming, coming up with new and creative ways to torture Special Agent Mike Ramirez. The Molotov was too good for him.

• • •

The waiting room at the Metropolitan Correctional Center is a lot like the waiting room at the DMV, if you add a collection of convicts in fancy bracelets awaiting processing.

Seeing so many people in custody makes me jumpy. Living on the edge of eventual incarceration gives a person a preemptive claustrophobia for confined spaces. Especially confined spaces crawling with cops.

"Who are you here for?" the booking officer asks, looking over the rims of his reading glasses at me.

"Samuel Seward," I say. "Is bail set yet?"

"Hold on," he says. A few computer clicks later, he tells me he'll be right back.

Sam needs a lawyer, which means parents. His mom is going to have an apoplectic fit, and she sure as hell is never going to let Sam within a football field of me after this. But then, that might be in his best interest.

I pace between the plastic chairs bolted to metal frames and the hallway leading to the interrogation rooms while I wait for the booking officer to come back. Tyler knows better than to try to comfort me. He sits patiently, brooding and watching me.

But the booking officer doesn't come back. At least, not

until after Sam's dad marches through the lobby door at the same time Mike ushers Sam out of one of the interrogation rooms.

"Mr. Seward," I say, moving to intercept Sam's dad. "I fully intend to—"

"What are the charges?" Mr. Seward barks at Mike, ignoring me.

"No charges yet," Mike says. "But your son is still under investigation. I expect him to be available for further questioning."

I breathe a sigh of relief. Sam's off the hook for now. But he still looks miserable, and he hasn't looked at me once. He and his father seem to be engaged in a silent battle of wills.

"Sam—" I say. But the only acknowledgment I get is him shrugging off the hand I put on his arm as he passes. Which hurts. But it's the least I deserve for getting him into this.

"I'm sorry," I whisper at his retreating back, though I doubt he hears me. He follows his dad out of the building, and I break out in a sickly sweat at the thought that it might be the last time I ever see him.

But there's another person I still need to deal with, and it doesn't matter one bit to me that he's a federal officer and about twenty years my senior.

I fix a cop-killer glare on Mike, fury rolling off me in waves. I'm cognizant of the fact that my rage, hair spikes, and smudged makeup make me look like a post-battle Marvel mutant. But I can't make myself care in the wake of Mike's betrayal.

"Congratulations, Mike. You've caught yourself a criminal. Bravo."

He just stands there, not taking me as seriously as he should.

"I'd ask why you bothered with the sidekick when you could have collared the ringleader, but I'm guessing you didn't have the basic competence to gather the evidence you needed. If you think Sam's going to give it to you, you're sadly mistaken."

"Julep, this isn't personal."

"It's personal now."

He motions me into the room he and Sam just vacated. I have far too much to say to storm out. So I storm in. Mike closes the door behind me.

The room is pretty much what you'd expect from an interrogation room. Spare, government-issue table, two pointedly uncomfortable chairs arranged across the table from each other, and a long "mirror" on one wall. The room is carpeted, though, and there's a small barred window near the ceiling that is letting the neon night spill onto the floor.

"Sit down," Mike says. "Would you like some coffee?"

The offer reminds me of our conversations at the Ballou, which enrages me further. I sit in the seat nearest the door. I'm not the one being interrogated here.

"Everything you ever told me is a lie."

Mike takes the seat across from me. "Would you have given me the time of day if I'd told you I was undercover?"

"I might have," I say. "When the time was right. And it's not like I told you much as Mike the PI."

"When the time was right?" Mike's expression is a mixture of anger and incredulity. "If I hadn't tackled you out of the way of that Molotov, you'd be a Jane Doe charcoal briquette in the morgue right now."

"I'll get you your information," I say. "That's what this is about, isn't it? You want the evidence my dad found." And as soon as the observation is out of my mouth, my head fills with questions I didn't even consider while Sam was in custody. "How did you even know about that?"

Mike sighs and rubs his eyes. "Your dad told me."

"You're lying. My dad would never go to the authorities, not for any reason, ever."

"I don't know what to tell you, kid. All I know is I got a series of phone calls from a guy claiming he had evidence to link Petrov's gang to an extensive smuggling ring. That some top brass were involved, so he couldn't take it to the local PD."

"You knew all that and you didn't tell me? I would never have—" I literally bite my tongue to stop myself from admitting that I asked Sam to hack the FBI database. The last thing Sam needs is my confession added to whatever evidence Mike has against him.

"You didn't need to know who was pulling the strings to follow your dad's clues to the evidence he stashed. And I didn't need you getting pulled off course. If you'd known it was Petrov, you'd have gone straight to him."

"Why didn't *you* go after him? Why were you tracking me instead of Petrov in the first place?"

"I *have* been tracking Petrov," he says. "I've tapped his phone,

I've analyzed his financial records, I've had him followed, but nothing ever pans out. He's cagey enough to keep his business untraceable to him—money laundering, shell companies, the works. And I can't crack his inner circle. He only lets in people he's known for twenty years or more."

"Until my dad," I say, my shoulders slumping.

"Until your dad," he agrees. "He was the first contractor Petrov ever hired outside his internal crew."

"But why did my dad call you?" *Why didn't he tell me?*

"I think he was in over his head and needed help. He was going to give me the evidence the night your apartment was tossed, but he never showed."

"I still don't understand how you figured out who he was. Even if he did want your help, he'd never have given you his name."

"He didn't give me his name, Julep," Mike says softly. "He gave me yours."

I close my eyes. "He wanted you to protect me."

"Yes, though if he'd cut you out of the equation, sent me a direct location for whatever it is he found, you'd have been safer than with me just watching out for you."

I shake my head, resting my hands flat on the metal table between us. "He couldn't send you the evidence or its location without risking interception. That's why he hid it so only I could find it. It was his insurance policy against Petrov taking me out on the mere chance that I know too much. Besides, you're not the only one he put on Julep detail."

The chill of the table seeps into my hands, making them

feel disconnected, heavier. But I can't dredge up the desire to move them. They're the only part of me that isn't numb.

"Why did you arrest Sam?" I ask.

"He broke the law."

"Why did you really arrest him?"

Mike looks down, the only sign that I've unsettled him at all during this conversation. "You were getting too close to Petrov. Anytime you've made any leaps in that direction, it was because Sam made it possible. I took him out to protect both of you."

Something else clicks into place. "You told the dean. About my dad. So she would bring in the social worker and set me up in foster care—get me out of your way."

He doesn't answer, which is all the answer I need.

"You ruined my life," I say.

"I know," he says.

I push myself up, the cold in my hands spreading to my wrists. I hope it reaches my heart before I forget what sensation is like altogether. I'd rather be cold than feel nothing.

I walk through the door into the too-bright hallway. Mike follows me out.

"One more thing," I say, looking back. "Why tell me Sam hired you? Why not tell me my dad did?"

Mike's hands are in his pockets, his face a picture of chagrin. "I needed you to feel sorry for me, so you'd keep me in the loop. With your dad gone, I didn't have the excuse of a paycheck."

Classic Spanish Prisoner con, and I fell for it like a total rookie. I nod at Mike, acknowledging his victory.

I slink into the waiting room, my wrath now tempered with regret and ignominy. Tyler takes one look at me and jumps to his feet.

"Are you—?"

"Let's just go."

I don't look back at Mike as I walk out the door. I won't give him the satisfaction.

Tyler follows me to the parking lot. "Julep," he says, grabbing my arm and turning me to face him, "talk to me."

"There's too much at stake, Tyler—too much at stake, and I keep making boneheaded decisions."

I lean against the R8, away from him. I can tell I'm hurting his feelings, but I don't deserve him. And I won't believe him when he says everything's going to be okay.

"Then stop."

I blink at him, disoriented.

"Stop making boneheaded decisions." He opens his passenger's-side door for me. "You can't do anything about what's already happened. Adapt."

I give him a weak smile. "That sounds like something my dad would say."

He smiles back, though worry still clouds his eyes. "I read it on the back of a cereal box."

"Thanks," I say. "I needed that."

"So? What next?"

I need to sort things out with Sam. I need to find the evidence against Petrov. I need to rescue Petrov's prisoners. But first things first.

"The clue," I say. "Time is running out."

• • •

When we get back to the hangar, the dance is in full swing. I thread my way through couples convulsing on the dance floor to strobe lights and the sounds of a DJ remixing the music of our generation. I'm grateful I managed to at least minimize the damage to Sam's reputation, though I'd be a fool to think word won't get around, and soon.

Tyler and I pick up the search where I left off, hunting through bins and cabinets, combing through tools and propeller parts. But nothing looks remotely out of the ordinary.

The music is too loud for us to carry on much of a conversation. Tyler's acting like his usual Tyler self, despite everything that's happened tonight. But I sense a space between us that wasn't there before, like he's holding something back.

We work our way to the small corner office where they must keep the majority of the paperwork for hangar operations. I pick the lock on the door, hoping that the chaperones are deep enough in their flasks by now that they won't notice.

The hangar is warm from bodies and space heaters, but the office itself is less so, since the door has been shut and locked all night. When we get inside, my eyes settle on the exact hiding spot of the last clue. He's made it so obvious I'm shocked it's still here. Anyone with even a hint of delinquency knows a *Carlito's Way* poster is always a hiding place for contraband. He meant it as a message: Once you're in the game, you're in until the big sleep.

My anger returns—at my dad for this ridiculous charade, at Mike for his betrayal, at Petrov for ruining all my chances at a decent life, at myself for leaving those girls behind out of fear for my own safety. I stalk across the small room and rip the poster from the wall.

I'm not sure what I expected. A piece of paper with another clue, I guess. But instead, there's a hole punched into the wall. Taking a deep breath, I start pulling out the bigger chunks of Sheetrock, dropping them on the floor. When I reach in, my hand brushes a thin, delicate stem. Carefully, I draw out the dried husk of a rose, beautifully preserved but thoroughly dead. And worse, no note.

As soon as I see it, everything becomes devastatingly clear, like a rope around my throat. Like a smoking gun.

"Julep?" Tyler says, steadying me with a hand on my arm.

"I know where the evidence is."

Tyler freezes. "Where?"

I look at him, my heart beating and shattering. I crumple, and Tyler sinks to the floor next to me, wrapping me in his arms as I cry.

The reason the clues never seemed to be leading me anywhere is because there was never anywhere to go. My father never found anything. There was never a hidden ledger or a recorded confession or a wiretap or anything.

The clues he left weren't a trail to a prize. They were a

message, and the rose is the final sentence. Even without a note, without any words at all, it says everything important, everything there is to say between my father and me.

It says he loves me. More than anything. And he's never coming back.

THE FOLD

I scoop another forkful of the greasy diner eggs into my mouth and force myself to chew and swallow. I haven't consumed anything more substantial than a bag of Cheetos and some coffee in the two-plus days since the dance, and my mind is starting to go dull around the edges. As far as last meals go, it could be worse.

Not that I can afford to pay for it. I had a long, discouraging talk with my wallet this morning. I'm looking at a dollar thirty-seven to cover this bounteous feast. Mike froze my bank account—some bull about it being "evidence" in the case against Sam. He's trying to keep me from doing anything stupid, but sadly for him, I don't need money to do something stupid.

The door jingles as another patron enters the diner. I peek

over my shoulder and notice his heavy horn-rimmed glasses, trucker hat, I HEART IRONY T-shirt, and outrageous mustache. He makes his way over to the counter where I happen to be sitting. He's perfect.

I paste on a smile and pick up my coffee while he orders the blue-plate special.

"At least it's hot," I say, and take a sip.

"Pardon?" he says, looking around to be sure I'm not addressing someone else.

"The coffee." I make a face. "If this wind ever lets up, it'll be a miracle. But getting a decent cup of joe from this place? That would take the second coming of Christ."

He laughs. It sounds free, open—innocent of irony, despite the T-shirt.

I flick my eyes to his hat and smile, feigning an innocence to match his.

"Well, it isn't Agrippa, that's for sure," he agrees. The waitress gives him a sour look but sweeps by without comment.

"Ah, Agrippa. Temple of the coffee gods. Too bad it's on the other side of town."

We chitchat for a few minutes as we wait for his breakfast to arrive—weather and other inanities. I'm going for a light-hearted mood here, so I steer clear of topics like politics and work, and focus more on witty remarks designed to amuse.

When the waitress hands him his plate, I set my cup down on the counter between us.

"I've got a proposition for you," I say, smiling. "But I'll need to borrow your hat."

"My hat?"

I extend my hand for it. He looks puzzled but curious. When he hands me the hat, I set it down over my still mostly full cup.

"I'll bet you the price of breakfast that I can drink that entire cup of coffee without touching your hat."

"No way."

"Yep, I can. It's really quite something. I learned it from a swami on a book tour."

"Okay, you're on."

I close my eyes and affect my best imitation-swami pose—thumbs touching middle fingers, face lifted up to nirvana—and make a humming noise deep in my throat. Then I swallow three times. I open my eyes and smile at him.

"All done."

"Right."

I shrug. "It's true. I can't help it if you don't believe me."

He narrows his eyes, but he's still smiling. "You didn't do anything."

"There's only one way to find out."

"Fine."

He lifts the hat off the counter, revealing the still nearly full cup. I calmly pick it up and drink the contents.

"Hey!"

I smile at him. "I never touched the hat."

I get up to go, signaling to the waitress that my patsy is paying the bill.

"I walked right into that one, didn't I?" he says, already shouldering the responsibility for me fleecing him.

I pull out the dollar thirty-seven and lay it on the counter.

"For the coffee," I say and walk out the door.

I catch the "L" and head to school. I haven't done any of my weekend homework, but then, I don't plan on attending any of my classes. I figure what's the point when there's a pretty decent chance I won't live beyond the next twenty-four hours? But I do have a batch of IDs to deliver. Seems like all I do these days is make these ridiculous cards. It's not like pretending to be someone you're not is going to get you anywhere good. *Look at me,* I want to tell them. *Don't make the same mistake.* But their money is green, and they wouldn't listen to me, anyway.

It's been more than two days since Sam got pinched, and he won't answer any of my texts, emails, or calls. I've never gone this long without at least a text from him. I'm not sure how to give him space, or if I should, or if I've ruined his life. In one long, rambling voice-mail message, I filled him in on my discovery of the rose. I don't know if he wants to know, if he's even getting my messages. But I figured I owed him closure.

Meanwhile, Tyler's been out of town for the championships. He offered to invent some sort of illness and stay with me because of how upset I was about the rose.

I told him what it meant as he was driving me home that night. He asked me several times if I was sure. But of course I'm sure. The only time my dad would ever call me by my real name is if he was saying good-bye.

In any case, I wouldn't let Tyler skip the game. I'm not going to be responsible for ruining his life, too. With Petrov breathing down my neck, he's better off as far away from me as he can get. Besides, I'm a con artist. As much as I wish I weren't, I'm still all smoke and mirrors. You can love an illusion, but the illusion can't love you back. Even if it wants to.

I stare out the "L" window as the train passes all the familiar landmarks. I'm pretty sure once I pull off the biggest con of my life, I won't be seeing them again. And that goes for both Tyler and Sam as well. Even if I manage to keep from getting shot during the next twenty-four hours, my life will still be over.

I send a text to Heather. A few seconds later, my phone pings with a return text. I scroll through the message and then delete it.

When I reach my stop, I walk through the sliding doors and toss the phone onto the tracks.

Ten minutes later, I stroll through campus, ignoring the blowing leaves, the chattering of my classmates, the fluttery feeling I get right before I bite off more than I can chew. Remember how I explained at the beginning that everyone has something in their past they're not proud of? Well, I'm about to become a glass house. Let's hope that stoning isn't as painful as it sounds.

My plan is simple enough, but as with most cons, it involves betting heavily on one's ability to foresee all possible reactions on the part of other people without them suspecting a thing. Easy enough with strangers, harder with people you know. If that seems backward, don't look at me. I call it like I see it.

When I reach the second floor, my feet slow of their own

accord. But it's time and past to get this over with. People are counting on me. Sam deserves someone better than me. And Tyler will land on his feet.

I step into the dean's outer office; my backpack, filled with illegal IDs, bumps against the doorframe. Heather is standing at the copy machine, and her eyes get huge when she sees me. *What are you doing here?* she mouths at me. I give her a small smile of apology but otherwise ignore her as I push open the dean's inner office door and stride into the lion's den.

I empty my bag of cards onto her desk.

"I have a confession to make."

Twenty minutes later, I'm sitting outside the president's office as the dean, the head of security, and various assorted board members decide what to do with me. I imagine my phone, under the "L," lighting up like a Christmas tree with texts from Heather.

I feel bad—I do—for throwing her and the rest of them under the bus. But there's more at stake here than partying privileges. And yes, I know it's more than that. I'm gambling with their future, our future. But it's the only way I'll be able to live with myself. I have to finish what my father started.

"Ms. Dupree?"

Finally. I follow the executive assistant into Sister Rasmussen's office, the plush carpet masking the footsteps of doom, as Sam would say. The door closes behind me with a click, and the stares of five adults in various stages of appalled settle on me.

Of all of them, Sister Rasmussen should be the most irate. Ultimately, the behavior of the students, the reputation of the school, and most important, the robustness of the endowment fall on her shoulders. But she seems the least upset of the five. Her expression says concerned but curious. Which is not what I'd hoped for. It would be better for me if she were furious. Anger is almost always based on fear, and fear is the easiest emotion to manipulate. Ask any politician or pastor.

The dean is the first to speak. "This is your chance to plead your case. I wouldn't—"

"I think it would be advantageous for me to speak to Ms. Dupree first," the president interrupts her, coming out from behind her desk and gently ushering the other board members, including the dean, out into the hall. "Thank you. I'll call you all back in a moment."

Then she shuts the door and calmly returns to her chair. I force myself to unclench my fists. I won't gain anything by acting nervous. But Sister Rasmussen is one of too many linchpins in my shaky plan. And she's the one I have the least power over.

"You may speak freely," she says, gesturing to a recently vacated chair.

I sit, because she's asked me to. "I have a favor to ask," I say.

She laughs. "You break three major school rules, not to mention the law, on this grand a scale, and the first thing you say is you need a favor?"

"According to those same rules, you'd have to expel every

one of the students on those forged driver's licenses. Plus the fifty or so other students I can name who I've also created forgeries for. Am I right?"

The president leans back in her chair, folding her hands and looking at me like she's trying to solve a riddle.

"Why are you doing this?" she asks.

I ignore the question. "If you expel more than a hundred students, that's nearly a tenth of the school population. You'd have to close the school without that tuition money."

"We have enough to cover the shortfall until we enroll more students."

"Even if that's true, the school's reputation would be ruined. Or would at least take a serious hit. Alums would pull their financial support, parents would take their kids elsewhere, you'd have a harder time recruiting new students. And it would all be for nothing."

The president absorbs this, still unruffled. She must have considered all of this already. Does that mean she has another plan in place? She needs to accept my alternative, or none of this is going to work.

"I assume you're bringing this up because you wish to offer a solution."

"Don't expel anyone yet," I say. "I know a way they can pay their debt to St. Agatha's and keep the honor, and the finances, of the school intact."

"I will have to expel someone. The board is out for blood, and the dean has more power with them than I think you bargained for."

"Give the dean what she really wants, and you won't have to expel any of them."

"Give her you, you mean?"

I don't say anything, but I don't have to.

"I ask again, why are you doing this?"

"I have a debt to pay, too," I say. "Can you keep them at bay until I set something else in motion? A couple of days at most. If I can't do it by then, you can do whatever you deem best for the school."

"I always do," she says. "I'll give you till the end of the day tomorrow."

I nod and sit a little straighter in my chair. "Now, about that favor . . ."

"That wasn't the favor?"

"That was a solution to your problem," I say. "That was my favor to you. Now I have a favor to ask in return."

"I'm eager to hear it," she says.

"I need five hundred thousand dollars."

• • •

Ten minutes later, Sister Rasmussen lets me out the rarely used door leading from her office directly to the hallway, bypassing the sitting room and its livid inhabitants. I feel like I've been poking a wasp's nest with a stick. Sometimes you can get away without getting stung if you're bold enough. Of course, in my case, the sting will come later.

I collar my next victim on his way to the dining hall.

"Murphy," I call, waving him over to an alcove off the main

hallway. When he gets close enough to hear without me shouting, I say, "Did you get it?"

He nods and hands me the package. "You owe me fifty bucks, on top of the two hundred for the converter you quote-misplaced-unquote."

As much as I'd like to make it square, I'll probably have to owe him for a while. "Did you set it up?"

He sighs, looking worried. "Yes, but I really don't think it's a good idea. It's not precise enough, and you have to be close."

"Thanks, Murphy." I squeeze his arm. "You're a lifesaver."

Murphy mumbles something back, his eyes wary. But I'm already past him and on to my next errand.

I leave campus and take an assortment of buses to a dumpy strip mall on the midline between downtown and the poorer districts. Disregarding the packed waiting room, I breeze past the receptionist's desk without signing in. It's a testament to how overworked the office is that the receptionist doesn't even look up, much less protest.

The rows of desks crowded with paper and separated by cubicle walls in a superficial attempt at preserving client privacy do nothing to obscure my objective. Even without directions, I know her desk immediately. I can see her all-over brown exterior from here.

I sit in the empty chair next to her desk, and she looks up in surprise.

"Can I—?"

"Ms. Fairchild, right? My name is Julep Dupree. Actually,

it isn't. But that's neither here nor there. I'm hoping you can help me."

A twenty-minute conversation later, and I'm another to-do task closer to meeting Petrov's ultimatum. One more stop before I take the hunt home to the hunter.

• • •

Apparently, one can walk straight into the FBI's elevator, punch a button, and walk into the organized-crime wing of the building without so much as a blink from any of the suits circling the floor. I didn't expect that, to tell you the truth. But I'm not complaining, either.

I walk into Mike's office and shut the door, all my rage at his betrayal still present and accounted for. But despite the hurt and anger roiling in my chest, I need him as much as he needs me. I hate that I need him, but there it is.

"I can get you the Ukrainian mob," I say.

"Julep," he says, spilling coffee on his white button-down. "Damn it."

He mops up the mess with a McDonald's napkin he pulls from a drawer, which only makes the stain worse.

"How did you get in here?" he grumbles.

"I walked. Do you want the mob or not?"

Mike picks up his phone receiver. I yank the cable out of the phone before he can call anyone.

"What the hell?" Mike yells at me, replacing the now useless handset.

"You can call in the cavalry after we're done here."

"You don't get to make that decision."

"I do if you want what I have."

Mike stands and crosses his arms, his scowl intimidating. I see why the FBI uses him for undercover. But there's enough riding on this that his scowl rolls right off me. I have to throw him off balance to keep him from taking over. I need his help, but I can't let him call the shots. Not on this.

"Where is it?"

"Safe," I say. "For now."

"What do you want?"

I pull a pen out of the holder on his desk and hand it to him. "You're going to need to write this down."

• • •

Feeling lighter, I walk out of the FBI building a mere ten minutes later, congratulating myself that thus far everything is going according to plan. If this keeps up, I might actually get all of us through this with minimal collateral damage.

As soon as the thought enters my head, I know I've jinxed everything all to hell. And sure enough, in the very next moment, I bump into a familiar black-coated criminal. I look up into Dani's blue eyes, stony as always but betraying her worry.

"What is it?" I ask, though I'm pretty sure I don't want to know the answer.

"Petrov has your friend Sam."

THE STING

"Can we please talk about this?"

Dani ignores me, pushing the Chevelle to greater acceleration than is advisable on surface streets. I've been trying to reason with her for the last ten minutes, but logic, bribery, and manipulation don't seem to be working. At this point, I've resorted to pleading.

She cuts the wheel to the left and merges onto I-90.

"There's no place you can take me that he won't find me once he knows I have the evidence. You know that."

"Better to take you straight to him? This is your better plan?"

She heads for the nearest state line, either not knowing or not caring that transporting me over it constitutes kidnapping.

"All I need is ten minutes with him and all this goes away. I swear, Dani."

"It takes less than ten seconds to put a bullet in your brain."

"It won't come to that. He won't do anything drastic until he has the evidence in his own hands."

Her answer is a roar from the engine as she pushes the pedal closer to the floor.

"This is ridiculous. You're risking your own life for nothing."

"Not for nothing," she mutters, almost too low for me to hear over the engine. "I cannot save them, but you—you I can save."

"But you *can* save them." I seize the small opening. "I have it all figured out. You can save all of us. Just take me to the warehouse."

"Even if you manage to bring down Petrov and all of his people, no one can save those girls. I told you this. Deportation, prison, refugee camps if they are lucky—"

"We can save them." I touch her arm. "Do you trust me?"

She eases up on the pedal. "Your father did not want you involved. You must respect his wishes."

"You obviously don't know anything about American teenagers," I say, hiding my hurt behind a sardonic smile. "I can do this, Dani. I'm the only one who can."

I can tell from the slope of her shoulders, her small frown, the way she won't look at me, that she's giving in. I sink into my seat as she switches lanes to exit and heads toward the warehouse. We spend the rest of the trip in silence, giving me plenty of time to rehearse the game.

Sam I didn't plan for. At least, not in terms of bargaining with Petrov. The mob boss has stepped up his game, which means he's tired of waiting for me. He's probably worried that I reneged on our deal and am pulling in the feds. He's right, but as long as he doesn't know for sure, Sam is safe.

Unfortunately, that doesn't make me feel much better. All of this is my fault. Sam is in the line of fire because of me. If I'd kept him out of this, he'd never have gotten arrested, he'd never have been on Petrov's radar, and he wouldn't be in this mess now. He'll likely never speak to me again, and it will break what's left of my heart.

"You haven't asked me what my plan is," I say as we pull into the alley next to Petrov's warehouse half an hour later.

"I don't need to know it to keep you from getting shot. I just need to keep you out of the way of the bullets."

She opens her door with a creak and gets out, quietly drawing her gun. I get out, too, and twist my hair into a messy bun, pinning it to the back of my head with the pen in my pocket. I try not to focus too much on the weapon in Dani's hand.

I follow her, but not into the warehouse we were in before. Instead, she leads me into the smaller one next to it. We sneak through the rows of stacked wooden crates toward the back of the building, where the offices are. As she walks, her gaze seems to be everywhere at once. She holds her gun low but ready. I want to tell her to put it away, that Petrov's enforcer drawing a gun on him will only get in the way of my plan, but I don't want to risk another time-wasting argument.

I hear the faint buzzing a split second before all the lights in the building kick on. I resist the urge to duck behind the nearest stack of crates. I'm here to confront Petrov, not skulk around hoping to take him by surprise. Besides, the lights are bright enough to dissolve all shadows, leaving us rats no place to run.

"How nice to see you again, my dear," Petrov says from somewhere above us. Six of his goons walk out from the stacks and surround us. They keep their distance, but their presence is meant as a threat. Petrov likes to flaunt his power. And yes, I intend to use that to my advantage.

I squint against the glare of two spotlights clamped to a catwalk about fifteen feet up. Standing between them, Petrov leans against the railing.

"Nice entrance," I say. "How much practice did that take?"

"Tsk, tsk. Opening with sarcasm is hardly an effective negotiation strategy. But then, neither is turning one of my own people against me."

"Let go!" Dani struggles against two of Petrov's suits, who are pinning her arms behind her back.

"Now that my treacherous pit bull is restrained," he continues, "I feel more comfortable proceeding with the conversation."

Petrov's silhouette detaches from the catwalk railing and moves down the thin metal staircase near the corner of the room. He nods to a skinny man with red hair and freckles, who then rifles through my pockets and pats me down. There's nothing for him to find, since I ditched my phone, Sam still has my gun, and the dean confiscated my backpack. The ginger says something terse in Ukrainian that probably means

"She's clean." Then he backs up a respectful distance, awaiting his next order.

"I hope you'll forgive my rudeness," I say to Petrov. "I really should have knocked."

"I will if you forgive mine. I really shouldn't have shot your father."

A low blow, but one I anticipated. I keep it from decimating me by countering it with my last shred of hope that he's still alive, a hope that's not even really a feeling anymore so much as a conscious decision to believe.

Petrov smirks as he sees the emotional skirmish on my face. I lift my chin and affect an expression of contempt. He may have the power to kill me, but I'm still holding all the cards.

"I believe you have something of mine," he says.

"And you have something of mine. How about a trade?"

Petrov shrugs. "It depends on how valuable the thing you have is. If it's not worth much, I can throw your friend in the canal with the rest of the trash."

His jab has less muscle this time. Words have power—nobody knows that better than a grifter—but harping on the same idea diminishes its strength. The first time you're exposed to a virus, it can kill you. But if you're exposed to small doses of the virus over time, you develop immunity. Besides, if Petrov had anything else to batter me with, he'd have used it by now. Which means Sam is probably fine. That knowledge acts as a shield against any further barbs from Petrov about my father.

"Oh, I think you'll appreciate the significance of the message my father left me." Which is true. Petrov would appreciate it, just not in the sense I'm implying.

"Again, it depends on the content. Most information is easy enough to bury. It helps to have friends in high places."

"Friends are important," I agree. "Which is why I'd like mine back."

"Tell me what your father took from me and maybe it will be worth a limb or two."

"He found out why you need the forged documents. He made a video of your warehouse of hostages."

Petrov snorts. "The warehouse is not in my name, nor can it be connected to me in any way. Besides, now that I know, I can move the product before you have a chance to turn the video over to the authorities."

"He also taped a phone call between you and one of your distributors. I haven't listened to it yet, but I imagine there's a whole lot of you being refreshingly open and honest about your business practices."

"That might get you an arm or leg. But with all the editing software these days, as well as the justice system's insistence on pesky things like chain of custody for electronic evidence, it would be a generous gesture on my part."

"All right, then. What about bank statements?"

Petrov doesn't move, but his face turns pale. "I want to see them."

"I'm not stupid enough to have brought them with me. And anyway, I think I've earned proof of life."

Petrov snaps and Ginger leaves. I'll never understand how

really bad bad guys can communicate with just a series of small signals like that. I always have to explain everything in agonizing detail to get my minions to do my bidding. Maybe I have faulty minions. Or maybe I'm losing my mind. *Focus, Julep.*

Ginger returns with a roughed-up Sam, his hands bound in front of him with a zip-tie.

"Sam," I say, moving a step in his direction before I can stop myself.

"What are you doing here?" One of Sam's cheeks is swollen and his jaw shows the beginnings of a sizable bruise, but otherwise he seems intact. No visible broken bones, thank god.

"Enough." Petrov says, demanding my attention. Once I've turned it back to him, his scowl melts into a psychotic smile. "I am sorry for damaging your property, my dear, but I caught him impersonating a computer-repair technician with the intention of stealing my files."

Sam, you moron. He's lucky I'm probably not getting out of this alive. If I do, I'm going to murder him.

"Let him go and you can have your bank statements," I say.

Petrov's grin deepens. "Shouldn't you be bargaining for your own release as well?"

"I know the game. I know I'm as potentially damaging as those statements. I've seen them; he hasn't. Let him walk, and you can keep me and the evidence."

"No!" Dani renews her struggle against her captors. Sam wisely stays quiet. He knows I have an ace or two I haven't played yet.

"Dani," I say, giving her a stern look. She settles down but is scowling at me as much as at anyone else.

"Do we have a deal?" I ask Petrov. "This is a limited-time offer."

"Don't do it, Petrov." A familiar authoritarian voice joins the party. "She doesn't have anything. She's lying."

Senator Richland strides into the light from the shelter of the doorway, Tyler by his side.

THE ULTIMATE CON

*T*yler.

There is no word strong enough in the English language to describe how I feel at this moment. *Betrayed* isn't quite right, because I should have known better. *Humiliated* is close, but doesn't cover the heartbreak ripping through my chest. *Furious* might work, if it weren't for the fact that despite everything, I still want to throw myself into Tyler's arms and have him tell me everything is going to be fine.

But everything is not going to be fine. Everything is shot to hell. My inner grifter is scrambling to come up with some kind of spin to salvage the situation. But with my heart skidding into the wall, all my confidence—and with it my grifter superpower—is simply gone.

It's both hilarious and awful, when you think about it. I

suck at picking the right people to trust. I knew better. I knew it made no sense that Tyler kept insisting on helping me. Well, now it makes perfect sense. He was spying on me for his father, and by extension for Petrov, this whole time.

Tyler's brown eyes, usually soft, bore into mine. He's trying to tell me something, willing me to understand. But knights in shining armor don't appear at the point of no return and betray their damsels in distress. They just don't. And all I can think for several heartbeats is *But you yelled at me for not trusting you.* Is it really possible to be that much of a hypocrite? Then I think back to all the lies I've told to gain people's trust and realize that yes, it is possible.

I try desperately to stuff all the hurt back down my throat as I come to grips with the knowledge that Tyler's betrayal, and my inability to recover from it, means I've lost all leverage with Petrov. Bargaining for Sam is now out of the question. The only option I have left is to stall.

Petrov gestures at the senator. "May I introduce my friend Senator Richland? I believe you've already met his son, Tyler."

"I've also met the senator," I say, not bothering to hide my bitterness.

"Well then, shall we conclude our business? I believe you were just countered, my dear."

"She doesn't have anything and hasn't seen anything," Tyler says, stepping out of his father's shadow. "You were about to let Sam go for not being a threat. Now you can let her go, too."

He's still trying to be a hero, the idiot. Despite lying to me for a month, faking most, if not all, of his feelings for me, and working for a sociopath, he's actually trying to save me. I can't decide if that makes me feel better or worse. Not that it matters. His interference has doomed us all.

"Shut up, Tyler," I say.

"You'd be wise to listen to her, boy. You have even less to bargain with than she does."

I close my eyes and take a breath. A strange peace seeps across my shoulders and into my core, as if someone has wrapped me in an invisible blanket. My erratic heartbeat slows and my scattered thoughts assemble.

It is simply time for Plan B.

I open my eyes, pulling my gaze from Tyler to Petrov.

"Okay," I say, my voice gaining strength. "You got me. My father lied. He never had any evidence against you. You killed him for nothing."

Petrov smirks. "Not for nothing, my dear. He was still disloyal. Besides, I didn't kill him." He looks meaningfully at Ginger.

I grit my teeth, trembling with frustration. "You could have picked any forger in the country. Why did you pick my dad?"

"I prefer to get referrals," he says, indicating the senator. "Your father came highly recommended."

I direct the next question to the senator. "How did you even know my dad?"

The senator is sweating, his eyes shifting and nervous. He's not going to answer me, so I answer myself.

"From the racetrack, right?" I'm drawing connections quickly now that I have all the information. "I saw your name on the list of donors. You were a regular, weren't you?"

"Yes," he confirms reluctantly. "But I had no idea this would happen."

"Of course you didn't," I say, feigning a sympathy I don't feel in the least. "But Petrov has his hooks in you somehow. You didn't have a choice."

The senator takes the bait. "Exactly," he says. "Petrov threatened my family."

Petrov rolls his eyes. "What I threatened was to cut off my illegal contributions to your campaign fund, as well as tarnish your pristine public reputation with allegations of fraud. The truth is, you didn't want to go down with me if Dupree had the evidence he claimed."

Ding.

"The evidence that never existed in the first place," I say.

Petrov shrugs. "He said he'd hidden it. That the only person who could find it besides him was you."

Which is why Petrov ordered the senator to have his son spy on me. I can't stop my gaze from flicking to Tyler.

"For all his criminal brilliance, your father had a fatal weakness," Petrov says. "You. Or rather, a regrettable bleeding-heart sympathy for the innocent, which he no doubt contracted from his ongoing proximity to you."

This time, Petrov hits the mark. My dad knew what it took to succeed in this business. Just as I now know what it means to fail.

"I knew I couldn't trust him, so I had Yenko follow him," he says, gesturing to Ginger. "Yenko overheard a call he made to the FBI. When he was less than forthcoming about the information he'd supposedly stolen, I gambled that he'd left that information with you. And then I may have shot him a little."

Ding.

"If only I'd known how much more of a pain in the ass you are," he adds.

"He called the FBI to save your victims," I say.

"Save them," Petrov scoffs. "As if I haven't given them everything—a chance at a new life in the land of plenty. It's a business arrangement. There is nothing to save them from."

"Yet they live piled on top of one another in an abandoned warehouse," I say. I'm pushing it, but I need to be sure. "How long does it take one of them to work off their debt to you?"

"I provide an affordable workforce for an elite clientele. I feed them and train them. It would be a shame to squander such effort."

"So none of them have ever earned their way out?"

At first, it doesn't seem like he's going to answer the question.

"Not as such, no."

Ding.

My work here is done. *Damn it, Mike, where are you?*

"What about the crates?" I say, improvising.

But I've pushed it too far. Petrov narrows his eyes and pulls out his .45, leveling it at my forehead.

Then several things happen in rapid succession, the first being the catalyst for everything that happens after.

All the lights go out.

THE O.K. CORRAL

Someone knocks into me from behind, taking me to the floor right before Petrov's gun goes off, shattering the stillness.

By the time the red security lights blink on, everyone has dashed for cover. Sam pulls me to my feet, his hands still bound. Tyler signals to us from behind a nearby stack of crates. I'm not wild about trusting him, even if he did try to save me. But given a choice between Tyler's crate and Petrov's, I'll take Tyler's.

I tug Sam in Tyler's direction and do a quick check for Dani in the semidarkness. If she's here, she's hiding, and that's good enough for now. Of all of us, she's the one most capable of taking care of herself.

We duck behind the crate as the Ukrainians open fire. One

of the bullets splinters the edge of the crate I'm huddling behind. I scramble backward into Tyler.

"We have to get out of here," Tyler says. "These crates aren't going to last long against bullets, and we have no idea what's in them. Could be explosives for all we know."

"I'm open to suggestions," Sam replies, ducking a volley from another of Petrov's henchmen.

"There's a side door farther down this wall," Tyler says.

More bullets clip the crate, and all discussion halts as we cluster as near to the center as possible. Then Dani darts from out of nowhere to join us. She drops into a crouch, gun raised. She hands me Sam's pocketknife, which she must have liberated from whatever backroom they took him to when they frisked him.

I saw through Sam's zip-tie with the serrated blade and more desperation than strength. I think I may be nicking him in my haste, but finally the zip-tie falls to the floor. I pocket the knife as more shots ring out.

Dani takes a shot at Ginger, who scuttles into a better position away from the line of fire. The reverberation from her gunshot is deafening in the cavernous warehouse. I clap my hands to my ears too late.

Then Dani pulls out another gun, this one familiar, and hands it to Sam.

"*No.*" I try to take the gun away from him, but he shoves me back into Tyler.

"Get her out of here," Sam says to Tyler as he slides the chamber back on the gun and lets it go. "We'll cover you."

"The hell you will! You're not a SWAT team, Sam. Shooting at the gun range with your dad is not the same as shooting people."

Sam gives Tyler a meaningful look, and Tyler wraps a hand around my arm.

"If we don't cover you, you'll never make it out of here," Sam shouts above the noise.

"We could just wait. The FBI will be here any minute," I shout back.

Sam grabs my chin so I can't look away, so I'll take what he's saying seriously.

"No one can get in as long as we're in a firefight. And unless Dani has some kind of miracle up her sleeve, our side is running out of bullets. If there's any hope for any of us getting out, you have to go now."

I try to shake my jaw loose from his grip. "I'm not leaving without y—"

He kisses me hard, cutting me off.

"Go," he says, nodding at Tyler. Then, despite my struggling, Tyler hauls me behind the next row of crates before stopping long enough to shake me.

"They'll follow us out. But they can't leave until we're out of their way."

"What makes you think I'm going anywhere with you?"

"I came here to save you, and that's exactly what I'm going to do."

I yank my arm out of his grip. "I came here to save Sam, and that's exactly what *I'm* going to do."

"By getting shot?" He backs me against the crate, his nose an inch from mine. "Because that's all you'll accomplish by going back."

"Why are you even here? You could have just left it alone! I know I mean nothing to you, but you could have kept out of my way."

"You mean *everything* to me. And that means I do whatever it takes to save you. Even if saving you means losing you."

I stop arguing, but I'm breathing hard and glaring at him.

Tyler's gaze softens. "Sam is not the only one who loves you," he says.

Should I believe him? Does it even matter now? I can't go back to the Julep I was before I found out he was double-crossing me.

"Fine, I'll go," I say, straightening. "But if you betray me again, I will demolish you."

"Deal," he says, relieved.

I didn't plan for things to get this dire. Sam was supposed to leave. He was supposed to be safe. And Dani. She didn't ask for any of this. What if she dies tonight? How do I deal with that? She saved my life.

Tyler's solid presence ahead of me is the only anchor I have at the moment, and despite my faith in him being shaken to its foundation, I reach out to touch his back. He looks over his shoulder and gives me a reassuring smile. Then he takes my hand gently and leads me through the door.

As soon as we step into the frigid night, I hear a crack and feel the wet on my face. For a split second, I think it's tears I didn't notice I was leaking. But then Tyler seems to hang suspended midstep for an interminable moment before dropping boneless to the ground. I wipe my face with sudden dread and, as I feared, my hand is stained red. I look down at Tyler's too-still body. His eyes are open and vacant, and blood is pooling under his head.

I blink, unable to process at first what my eyes are telling me. It takes several moments for Tyler's death to sink in. *Tyler's death.* And when it does, a tsunami of anguish slams into me. I collapse next to him, tugging his arm and shouting his name, my voice sounding to my own ears as if it were coming from down a well. I don't know what I expect. That he'll get up and shake it off? That the movement will wake me up from a nightmare?

My vision starts to speckle and I feel light-headed. But before I can tumble into oblivion, I am yanked up and away from where Tyler is lying, staring vacantly from a puddle of his blood. I can't seem to tear my gaze away from him, even as my captor jerks my arm painfully.

"Do you have any idea how hard it is to find corruptible officials?" Petrov spits at me.

"You . . . you killed him." *Get it together, Julep, or you're next.* "Why did you kill him?"

"I only need one body shield, and you were the smaller, easier-to-maneuver option."

I hammer through my nauseated, terrified haze enough to notice unmarked black SUVs filling the side parking lot. He's noticed them, too, of course, and he digs the business end of his silencer between my shoulder blades.

I follow his prompting, blind and stumbling, trying to gather my wits before I lose my life. I have only one shot left now, my nuclear option, and there's pretty much no chance I'll survive it. But if he makes it where I think he's headed, he'll have no further need of me, and I'm dead just the same. So if I have to go down, I'm damn well taking the murdering bastard with me.

I wipe Tyler's blood from my cheek and wish like hell he had never interfered, that I had never met him, that he'd never talked to me that day in the hallway. I gather my anger at him for betraying me, for fooling me, for dying, and fuse it into a ball of rage I can focus on to get myself through this.

We've passed the trees and reached the docks. An unassuming motorboat bobs serenely in its mooring. Petrov points me toward it and I slow my steps, searching for something to delay us.

"A boat's a good idea," I croak past the knives in my chest. If I want even a chance at taking him down, I'll need to grift for all I'm worth. "It'll take them time to rally the resources to chase you. It's not how I'd do it—"

"Shut up," he says, digging the .45 deeper into my back. "Whatever trick you're planning isn't going to work."

"No trick," I say, my mouth dry. "I admire your preparedness, that's all."

"You knew, didn't you? That I'd have an escape plan."

"Well, it makes sense. Picking property on the edge of a canal is a tell."

Petrov considers this, allowing me to restrict our pace to a crawl. "You set some kind of trap."

I keep silent, letting him process the seeds I've planted. I put a hand in my pocket, moving my arm as imperceptibly as possible. With luck, the shadows will help obscure the shift. My fingers bypass Sam's pocketknife and close on the small kitchen timer Murphy gave me, harmless-looking enough to leave during a pat-down. But with slight modifications—

"No, you just want me to think there's a trap. Like the evidence."

We slow to a stop and my grip tightens on the timer. I'll only have one shot at this, and it's not going to be a very good shot.

He hesitates, eyeing the boat with suspicion. Spotlights click on in the parking lot, lighting up the night like it's noon. They're all pointed at the warehouse, but it's enough to spook Petrov into action.

He sets foot on the boat just as the engine explodes into a fireball. The blast knocks Petrov back several feet, but alas, safely onto the dock rather than into the water or a wooden stake. Murphy was right—the timer's delay was too unpredictable. I should have risked the cell phone.

Plan C it is, then.

Petrov jumps up, leveling his gun at me before I can run. My hands are trembling so much I can barely pull the knife out of my pocket.

"Bitch!" he screams at me.

There are shouts behind me. No doubt the feds have noticed Murphy's light show. Whether they can get to me before Petrov pulls the trigger is doubtful.

"You, me, and sixty-three," I whisper, and whip the knife out of my pocket, aiming for an eye. But not having any experience in any kind of martial art, I only manage to jab his shoulder.

He howls in pain and knocks me down. My elbow hits the deck hard as I land, which sends the knife flying. With a plop, my only hope of self-preservation falls into the water.

Petrov stanches the blood with one hand while taking aim at me with the other. I close my eyes and think of my dad, of Sam, of Tyler.

"Freeze!" Mike shouts from too far away. He won't make it in time.

Then Dani leaps onto the dock, the boat fire behind her casting her in shadow. She lands between me and Petrov, her gun pointed at his heart.

Never taking her eyes off him, she bends down just enough to help me to my feet.

"Are you hurt, *milaya?*" she asks softly.

"No, I'm not hurt," I say, the trembling in my hands infecting the rest of me. *I'm destroyed.*

Petrov snarls a few guttural words at Dani. But instead of answering, Dani shoots him in the chest. He collapses to the ground, dropping his gun, his fingers curled into claws. She steps a pace closer and kicks his gun into the canal. Then she aims the barrel of her gun at his head.

"Dani, don't!" I hear myself say.

She stands still, not acknowledging that she's heard me, though the stiffness in her shoulders suggests that she has. She shifts the gun slightly and fires again, its roar followed by the sound of wood splintering. Petrov cowers away from the shrapnel, and I breathe a sigh of relief. Dani lowers her gun but doesn't holster it. Her expression is calm, but her eyes are an ocean of loathing.

I sink to my knees and grab the edge of the dock, losing what's left of the diner eggs over the side of it. When I pull myself back up to sitting, Dani is gone.

THE FINAL SCORE

Sam is sitting on the back bumper of an ambulance, a gray wool blanket wrapped around his shoulders, when Mike leads me back to the parking lot. A tidal wave of relief crashes against the flood of pain and terror filling me, and I throw myself at him, bawling like a baby.

He drops the blanket and pushes me back to arm's length, his face filled with worry.

"My god, Julep, you look like you've been through the Texas Chainsaw Massacre."

I tell him about Tyler through hiccupping sobs, punctuated by a confessional litany of apologies.

He pulls me close, warming my hair with shushing noises. "There was nothing you could do."

"I could have forced him to go back," I say.

"Then we'd all be dead," Sam says. "When Petrov left the fight to follow you, his thugs lost interest and took off. The FBI caught them, of course, but if they hadn't run, they'd have won."

"Still," I whisper, my sobs quieting but the tears still streaming.

I close my eyes and Tyler's there. A slideshow of smiles, touches, and blood. No sound track, just sirens. And guilt—an everglade of guilt.

"When I heard the explosion, I was so afraid you'd . . ."

I press my face into his chest and feel him flinch.

"What is it?" I ask, exploring his chest with my fingers, searching for wounds.

"It's nothing," he says. "I'm just banged up. No permanent damage."

"I'm so sorry, Sam. I should have gone to the police when you told me to."

"You had your reasons," he says. "I'm just glad the feds are here now."

I shudder at how close I came to losing him, too.

"Listen, Julep—about your dad . . ."

The look on his face sends what's left of my adrenaline surging.

"Where is he?" I whisper.

But before Sam can answer, a team of paramedics rolls an occupied gurney out of the warehouse. The IV bag and oxygen mask obscure the patient's identity from this distance, so I rush over to see for myself.

"Miss, step back," says the medic closest to me. But I burst past him, bumping him out of the way as I scoop up my dad's hand. I squeeze it hard and he turns his head, opening his eyes and smiling at me. With his other hand, he pulls off the mask.

"You're . . . grounded," he says, wheezing.

In my head, I'm saying *I love you* and *How could you?* over and over, but nothing comes out of my mouth.

"I'm going to be fine, Jules. It's all going to be okay," he says, returning my squeeze. We've reached the ambulance without my noticing. They're lifting the gurney into the back, and our hands are coming apart. I try to climb up after him, but the medics push me back.

"I'm family," I manage to croak, but they don't listen.

"Let us do our jobs," says the EMT who told me to step back. "We're taking him to Mercy. You can meet us there."

"But—"

Then they're closing the doors, and Sam's pulling me away. I sag into him again. My dad's alive. Dani must have seen Petrov shoot him and assumed he was dead.

Dad's alive. Tyler's dead. My brain is short-circuiting with too many conflicting emotions. I have no idea how much time has passed when I finally realize I'm sniveling all over Sam, and I start pressing myself back together into some semblance of a human being. Sam hands me a tissue he got from who knows where.

"You okay?" he asks.

I nod, gripping the tissue like a lifeline. "Yeah, I'll be all right. I just need to"—I make a gesture like a ball rolling down a hill—"you know, process. You okay?"

"Not even remotely," he says. "But I'll manage as long as I know you're all right."

I lean my head against his shoulder, exhausted.

"Agent Ramirez isn't disclosing much. You cut a deal with him?" Sam asks.

I nod again.

"What about St. Agatha's? Foster care?"

I don't answer directly, not wanting to face my future now that I actually have one. I didn't dwell on the consequences of my crazy plan when I was crafting it, because my coming out alive wasn't likely. But I'd already lost everything when Mike ratted me out to the dean anyway. I just didn't know it at the time.

"There's more to Mike," I say, feeling compelled to get it off my chest while I still can. So I tell him everything—about Mike the PI, how he claimed Sam had hired him, how I stupidly kept his secret out of misplaced loyalty and a grievous lapse in judgment. I apologize again, and Sam responds with a heavy sigh and silence. Then Mike makes his way over to us as if his ears have been burning.

"All right, Julep," Mike says, flipping open a black FBI notebook. "Bad guys have been dealt with. Time for your statement."

I pull the pen from my hair and hand it to Mike. "Will Petrov live?"

"Hard to say. Chest wounds are dicey," he says, taking the pen from me. "But if he does make it, we're going to need more than the testimony of a con man and a couple of teenage reprobates to put him away. Where's your dad's evidence? You said it would be here."

"There isn't any," I say, my head as heavy as a boulder. Exhaustion settles into my every sinew, muscle, and bone.

"What?" Mike says.

So I tell Mike about the rose, about the spectacular lack of anything useful my dad left me.

Mike tucks his notebook under his arm and rubs his forehead. "What are you doing here, Seward?" he asks.

"I posed as a computer technician so I could get a look at their files, see if there was anything useful."

"And was there?"

"Petrov figured it out before I could get anywhere. I can look at the computers now, though."

"We have analysts for that. And you'd better pray they find something, or I'm handing each of you over to the prosecuting attorney, and probably the Witness Protection Program." He turns a baleful eye on me. "If you think foster care is bad, wait till they assign you a marshal."

I shrug, taking Sam's hand and leading him away from the ambulance.

"Hey, I'm not finished with you. I still need your statement."

"You're holding it," I say.

Mike's expression morphs from confused to shocked to

excited. We leave him holding the pen with a goofy smile on his face as he barks for one of his analysts over the walkie.

"You recorded the whole thing on a spy pen?" Sam says.

"Sometimes the most obvious method is the one they least expect," I say. "I took a chance."

"If there were a standardized test for wicked genius, you'd score in the ninety-ninth percentile. You know that, right?"

I swallow against an upwelling of guilt. "All the evidence in the world doesn't undo what I did to Tyler."

I lead Sam over to a knot of police officers, nurses, social workers, and bewildered Ukrainians. The social workers are trying to calm the girls, a couple of translators flitting from group to group to help with communication. The nurses are examining them, handing out blankets and writing on clipboards, while the officers make notes in small notebooks and occasionally jabber into their walkies.

A familiar brown figure detaches from a group of girls babbling anxiously to a translator. "When you asked me all those questions about how we choose foster families, I assumed you were asking me for yourself—not ninety-three illegal aliens."

"Ninety-three survivors," I correct her. "Are there really ninety-three?"

"Yes," Ms. Fairchild confirms. "None of whom speak English, by the way. You could have warned me, so I'd have been more prepared."

"I figured Agent Ramirez would fill you in when he called you."

"He did. But do you have any idea how hard it is to track

down multiple Ukrainian translators in the middle of the night?"

"You said I could suggest housing for them," I say.

"I said you could suggest a family for yourself— Wait, you have ninety-three homes already lined up?" She raises her brown eyebrows in disbelief.

"I have a hundred and twenty, give or take," I say. "And some could probably take more than one."

"How could you possibly—?"

"I'm calling in a few favors," I say. "Have you got a place for them all till I can arrange it? A day at most."

"Yes." She's looking at me like I've grown a second head.

"I'll be in touch," I say and pull Sam in the direction of the SUVs.

Sam turns to me as soon as we're out of earshot. "How could you possibly have a hundred and twenty families that owe you favors? I've known you since fourth grade. I'd remember if you had that many people on the hook. Are you conning her?"

"Not a con. I actually tried the truth this time. Seems to be working so far, but it'll cost me."

"What do you mean? Cost you how?"

I pull open the door to one of the SUVs and climb in. It's cold and I want out of this wind. If the suits have a problem with it, they can arrest me. After a moment's hesitation, Sam follows me in and shuts the door. The SUV smells like old cigarettes and aftershave.

Sam circles an arm around my shoulders. I don't push away from him, though the touch reminds me painfully of Tyler. Will

I relive the ache of losing him every time someone touches me from now on? I suspect I already know the answer.

"They're expelling me," I say to distract myself.

"Oh, Julep," he says into my hair.

"I couldn't just leave them."

Then I tell him the rest of everything—my crazy plan to get the Ukrainians out of Petrov's cage without getting them deported, or worse. How I used the fake IDs I made to blackmail more than a hundred of Chicago's wealthiest families into offering their homes and resources. How I persuaded the president of the best private school in Chicago to spend five hundred thousand dollars on a special program to help the victims integrate into American society.

He listens, whistling softly at my description of dumping the IDs on the dean's desk.

"You're crazy," he says. "And wonderful. But mostly crazy."

"Your turn for confession. What the hell were you thinking, going to Petrov alone like that? And how did Dani end up with my mother's gun?"

He sighs. "After Agent Ramirez let me go, I was so angry—mostly at myself, for getting caught. I wanted to make it up to you and break Petrov's hold on you, so I tried to pull the Franklin job on him. I disabled his WiFi access and intercepted his call to the phone company. I took your mom's gun with me just in case. I made it all the way into Petrov's office. But then you texted me, and he saw your name on my phone."

I squeeze my eyes closed, blocking the scene playing in my head.

"I didn't answer your calls because I knew you'd figure out my plan as soon as you heard my voice. And speaking of . . . here."

He pulls an object wrapped in a towel out of his laptop bag and hands it to me. I peel back a corner just enough to confirm it's my mother's gun before wrapping it up again and handing it back.

"You keep it for a while, Sam. Just until I feel like you're safe again."

He doesn't argue, which is a relief.

"I negotiated for you, too," I continue. "You're free of the FBI. And the dean doesn't know I made you an ID."

"What about you? What are you going to do?"

"I don't know. Public school, I guess. Yale is for sissies, anyway."

"You can still get in," he says, knowing full well that even if I could convince them to admit me with an expulsion on my record I'd never be able to afford it.

"I know," I say.

"Yale is for sissies," he agrees, resting his cheek against my head.

I'd be lying if I said I don't regret falling on my sword to rescue a bunch of strangers. Tyler's dead because I thought I could save the world. I've destroyed my life here. And though I'd be an idiot to stick around, trying to scratch out an existence in the crumbling ruins of my broken castle, a fresh start is not something I really deserve, or want.

"Will you stay in Chicago?" he asks, reading my mind.

"You're here."

He stiffens. I feel it all along my side, though he doesn't actually move.

"You're leaving," I say in a small voice.

Sam sighs. "My dad is shipping me off to military school."

"What?" I say, wilting further.

"I got arrested, Julep. That kind of thing doesn't fly with my dad."

"Blame me. Tell him I lied to you, that you had no idea what you were doing. Tell him you'll never see me again—we can come up with something."

He takes my hand and shifts so that he's facing me. His eyes look sad and uncertain. "I think I need to go, Julep."

"Why?" The golf ball lodged in my throat makes it hard to get the words out.

Sam looks down. "I love you. I have for years. But so much of who I am is wrapped up in us. I don't know who I am without you. I need to find that out before I have anything to offer you. Tyler taught me that."

My heart beats slowly, painfully, as I try to imagine my life without Tyler, my dreams, and my Sam.

Sam takes my hand. The way Tyler used to. The twin aches are almost unbearable.

"Just don't leave, okay?" he says. "When I come back to you, I need to be able to find you."

I close my eyes, letting out a shaky breath.

"Okay, break it up," Mike says after opening the SUV door and letting in all the wind. "Your folks want to talk to you."

Mike hands Sam a phone. Sam takes it and steps out into the night, leaving a gaping hole behind him.

"You all right?" Mike asks me.

I shake my head. I'm so tired of lying. But I'm not any happier telling the truth.

"You know I have to charge you, right?" He sounds regretful, which is something, I guess. If I can't get amnesty, I'll take pity.

"Yeah," I say.

Mike leans against the door, dropping his official demeanor. "Why'd you do it?"

"Because you couldn't."

He chews on that for a moment but doesn't argue.

"Can you wait till after we drop Sam off?" I ask.

"Sure, kid."

The ride home starts off fairly sober as I consider my bleak future. But then I realize I'm wasting what precious time I have left with Sam. So I paste on a smile until I start to feel the loss a little less, and I reach past the pain to take his hand.

When we get to Sam's house, Sam slides out of the car, his shoulders slumped in weariness.

"I'll call you," he says, letting my fingers slide through his.

I don't say anything as he walks up the drive and into the house. Then Mike opens the door and I get out, sliding my wrists together in front of me.

"Julep Dupree, you're under arrest for identification fraud. You have the right to remain silent. Anything you say or do may be used against you . . ."

I tune out the rest of Mike's monologue as he fastens a pair of cold metal cuffs onto my wrists. It might be what my father feared the most, but I think he's proud of me anyway. Despite everything, I think he's the only one who really understands why I threw away everything to save a handful of strays.

I did it because it's who I am.

I smile for real this time.

THE AFTERMATH

The Graceland Cemetery is as well manicured and picturesque as the bereaved among Chicago's aristocracy could wish. Grassy knolls slope elegantly toward still waters. Sun-stained statues guard against the ravages of time, eyes downcast, hands clasped as if to hold the lost to this plane.

I stand at the edge, an interloper with a pink chrysanthemum.

My foster-care provider—I can't think of him as a father—is waiting for me in the car. I ask him to bring me here, and he always agrees, though the jury's still out on whether or not I belong in Witness Protection. He's worried that my visits to Tyler's grave make me an easy target for any unaccounted-for malcontents from Petrov's crew. But the downside of having such a tight-knit cabal is that no one's really left when the big man falls. There is one still on the run, but she wouldn't hurt me.

A slow twenty-minute meandering brings me to the Richland family plot, complete with moss-covered mausoleum. Tyler's not in the mausoleum, though. He's here, under my feet. And the thought is still so foreign that my brain dismisses it. Tyler is the essence of what it is to be alive. He's the kind of guy who every good thing comes to naturally. He belongs in the world, not under it.

I kneel next to the frost-covered earth stretching eight feet west from his gravestone, the chrysanthemum in my lap. It's been nearly three months since his death, and the grass still hasn't grown over the grave. He was buried too late in the fall, I guess. He'll have to wait until spring. It's a silly thing, but it bothers me.

I start the conversation the way I always do, telling him I miss him, telling him about my trial, telling him about how Sam still hasn't called. But all too quickly I run out of things to say, except for the thing I came here to say. This is my last visit to Graceland Cemetery. I'm here to say good-bye.

"Our dads have a lot to answer for," I say, directing the conversation to the stone rather than to the dirt. "We should have been kids a little longer. Even if we didn't want to be."

The Tyler in my head answers me: *We all have things in our past we're not proud of.*

I sigh, because this is a sage response, both apologetic and forgiving. It's exactly what Tyler would say.

I lay the chrysanthemum across the stone, letting my fingers trail across the cut of his name and ignoring the tears that never seem far from my eyes these days. Even three months later, I have nightmares about him. Not his death, though I still have day-mares about that. My nightmares are much worse.

"Don't worry," I say. "I'll watch the world while you sleep."

When I get back to the car, Mike is leaning against the fender instead of sitting inside, behind the wheel. Still the protector, even though there's nothing left to protect me from. Well, nothing mob-related. I could still use protection from Tyler's friends and family. I haven't seen any of them since being officially suspended from school pending a lengthy investigation. But I know that the senator has been indicted and is on his way to prison. I can only imagine how Mrs. Richland must feel about me now.

"Ready?" he says.

I'm grateful that he doesn't add "to go home." I may be in his custody for the foreseeable future, but his home is not mine.

We pull out of the circular drive onto Irving Park Road in relative silence. Mike is giving me space, and I appreciate it.

You may be wondering a) how I got sucked into foster care despite finding my dad, b) why Mike of all people volunteered to foster me, and c) why I agreed to let him.

To answer the first, my father is in Cook County jail awaiting sentencing, though the deal he made with the district attorney pretty much guarantees he'll get four years in the pen (medium-security facility, thanks to Mike pulling some strings). But with my mom out of the picture and my dad in prison, foster care is my only option.

As for why Mike willingly volunteered to put up a kid who's given him as much trouble as I have, I honestly couldn't tell you. He probably feels sorry for me. Which is not the best reason in the world to invite somebody into your home, but it's better than putting up with the guilt, I guess.

I'll be honest: I was not wild about the idea when he first proposed it. I'm still mad at him for lying to me, and for Pete's sake, he's an FBI agent. Talk about incompatible. But Mike understands what I've lost, and it's important to me that my handler gets that. Besides, it's either Mike or juvie, and Mike's wife, Angela, serves much better food.

Heather and Murphy surprised me by showing up at my apartment with boxes the day the judge ruled that my temporary housing with Mike would turn permanent. I never asked how they knew, but I'd bet Sam called them after I texted him my new address. In any case, the afternoon I crated up and stored all my belongings—including a battered trunk holding a cream-colored dress and two dried flowers—was rendered a little less heartbreaking by a couple of inadvertent friends.

"Sister Rasmussen called," Mike says now, breaking into my thoughts. "They're just about to start winter break, and she wants to see you before the school closes. Are you up for it?"

"Sure," I say, my eyes fixed on the scenery stealing by. "I don't know what there is to talk about, though. They have to expel me. The investigation is just a formality."

"I think she wants to explain why."

I decide to go with it, though anything she says will only be painful and pointless. Maybe it will make her feel better, though. And this new Julep can't pretend any longer that other people's happiness doesn't matter.

Mike makes a U-turn and heads toward St. Agatha's.

When we pull into the parking lot and I step out of the car, I get the strangest feeling. Like I'm looking at a house I grew up in that belongs to somebody else now.

"Do you want me to go with you?" he asks.

"No thanks," I say through the window. "I can find my way back to the house from here."

The halls are blessedly empty as I make my way to the administrative wing. The lockers cling to the walls with feigned innocence, as if none of them had ever harbored an illegal ID or a dead messenger. I assume the Brockman Room with its row of portraits will reek of smug satisfaction when I pass through it. But though the men in the portraits are as somber as always, this time they seem to judge me a little less.

When I enter the waiting room outside the president's office, her mousy aide pops up at once and scurries in to announce my arrival. She comes back more subdued, leaving the door open for me. But before I can walk through, Dean Porter comes out, glaring at me as if the devil is spitting on her shoes.

"Ah, Ms. Dupree," says Sister Rasmussen, who is just a step behind the dean. She is holding a heavy black coat in one hand and an envelope in the other. "Let's go for a walk."

I fall into step beside her when the dean heads down the opposite corridor.

"I hear that the judge was fairly lenient, considering the widespread nature of your crimes," she says as she settles her coat onto her shoulders. "Community service, FBI supervision, a number of fines, and an apology letter, am I right?"

"Yes," I say. "I suppose he thought I'd suffered enough."

"Or perhaps that your extreme efforts toward rescuing others showed a redemption of character he wanted to encourage." She opens the door to the quad and I walk out. I'm not sure where this is leading, but I am curious about the envelope. Is it for me? Is it my official expulsion letter?

"I guess we'll never know for sure," I say, zipping my jacket against the chill.

"Actually, Judge Collodi is a friend of mine. I'll likely ask him during our next tennis match."

"Oh." What do I say to that? What am I even doing here?

"No doubt you're wondering why I called you here."

She takes a pair of thick knitted mittens from her pocket and puts them on. Her breath is a fog on the frigid air. This far north this late in the year, the sun is already shedding the golden light of sunset as early as two o'clock in the afternoon.

She hands me the envelope.

Inside are two sheets of paper folded into thirds. The first is indeed an official letter from the administration board. But instead of expelling me, it says that they're rescinding my suspension, that I can return to St. Agatha's at the beginning of the term.

"I don't understand . . . ," I say.

"You may need to examine the second page."

I flip to the next page—a statement of payment in full for the rest of my education at St. Aggie's. Not just for the rest of the year, but for the whole of junior and senior years as well.

"Holy crap!" I say, realizing belatedly that Sister Rasmussen is still standing here. "Sorry."

"Don't be. I have once or twice said *crap* myself. Three times now."

"I— Where did this money come from?"

"Your guess is as good as mine. Likely better, actually. The tuition came in as a cashier's check from an anonymous donor with your name and a perplexing note in the memo line."

"What note?"

She points to the bottom-right portion of the statement under the heading ADDITIONAL INFORMATION.

TROVA LA FATA TURCHINA.

"Any idea what it refers to?" she asks.

I shake my head, though that's at least partially a lie. I've seen *fata turchina* before—on an unloaded gun in a car stuck in a ditch. It must be from my father. Which means Petrov must have paid him in advance. No wonder Petrov was so peeved. Then I finally get it, what this really is, what it means. It's my dad's final score. And he's just given it to me.

"The truth is, the board didn't really have a choice," the president continues. "The tuition check may have been the final push, but the decision was already on a knife's edge.

313

During the investigation, scores of students spoke voluntarily on your behalf. Teachers as well. Ms. Shirley was particularly vocal in your defense."

"Ms. Shirley, my computer-science teacher?" I say, wincing. I think I may owe her an IRA contribution, and an apology. And the students? I thought for sure everyone blamed me for Tyler's death. I certainly blame myself.

"And then there's the national publicity the school's received for its unprecedented efforts at integrating displaced young people. Our admissions applications numbers have tripled in the last month from what they were a year ago. None of which would have been possible were it not for you."

"But I didn't do it for the school. I did it to save myself."

"We both know it was more complicated than that."

I look down again at the pardon I'm holding, feeling overwhelmed. It's too much to take in at once. The tuition, the outpouring of support, the unexpected positive outcomes. I didn't intend any of it, so it doesn't really feel like I deserve it. I certainly don't deserve the credit. Any more than I deserve the second chance.

"You look sad," she says with concern.

"It's just—I think this dream has already sailed without me."

She smiles and takes my arm. "Come with me. I'd like to show you something."

We walk across the quad, past the triumphal arch, to an auxiliary building. She opens the door for me and then leads me to a small classroom holding about thirty girls in school uniforms, with a teacher and a few aides circling the desks. We stand unnoticed at the back of the room.

"I thought you'd like to see what your five-hundred-thousand-dollar favor has done," she says softly.

One girl a little older than I am raises a hand and says, "I catch the red ball," in a tentative, heavily accented voice. The teacher praises her and moves to the next exercise.

Sister Rasmussen leads me out of the room, closing the door behind us. "Their American student ambassadors are in the room next door, learning rudimentary Ukrainian. Most of them willingly enough, though there was some grumbling on the part of the parents. When I told them they had a choice between taking in an émigré or having their children expelled for a breach of honor code, they fell in line reasonably quickly. They even reframed the situation to their advantage by forming an organization around it. That's where all the publicity came from."

"Wow," I say. It's more than I'd hoped for. And I'm sure it costs more than the five thousand dollars per survivor I initially estimated. The families I blackmailed into taking the girls, and St. Agatha's itself, must be ponying up the rest. "I don't know what to say."

"Ms. Dupree, you have been blessed with a very special skill set, and a brain and a heart to use it to benefit others. Promise me you won't squander it."

I smile. "I promise."

THE CLEAN SLATE

Three weeks later, I push against the small stack of junk mail that has piled up in my weekend absence and open the door to my new office. I gather up the ads for carpet cleaning and furnace maintenance and local pizza, dumping them in a wastebasket I picked up at the Goodwill along with the partially broken desk chair and the faded upholstered chair across the desk from it.

Despite the tuition check my father sent, a girl can't live on education alone. Especially a girl in the foster system. Mike might be responsible for feeding me, but I'm responsible for the rest. And since I'm officially a domesticated grifter now, I'm supposed to avoid anything even remotely resembling the shadier side of the law. That leaves gainful employment.

I considered a coffee-shop gig. Briefly. But we all know what a waste that would be, so I decided to hang out a shingle as a security investigator, which is just a fancy way of saying "PI with a specialty in security systems." You build 'em, we test 'em. If something's already gone, we can try to track it down, but mostly we deal in prevention. Not that we won't take a few odd jobs for insurance companies and such. Anything to make the rent.

All in all, not bad for an after-school job. And if I have to slip into Ms. Jena Scott mode from time to time to lead clients to believe that I'm older than I really am, well, there's nothing exactly illegal about that, is there?

"You couldn't pick up the mail, Murph?" I ask as I slide my bag off my shoulder and onto the desk next to my keys.

Murphy looks up from his much nicer desk under the window. "What? Oh. That's the boss's job."

I can already see this is going to be an equitable partnership. "Everything's the boss's job."

"I'm a sound and lighting expert, not a maid." He dives back into his laptop, and it reminds me so much of Sam that my insides twist for a moment.

"I'm going down to get a latte. You want anything?" I say as I dig through my bag to find my wallet. Yes, I pay for coffee now—try not to fall over.

Murphy waves me off, and I tromp down the steps and around to the front, where the Ballou's inviting vapors seep through the cracks around its door and out into the street.

"Two double vanilla lattes, one iced," I say to the not-Mike barista. I think his name is Yaji, or something like that. He takes my cash and starts the lattes.

When it turned out that the office space above the Ballou was tenantless and available for rent, I jumped on it. Sure, it has a strange moldy-coffee smell baked into the walls, a closet full of old paint cans from the 1960s, and a generous sprinkling of mouse droppings all over the floor. But it also has a lockable door, working lights, and free Internet connectivity. And it's cheap—the meager funds left in my account after I paid back the people who bought fake IDs from me actually managed to cover the deposit and the first month's rent.

It's perfect. I just wish my dad could see it. He'd probably dry-heave at the respectability of it all.

When I get back to the office, Murphy is packing up.

"Thanks," he says, taking the iced latte.

"You out for the day?" I ask.

"Yeah. Bryn's meeting me at the Logan for a showing of *Shaun of the Dead*."

"How's that going?" I ask, genuinely happy I was wrong about Bryn, at least so far.

"Great. Turns out geek is the new black."

"I wonder where she got that idea." I set my coffee down on my desk and shuffle through the remaining mail.

"I emailed you the financial analysis for the Covey job."

"Thanks. Now get out of here before Bryn starts the epic texting."

Just as Murphy reaches for the knob, the door smacks into him.

"Oops, sorry," Heather says as she slides past Murphy.

"Nice to see you, too, Heather," Murphy grumbles as he shuts the door behind him.

"I'm betting you're here for this." I take out a cashier's check from the desk drawer.

"I still can't believe it actually worked," she says.

"That's what everyone always says." I hand her the check. "This is my last act as grifter, and I'm only following through because I always finish a job. But"—this part is tricky, because I'm not preachy by nature and I don't have a moral leg to stand on—"you should consider coming clean to your mom."

"Are you joking? Who are you, and what have you done with Julep Dupree?"

"Look, I don't know a thing about modeling or New York, university or otherwise. But I do know a thing or two about losing parents. Trust me when I say that keeping secrets will drive you apart."

Heather affects the resentful expression guilty people usually get when called on their crap. "There are worse things."

"I can't think of any," I say.

"Noted," she says, tucking the check into her purse. Then she slings the purse over her shoulder and leaves without a good-bye.

I've done the best I can without compromising my seriously warped integrity. She'll either listen to me or she won't. In either case, we're square. And even as I contemplate the other debts I have yet to pay, my door opens again.

"An office makes you an easy target, you realize."

The familiar Eastern European accent sends a shiver down my spine.

"Dani, how nice of you to drop by."

She looks surprisingly good for someone on the run from cops and robbers alike. She's wearing her new black coat, since I still have her old one. She looks fed and washed, and she doesn't betray even a hint of the distress that someone being hunted would normally show. She's smiling at me, and I realize that I don't think I've ever seen her smile before. It's a small smile, but it transforms her face into that of an almost normal nineteen-year-old. I smile back.

"Mike would want me to ask: Are you here to kill me?" I say.

"If I am your only danger, then you are quite safe."

"Good to know." I offer her the client chair even though I already know she'd never sit with her back to a door.

"But just because I don't wish you dead doesn't mean others do not."

I sigh. It's Mike's argument, coming out of Dani's mouth. I'm lucky the two would never join forces, or I'd have a tougher time getting my way.

"I'm not important enough to be a target." I sit in my chair and prop my boot heels on the desk.

"Maybe," Dani says. "But you do have a way of pissing off dangerous people."

"Believe me, taking on another crime family is the last

thing on my to-do list. And when I say last, I mean below getting waterboarded and having my eyes gouged out."

Dani laughs, actually laughs, and then leans over the desk, a small card in her hand.

"In case you get past the waterboarding and eye-gouging."

She places the card on my desk and pulls back. I pick up the card to read it, but all that's on it is a phone number in small black print.

"What's this?"

"My cell. In case you need backup."

"Thanks," I say. "But my cases are going to be pretty boring from here on out—embezzlement, insurance fraud, testing security systems. Nothing involving bullets, I promise."

"I don't mind a little boring now and then."

"Aren't you worried you'll get caught?" I still don't know how to peg her. Every time I think I have a handle on her, she does something new and completely different.

"If the police were actually looking, they'd have found me by now. I am as I always was."

And she is. Something tells me she always will be.

On a whim, I pick up my keys and unhook one of them from the ring. I toss it to Dani, who catches it effortlessly.

"I know a guy at the impound lot," I say. I had planned on keeping the Chevelle myself, but it really belongs to her. Besides, now I get the Chevelle and a driver.

"You know a guy?"

"Okay, I know a guy *now*. It took almost no grifting at all. He was itching to give me the car."

"And now you're giving it back to me?"

"Today is a good day. Just go with it."

She nods, a somber look on her face. "If I'd known he was alive, I would have gotten him out," she says. "I honestly thought—"

"I know," I say, fidgeting with my keys. Then, out of nowhere, I say, "You up for a little boring right now?"

"What kind of boring?"

"The kind that involves driving into the lion's den?"

She shrugs and smiles. "Why not?"

Fifty minutes fly by as I try not to let my nerves get the best of me. I'm still a grifter at heart. Walking into a prison, even to visit, is enough to make my blood itch. As Dani pulls up to the entrance, she shoots me a concerned look.

"Would you like me to come with you?" she asks.

"Nah," I say. "It's just a silly phobia. I'll get over it."

"I'll be here when you get back," she says. And the emphasis she puts on *be here* seems to signify a deeper meaning, a longer promise.

"Thank you," I say, holding her gaze for a moment to add weight to my words in return. It's good to have friends. Even crooked ones.

Entering the prison is less like the movies and more like a hospital. A giant circulation desk with a heavyset man in a uniform behind it dominates the foyer. It's almost too easy to walk up and state my business. He leads me through a very nonthreatening vestibule, opening a door for me and pointing down a hallway.

I follow the signs labeled VISITORS and enter a fairly ordinary room with windows, tables, and chairs—no bars. My dad enters from another door a few seconds after I shut mine behind me, and I leap into his arms. He winces but catches me and hugs me back.

"How's your shoulder?" I ask as he lets me down.

"Fine. A little stiff."

There are so many questions I want to ask. So much fear and guilt and anger I haven't really processed. I know he did it for me. But that doesn't change everything I lost when it all went south. Something's been off between us since that night, and I guess it's true what they say—you can never go home again. You can miss it, you can visit, but you can't go back. Which is why I don't bother asking. His reasons and reassurances won't really change anything.

"Read any good books lately?" I ask.

"Best thing about prison—unlimited reading time." He smiles, almost hiding his knowledge of what's going on in my head.

"Worst thing?" I ask, because it follows.

"Not seeing you every day."

I hug him again, softer this time, keeping my feet on the floor. Even if he's no longer my parent, he's still my dad.

"Is Ramirez still insufferable?" he asks as we sit at a nearby table. He keeps hold of my hand, though.

"Is a bookie a safe bet?" I say with a sardonic smile, until I remember Ralph and the smile falls off my face. "Sorry, Dad."

He looks down at our hands. "Still no sign of Ralph?"

"Not yet. But I'm still looking."

He sighs. "No news is good news. He's probably just relocated."

"Yep," I say, and I'm pretty sure he's right. "Pretty sure" is not really good enough when you're talking about a friend, but it's better than nothing. To change the subject I say, "Dad. About Mom."

"Did you find her?" he says, perking up.

I shake my head. "Why can't you just tell me where to look?"

"I would if I knew, Jules, believe me. Bringing her back would mean you didn't have to stay with Ramirez." He says it like I'm the one in prison.

"But what about the note you put on the check?" I say.

"What check?" he says, puzzled.

"The tuition check," I remind him. "The memo line: *Trova la fata turchina*. 'Find the blue fairy.'"

"I have no idea what you're talking about."

The bottom drops out of my stomach. "You didn't send the check."

He shakes his head slowly.

After a half hour of fruitless brainstorming, we admit defeat for the day. Neither of us has any clue who'd have paid my tuition or why, and my visiting hour is up. I say good-bye around a large lump in my throat. He hugs me and lets me go.

I tell Dani about my discovery on our way back to my office. Her fingers tighten on the wheel a few times, and she looks worried. But I can't see someone who means me harm paying for my educational betterment, so I tell her to stop fussing. Unfortunately, my rationalization doesn't stop her from walking me up the stairs and checking the office for boogeymen. Why am I so bad at picking minions? Seriously, it's a thing with me.

I finally convince her to leave with a promise that I'll text her when I get back to Mike's. And speaking of, I check my phone for the first time in hours. Three texts from Mike. Argh. Missed my check-in. I quickly text him back my whereabouts and my ETA. The last thing I need is another Mike Ramirez lecture about responsibility and follow-through.

In any case, I'm not going to solve the riddle of the mysterious check tonight, so I sit in my chair and breathe out a heavy sigh. I prop my boots up on the desk again. The stretch in my tired muscles feels good.

It's nice to have the office to myself once in a while. I like to hear the sound of cars passing by, of steaming milk and pretentious debate going on below. I leave the overhead light off, because I like the feel of the night around me, a soft blanket of shelter and possibility. Yeah, I might be a little abandoned, and I've lost more than I care to admit, but I'm surviving. One day at a time.

I lean back again in my chair just as a woman, midthirties with reddish-brown hair, pokes her head into my office.

"Are you Ms. Dupree?" she asks.

"Yes, come in. And you are—?"

The woman enters, worry tightening the fine lines on her face.

"Eliza Bancroft." She shakes her umbrella with one hand while extending the other toward me. "I think I need your help."

I stand and shake her hand, giving her a reassuring smile. Yep, today is a good day.

ACKNOWLEDGMENTS

The making of a book is as much a hero's journey as the story contained inside its pages. I would not have made it through the bumps and bends in the road without many wise friends lighting the way.

First, I want to thank my parents, Elizabeth Smith, Paul Smith, and Daryl Gibson, for giving me every advantage, including a lifelong love of reading, the example of their own fortitude in accomplishing the impossible, and an unending curiosity for things unseen. My brothers, James, Christopher, and Will, encouraged my developing imagination by putting up with my crazy ideas, like paddling across a pool in a massive stockpot to escape a herd of crocodiles. I thank Christopher in particular for spending summers watching *Star Wars* on repeat with me, and my mom for her unwavering excitement at every milestone.

Also, I can't thank my English and creative writing teachers enough for patiently explaining the Rules to me until I became savvy enough to properly break them. Specifically, thanks go to Mr. Giuliani, Mrs. McCormick, Mrs. Kinsley, Drs. Bennett and Garrett, and my beloved librarian, Mrs. Cooper.

Julep owes an eternal debt of gratitude to my cadre of beta readers. First, I absolutely must thank my wife and first reader, Miranda, who tells it like it is, good, bad, or ugly. Thanks also go to our daughter, Caelan, for putting up with the excruciating long hours a writer keeps. This book would not have been possible without their support and love and understanding.

My other beta readers have all contributed something to this story, and believe me when I say that I can look at every sentence and tell you which one of these lovely people helped me tweak it to perfection. Thank you to Laura Ferrel, my BFF and writing soul mate; my buddies in the Hawthorne Writers group—William Hertling, Debbie Steere, Jill Ahlstrand, and Jonathan Stone—who tactfully told me to ditch the Pomeranians; my buddies in the Pony Club—Kristen Ketchel-Bain, Ehren and Merri Vaughn, and Ethan Jones—who helped me plot Julep's adventures; Rachel Potts, YA expert and cover designer, who told me everything she loved and everything she didn't with love and thoughtfulness; and last but not least, Marie Langager, who came on at the end to help me massage the final edits. Special thanks go to Mary Kate Fellows Russell and her senior English class for giving me the invaluable teen perspective on the first three chapters.

And finally, this book is the best it could possibly be thanks to Laura Bradford, my agent and champion, who took a chance on an unpublished rookie, and my editor, Wendy Loggia, who took a piece-of-coal story and turned it into a diamond. I'd also like to thank the whole team at both the Bradford Literary Agency and Delacorte Press. So much goes on in the background that I don't even know about. Thank you all for your tireless efforts.

ABOUT THE AUTHOR

MARY ELIZABETH SUMMER contributes to the delinquency of minors by writing books about unruly teenagers with criminal leanings. She has a BA in creative writing from Wells College, and her philosophy on life is "You can never go wrong with sriracha sauce." She lives in Portland, Oregon, with her wife, their daughter, and their evil overlor—er, cat. *Trust Me, I'm Lying* is her debut novel. Follow Mary Elizabeth's latest exploits on mesummer.com, maryelizabethsummer .tumblr.com, and pinterest.com/mesummer, and on Twitter at @mesummerbooks.